Leanbh Pearson (Any) lives in Ngunnawal Country in Canberra, Australia. An award-winning LGBTQI and disability author of horror and dark fantasy, her writing is inspired by folklore, fairy tales, myth, history and climate. She's judged the Australian Shadows Awards, Aurealis Awards, and is an invited panelist and member of the ASA, AHWA, AFTS, BSFA, HWA and SFWA. Leanbh has been awarded AHWA and HWA mentorships, is a Ditmar Awards nominee and winner of HWA Diversity Grant and the AHWA Robert N Stephenson Flash Fiction Story Competition. Leanbh's alter-ego is an academic in archaeology, evolution and prehistory.

T0288539

IFWG Titles With Leanbh Pearson

Cursed Shards: Tales of Dark Folklore (Pearson, editor)
Three Curses and Other Dark Tales

Three Curses and Other Dark Tales

by Leanbh Pearson

Three Curses and Other Dark Tales

ISBN-13: 978-1-922856-76-0

V1.0

Story history can be found at the end of this book.

Printed in Palatino Linotype and Drakoheart Leiend.

IFWG Publishing International
Gold Coast
www.ifwgpublishing.com

Dedication

For Arwen. You taught me a love of tales, reading and history and you've been a constant inspiration since.

Table of Contents

Introduction...1

The Devil's Fool..3
Three Tasks For the Sidhe...........................5
A Thief In the Alhambra.............................13
Three Curses..19
The Black Hare...41
A Handful of Dead Leaves...........................43
The Hobgoblin's Lament.............................53
The Bull of Heaven......................................55
The Selkie Twins..69
Them..75
Pan's Dance...85
The Monsters We Become..........................87
Bones and Fur...99
Talismans..101
Maidens of the Bloody Brook.....................113
The Monster...117
A Night on Skye...127
Poisoned Fruit, Poisoned Reign..................131
The Dark Harpist...135
When Dead Gods Walk................................143
A Trail of Corpselights................................151
The Making of Hel.......................................157
The Dark Horseman.....................................161
Second Chances...171
The Order Sagittarius..................................173
Black Wings At Samhain..............................191

The Grave Robber and the Church-Grim.....193
The Eldritch Wood...201
Loki's Choices...203
The Bones of a Dead God...............................205
Hildur the Cursed Queen................................207
Selene and Endymion.......................................217
The Bargain...219

Publication Acknowledgments.....................233

Introduction

Three Curses and Other Dark Tales is a collection of fiction inspired by dark folklore from around the world. There are a range of short stories, novelettes, flash fiction and micro-fiction that explore bargains with guardian Fae, and tales of mortals led astray into the forests or the hollow hills never to be seen again. In writing these stories, these beings from an unseen Otherworld inspired me, these worlds defying explanation that exists alongside our own. This liminal plane has played an important role in many cultures throughout history; reflected in belief systems, made physical in items recovered by archaeologists, temples constructed to appease and implore beings.

All these stories are inspired by folklore, fairy tales and mythology but woven anew into re-imaginings with new settings, to create a new story that can be told beside the hearth on dark nights. I hope you enjoy them as much as I do.

Leanbh Pearson, 2023

The Devil's Fool

April 1171 was bitterly cold, remembered for empty granaries and larders.

In one hamlet, the arrival of the Stranger eclipsed all other promises, except to end the wintry curse and the witch who cast it. Fear plucked at the townsfolk, suspicion tainting those knowledgeable of any herb-lore or healing.

Now the townsfolk stared at the burnt corpse, ash and snowflakes frozen over the human form kneeling in agonised prayer. The Stranger had accused her witch, consort of demons, and yet none considered if the Devil himself had deceived them.

On the road, the Devil continued, dark amusement in his eyes.

'The Devil's Fool' was inspired by the 'mini-ice age' that occurred in Europe during the end of the dark ages where many crops failed. This time was the end of dark ages and the beginning of the Middle Ages and many marginalised individuals in communities were often blamed for the unexplained natural phenomena that was occurring.

Three Tasks For the Sidhe

There would never be a ballad sung about the three tasks you and Fianait endured. As a minstrel, you might have composed your own, but that right was taken from you and only those who witnessed your challenge to the Fair Folk know the truth of your tale. Though there are countless songs of mortal men who loved a lady of the Sidhe, none loved Fianait as she did you: a love to endure.

You and Fianait would meet in secret when the Fair Folk walked into the mortal realm. Those liminal hours betwixt day and night. Hidden in dense bracken, clinging vine and shadowed woodland, you would wait, watching those lords and ladies dance in the half-light, then follow Fianait from the grove into darker reaches of the forest. She, who among us, was always drawn to the meadows at the forest edges. You were a harpist, a minstrel and singer of the oldest songs. You knew the tales of mortal men obsessed with the ladies of the Sidhe. For Fianait was unlike any mortal woman, just as she was unlike any among the Folk. Although the daughter of the Winter Lord, she was unnatural, too often drawn to the forest fringe, her gaze lost to the horizon.

Yet your eyes never wavered from Fianait, her simple gown of moonlight and dew, unadorned by the gems of starlight that hung around the graceful necks of her ladies, gowns spun of spider silk, and laced with hoar frost and dew. You saw none but Fianait when you met that fateful time at the forest's edge. She, turning to you;

her violet eyes tinted with the blue of an evening sky.

"Fianait," you breathed, taking her slender form in your arms.

Her smile was summer itself, all warmth and gentleness, fit to make the Queen of the Summer enraged if she had witnessed it. "We should not meet here anymore," she murmured.

"Why?" you asked. "Why hide the love I bear you?"

She frowned then, delicate brows knitting, considering your words as she glanced back towards the dancing Fae.

"Leave with me, Fianait," you begged.

Perhaps you had never intended it to be serious, but once those words had left your lips, they found a truth of their own. When your gaze met Fianait's violet eyes, that truth sank roots of its own deep into the earth and she shook her head, black ringlets cascading around her shoulders, hiding her face from you.

"I cannot leave with you. You know the laws of my kind. You know who my father is."

"They're still dancing," you pressed, glancing back towards the grove, the gowns and frock coats of the Sidhe glittering in the pre-dawn light. "Your father need not know."

"You forget, I am not my mistress in these woods."

"You can't leave freely?" you asked, taking her pale hand in yours. "You're bound to your father's court?"

"We are beholden to our courts," she said. "If I am to leave with you, my father must release me."

"Then let me speak with him," you said, noticing several handmaidens now standing in the shadows.

"There is naught but tragedy awaiting you," she insisted. "But I release you, mortal. Leave these woods and our court to their moonlit revelries."

"Fianait, you never entrapped me. No magic binds our love that is not of the purest kind. But I will take my leave if you answer one question."

Her bottom lip trembled, and she hesitated. Tendrils of hoar frost uncurled across the forest floor and Fianait stared as dew froze along each stem and leaf. Reluctantly, she bowed her head in subservience, the Lord of the Winter approaching in near silence.

"Daughter," he said. "Introduce me to our mortal guest?"

Fianait lowered her eyes when her father spoke, then lifted her violet gaze to meet your own. "This is Matthew, a mortal man dear to me and one with whom I would leave our realm."

The Winter Lord's lips curled in contempt, and he glared at you, an intruder to his predawn revels. But resigned, he sighed, ejecting a puff of frozen air into the shadowy space between you and Fianait. "You trespass on my Court tonight, mortal," he spoke, revealing pointed teeth. "Does my daughter speak the truth? Do you seek to take one beholden to me?"

"The Lady Fianait speaks the truth. Our hearts are bound," you said, fists clenched, willing bravery into your words. "I would seek to fasten her hand to mine and take her from this realm as my wife."

Those still dancing among the dew and muted light now scattered at your words, their dance abandoned as the grove shivered with unspoken anticipation. The dispersed dancers peered from the half-shadow, eyes bright with interest.

Fianait stood motionless opposite you, brilliant eyes pleading where her lips would not betray her. She knew you were a skilled harpist, that very calling as a minstrel had led you to these woods for the first time, searching for truth in the oldest lores about the Fae. In those tales and legends of the Sidhe, with trickery and ill-bargains made, you knew the ground you walked upon was slick with ice, a single misstep would crack it and plunge you into peril.

"No mortal may challenge a claim on those beholden to me," the Winter Lord said, dark eyes glittering.

"Yet Fianait is our daughter," spoke the Winter Queen, her bare feet soundless on the frosty ground as she stopped beside her Lord. "It is prudent that Fianait discover how poor her choice of a mortal lover is, the weakness of his kind. If he seeks a hand-fasting with Fianait, let him prove the strength of their love."

The Winter Lord bowed in agreement to his Queen, then turned his black eyes on you. "Complete three tasks to my satisfaction without Fianait's aid, witnessed here by the Winter Court, and I will concede for Fianait to be your wife and she might leave our realm with you at dawn."

Glancing to Fianait, you met her gaze, an unspoken agreement passing between you. You wet your lips and declared your acceptance of the challenge put before you.

The Winter Lord bowed with rigid formality and, raising his hands, palms to the night sky, he flexed his long fingers as though clawing the air. The ground trembled, then pulled apart, saplings tearing from the soil, reaching skyward like twiggy fingers, mirroring those beseeching hands cast to the sky. Strengthening his command over the natural elements, he caused the saplings to grow with an uncanny speed, entwining their limbs, until a thorny arch awaited you.

"Your first task." The Winter Queen gestured to the hawthorn arch. "Only a love that is true and strong can stand beneath the thorns."

Paling, you tried to conceal your unease. You knew the old songs, those ancient tales of men broken beneath hawthorns and ensorcelled by the Fair Folk. Recognising the unmasked fear in Fianait's eyes—before she could protest, and your cowardice might lure you away—you walked beneath the thorny arch.

There was little space to stand without rounding your shoulders, exposing your back to the woody limbs above. The Winter Lord inclined his head once to his Queen, who, moving directly into your sight, raised her hands. Somewhere behind you, Fianait gave a piteous moan, the sound of her anguish nearly unmanning you. Shoulders tensed, you waited, body pressed against the boughs above. Hawthorn roots encircled your boots, creeping, thorny vines holding you firm. A slow, tremulous groan shuddered through the branches above, the wood sounding as if it were constricting, drawing itself inward to crush your bones.

Then, without warning, those slender hawthorn branches disentangled from the arch, unfolding limbs, long black thorns lining their length. The Winter Queen gestured, and rapid whip-like branches moved as though extensions of her body. They lashed your exposed shoulders, arms and back, slicing through leather jerkin, shirt beneath, and cutting bloody marks across your skin. A scream, ragged and piteous, broke your lips but you only bowed your shoulders, covered your unprotected eyes and face beneath your hands. Even as tears mingled with blood, and thorny blows struck you again and again, your refusal to fail Fianait remained unwavering.

The Winter King sighed and halted the blows. Pain lanced through your broken skin. The rawness of nerves exposed to air sent shivers of shock through you as if the thorns still lashed you.

"The second task is not as easy," the Winter Lord snarled. "You would not be the first mortal to value love until its absence."

Without comment, the Winter Queen gestured again and two handmaidens hurried forward, taking your already bleeding arms, and dragged you before her. Despite your earlier bravado, fear slithered inside you like a chill, and now, standing before the Winter Queen, your resolve began to fail. Before you could turn aside, her slender fingers tightened around your wrist, impossibly strong, like manacles that held you fast. Where she touched you, the skin burned with cold, icy tendrils spreading over you, shivers racking your body like the height of fever, your breath in hollow rasps. Then as numbness overwhelmed the pain, the callousness of the second task became clear, and you stared at the ruin of your harpist's hand, those once dextrous fingers unable to break your grip with the queen even as sensation returned. Looking at the imprint of her grip indelibly marked in black frost-bitten flesh, you met her dark eyes and refused to flinch.

"Has he completed the second task to satisfaction?" Fianait asked.

"Two tasks he's completed," the Winter Lord said. "But in life, as beyond death, love is an eternal flame that cannot be extinguished. Complete my third task and your love will be worthy of Fianait."

Discontent to watch you suffer but powerless to offer aid under the bindings of this bargain, Fianait struggled against her handmaidens, and breaking free, ran into the centre of the clearing. There, holding you in her embrace, she pleaded for mercy. Grimacing against the agony of your right hand, you held her, easing her wretched sobs, and glanced at the blue-grey flesh of your right arm, a memento from the Winter Queen's frigid touch.

Consoling Fianait, you stepped away from her embrace to

stand before the Winter Lord and his Queen. A tremor of fear shook your limbs as the Queen raised her hands once more. Between her outstretched fingers, a golden chalice appeared, its shining form hovering in the space before you. Long hours spent memorising the old tales gave you forewarning of what was to come. But with trembling hands, you took the proffered goblet.

A faint light emanated from the liquid sloshing against the sides. But this chalice held not wine, mead, nor ale; instead, an icy flame burned within.

The Winter Queen smiled and mimicked touching an imaginary goblet to her frost-rimed lips. Exhausted beyond endurance, your smile was weak, and not glancing at Fianait, you drank the icy liquid down. Gasping, Fianait rushed to your side as writhing pain spread outward from your core, igniting smaller fires as it travelled through your body. Where that icy flame had touched, the fire burned the skin to welts and blisters. Uttering a final broken sob, you fell, staring up at swaying forest branches, and listening to the breathless rattle in your lungs. Time and reason abandoned you, Fianait holding you in her arms on the forest floor, huddled and twitching. Finally, you opened your eyes, meeting the violet gaze of the woman you loved, trying to speak, to offer her comfort, but nothing came from your scarred throat.

Those three tasks might have broken the strength of your mortal body, crippled your harpist's hands and stolen your minstrel's voice, but when the Sidhe Lord and his Queen departed, Fianait remained beside you, cradled in your arms, and among the ferns and moss, her voice sang alone in the morning.

'Three Tasks for the Fae' was originally written in memory of Aiki Flinthart and many who are survivors of physical trauma, illness and disability. I was inspired by the Irish folklore of the Sidhe and the common appearance in legends involving the Sidhe setting of three tasks a mortal must complete to acquire a request made of the Sidhe. The three tasks are often impossible to complete. I was drawn to the idea of a mortal surviving the tasks but at a cost of their greatest abilities.

A Thief In the Alhambra

I was drinking in a tavern, a disreputable little bar in the Albaicin. Looking out the window, I gazed up at the Alhambra, the stone walls shining gold in the last light. A man approached from across the tavern and, sitting down on the window ledge, blocked my view. He regarded me with a frown.

"What?" I snarled, glaring from behind the veil that obscured much of my face.

"I need to hire you," he said, lip curling as if I were something disagreeable on his boot.

"You're obscuring my view," I said, gesturing at the window.

"I need this recovered," he said, moving from the window ledge and dropping a scrap of parchment on the table between us.

I regarded him cautiously. He was well dressed, gold thread embroidery visible beneath the plain robes he'd obviously stolen. *Probably from some washing rack*, I thought. *On his way from the Alhambra*. I hastily drained my glass, the sweet liquor burning my throat, and snatched up the discarded paper.

"Your insinuation is insulting," I said, waving the scrap of parchment.

"I know what you are," he hissed, his hand encircling my wrist, holding me firm. "Take the task offered you. Do it tonight and don't waste time. This is no common task."

I stared pointedly at the white-knuckled fingers gripping my wrist. He slowly loosened his grip and let go, stepping back.

"And I am no common thief," I growled.

He nodded curtly, dropping a heavy coin purse on the table,

the clink of coins audible.

I grabbed the coin purse and, still watching him, unfolded the parchment. I stared at the carefully drawn illustration of a birdcage and what looked like an angel. *Such common Christian items? But is it really an angel?* I wondered. Still frowning, I inspected the detailed layout of a wealthy house in the Alhambra.

"Recover what I need and bring it here before dawn, and I'll double your payment. Tomorrow, Queen Isobel and her Catholic court take residence and what I seek will be lost to me."

"I never fail," I said, hiding the pouch and parchment in my robes. "I'll find you before dawn."

He nodded in understanding, and without a backward glance, walked away. I watched him leave, a faint haze around him like heat from a flame. Frowning, I waited until he had disappeared into the twilit gloom of the narrow streets outside before leaving the tavern myself. The thought of that heat shimmer around the stranger sent shivers of unease through me. The jinn were more than legends; they were powerful beings to be feared. *Was I just hired to steal for a jinn?*

Outside the tavern, I hurried through the cobbled lanes of the Albaicin. My destination was the Alhambra, the palaces of the Nasrid kings built on the mountain above the crowded Albaicin where the common populous lived. Moving cautiously through the narrow lanes, I headed up the mountain slope toward the woods of the Alhambra itself. When certain I hadn't been followed, I ducked into a cluster of trees. I slipped off the flowing outer robes I wore during the day, loose ankle-length trousers and a simple jerkin beneath. This was the common garb for boys in the Albaicin and, with the dark headscarf hiding my long hair and face, it was difficult to tell I was a woman. Cinching the belt around my waist, I checked my curved dagger was secure before slipping through the dense woodland toward the fortress walls, my thin leather shoes silent on the path.

Ahead, the stone walls of the Alcazaba fortress shone in the moonlight, the silence broken by guards calling to the next post and monotone replies from further along the wall. When the guards turned away from the woods, I hurried from the shadows of the trees and through the arched gate and into the Alhambra.

The paved streets of the Medina, a labyrinth of walled gardens and the terraced houses of the wealthy, surrounded the royal palaces of the Alhambra. So long besieged by the Catholic forces, King Boabdil would finally surrender the city tomorrow. Already many in the Boabdil's court were fleeing, any who refused allegiance to Queen Isabel or conversion to Catholicism. Around me, many of the households were dark, likely abandoned already.

Checking my surroundings, I dusted my hands in the powdery lime from the crumbling mortar of the wall behind me. Glancing up and down the lane again, reassured the streets were empty, I walked to the tall garden wall. Flexing my fingers, I searched for handholds on the uneven stone surface and, hooking my fingers into a chink in the stonework, I started climbing. My toes gripped into the stone, unhindered by the thin leather boots I wore specifically for this purpose. Pressed close to the stone wall, my headscarf and dark clothing camouflaged me in the dark, making me nearly invisible unless someone was specifically looking for me. When I reached the top of the garden wall, I slipped carefully over the edge, dropping nimbly to the courtyard below. I paused, my breath seeming loud in the quiet night, but hearing no shouts of alarm, I crept from the shadows.

The courtyard was in a traditional layout. A shallow pool with small fountains ran down the middle, the garden walls adorned with espalier citrus trees, the air heavy with the perfume. But my attention was on two stone lions on either side of an arched doorway. *Had one of them moved?* Reflexively, my fingers curled around my dagger hilt. But nothing had moved. Inching nearer, I was nearly certain I'd fallen for a trick of moonlight and shadow. Reaching for the ornate doorknocker, I paused, staring in horror at the carved glyphs. A warning to potential thieves. *It's just superstition*, I reminded myself, and pushed on the enormous doors.

I hadn't expected the doors to be unlocked, but their massive bulk swung silently inward. Rolling my shoulders to ease the tension, perspiration already slicking the lime on my hands, I stepped into the cool interior of the house. *I should run, flee this cursed house, forget this task. No amount of money is worth this sorcery.*

But I ignored these worries, and looking around the large room, decided it seemed abandoned. Despite the low tables, silk floor rugs and embroidered cushions, I could see no trinkets, bowls of fruit, wine or oil jugs left out. Moving past stone pillars holding the stubs of extinguished candles, I withdrew the parchment from inside my jerkin. Checking the directions, I turned to the left and passed into a long, narrow room.

Moonlight poured through the windows; the delicate metal-work shutters open wide to the night. *This is not right,* I thought, agitated. *Just find what you're here for and leave.* Surveying the length of the room I saw the elaborate metal cage, not unlike many sold in bazaars to keep songbirds.

But the gossamer wings that flitted within, iridescent and brilliantly coloured in the moonlight, were not those of song-birds. I had been a storyteller's daughter and, after hours spent at my mother's hearth listening to her tales, I knew what these creatures were. These were peris. Unlike the jinn or ifrit, powerful beings owing their magic to air or fire, who blessed or cursed mortals as it amused them, peris belonged to neither group. *But why are they caged?* I thought again of the stranger who had hired me, the shimmer of heat around him. *Was he a jinn or an ifrit?* Watching the diminutive winged peris inside the cage, I recalled my mother's tales. *What had she told me about peris? In owing no allegiance to either air or fire, they made enemies of the ifrit and jinn both. They were rare but always hunted by the jinn and ifrit, captured and consumed like poultry.* I shivered. *Could I really steal this cage and give the peris to the jinn in return for coins?*

I was still my mother's daughter, and repulsed by the mercen-ary nature of such a bargain, I made a better one with the peris. For there were many legends after all, and peris could grant fortunes as freely as the jinn or ifrit.

Reaching for the cage, my fingertips brushed the edge of the lock. Pain like fire lanced up my arm, and I quickly pulled my hand away. Staring at my fingers, I saw part of the intricate script scorched into the skin, the original inscribed around the lock I had touched. Still shaking from the pain, I withdrew a lock-pick from my jerkin and started working on the complex mechanism.

"The jinn will hunt me to the end of my days," I said to the peris while I worked. "Grant me on thing in return: hide me from the jinn who intends me harm."

The peris gathered at the edge of the cage, voices soft as a summer breeze. "We have power only in the light. We grant you shelter from the jinn but only when in the light."

The last tumbler in the lock *snicked*. I unwound my headscarf and wrapped it about my hands.

"Keep me safe from the jinn. We've made our bargain," I said and, grasping the lock in my covered hands, threw open the cage door.

The peris darted toward the open windows, gossamer wings refracting moonlight in dazzling patterns. Smoke curled from the scarf still wrapped around my hands, and I dropped it to the ground. Peering at the sigils of a curse now burned into my skin, I thought about the agreement I had just broken. I had released the peris instead of stealing them for the jinn. Looking at the sprawling Albaicin below me, I knew the peris could only protect me in the light, and with each waning of the moon would come true darkness. Such a being as a jinn would never forget the insult I had delivered. But those were worries for another, darker night. I walked from the Alhambra, coin purse heavy at my hip and moonlight draped about me, and smiled. A thief had tricked a jinn.

The inspiration for 'A Thief in the Alhambra' came from a 2019 visit to Granada, Andalusia in Spain to the Alhambra world heritage site of the Nasrid Empire where the Alhambra court and gardens preserve the historic heritage of the last Islamic Caliphate in Spain. The rich Moorish history and culture of Granda inspired a reimagining of Arabic folklore and legend within the context of the Moorish culture of the Alhambra during the last decades of the Nasrid rule. My interest in the history of fairies and the winged representations so common today are found in the legends of peris. The legends of the jinn are widespread throughout Moorish and pre-Islamic cultures. The combination of the vibrant Alhambra and the Moorish culture inspired me with its rich folklore and legends.

Three Curses

The solid stone walls of the University of Aberdeen were a chill reminder of the surrounding civilisation. Ailsa hugged the shawl tighter around her shoulders and leant back against the wall. Where was Niall? He'd promised to be here when the courtyard clock struck noon, but the massive hands were ticking over ten past the hour and he hadn't shown.

"Good Lord, you're still here. Thank the heavens though, Ailsa."

She half-turned, dark hair around her face, a scowl darkening her expression. "Of course I'm still here. Where else would I be? You said this was urgent."

Niall looked chagrined, blonde hair falling across his face as he ducked his head. "I may have stressed the urgency to make sure you'd come."

"Is this about Conall again?"

"The other lads and I were going on a camping expedition. The reserve is at the foot of the O'Hanlon lands. I know you've mentioned more than once how they pushed out your ancestors from their ancestral homelands. I thought you might like to come along? And I was hoping to spend some time with Conall alone. I might need some company if it goes badly."

"You could get a bloody nose and beating if it goes badly, Niall."

He blushed, looked at the ground, then lifted his grey eyes to hers. "Please, Ailsa, say you'll come. Do it for me at least?"

She hugged her shawl tighter about herself. He was right, of course. If things went badly and Conall had no interest in Niall beyond a friendship, her presence could prevent a beating going out of control.

"All right, Niall. But I'm not stepping foot on my homelands. I've told you the reasons often enough."

He beamed and stepped closer, embracing her stiffly. "Thank you. It means the world to me."

"I'll pack bandages in case things go awry. Or whisky in case things go well?"

He grinned. "Both."

Ailsa knew these lands. She could feel the uncanny energy thrumming beneath the earth, the taste of the wildest magics on the breeze. To her and her ancestors, they were cursed. She had been reluctant to come here, to travel from Aberdeen and into these lands where she was as unwelcome as the plague. But Niall had insisted she accompany him. When she mentioned her grandmother had hailed from these very hills and told her never to venture here, Niall had only argued that was more reason she had come to see these lands that had once belonged to her bloodline. For these hills, groves and the loch had once belonged to the O'Hanlon women, but there was a very good reason none had called these lands home for generations. The way her grandmother told the tale, it had been her mother before her who had cursed O'Hanlon women and seen them cast from their homelands. Never again might an O'Hanlon woman step foot on these hills, walk beneath the boughs of the forest, or dip a toe in the loch without risking the wrath of the Unseelie.

Of course, Niall came from Aberdeen and did not believe in curses— neither those wrought by the Seelie courts nor their darker kin, the Unseelie. But Ailsa had grown up with hearthside tales of the Seelie and Unseelie courts and knew these hills were home to the Unseelie. Hoping Niall would change his mind, she'd listened to his increasingly excited chatter about the weekend away, and whether the other lads in his philosophy major would join them or not.

Now the weekend was here, and Niall had not forgotten nor changed his mind. His desire to visit these ancient O'Hanlon lands was stronger than before, but Ailsa wasn't a fool. She knew the reason Niall wanted to go camping for the weekend, and it had a lot more to do with Conall being there. Niall had been infatuated for a year now, but Ailsa doubted Conall returned any such sentiments. She'd seen the way Conall looked at her and the other lasses. But Niall was her friend, and her duty was to stave off any heartache. Now, looking at the mist-shrouded hills of her ancient homelands, Ailsa knew she'd taken Niall into danger, knew she was trespassing here. Queen Mab ruled the Unseelie Court.

The lads set up the camp, tents surrounding a campfire. Ailsa surveyed the site and couldn't help but notice her tent was next to Conall's and it made her feel physically sick. She hated the man, couldn't understand what Niall saw in such a swaggering boor. But they were here now, and she wasn't sure who she was protecting anymore, Niall or herself.

Conall met Ailsa's eyes. "Come sit with me by the fire."

She glanced around the campsite, but the other lads were all busy putting up the last tent, Niall among them. Without a way to escape Conall, Ailsa complied. She sat stiffly beside him, pulling her shawl around her shoulders.

"Are you cold, Ailsa? Come closer, I can keep you warm."

She half-turned to look at him, offering his arm in an embrace. She shook her head.

"Just a sudden chill. The fire is warmth enough."

He grunted and turned back to watching the flames. "Niall says these are your ancestral homelands. But you don't live here anymore?"

She shook her head, hair covering her face from him. "No. There was trouble for my ancestors many generations back. We don't come here anymore."

"Niall told me it was the uncanny folk," he chuckled.

"That's what I told him. But they also accused my ancestors of witchcraft and so they left these ungrateful lands behind them."

"They sound like intelligent women, just like you."

Ailsa repressed a shudder at his mild advances, hating the way he leaned closer to her. She could feel his body shift as he closed the distance between them.

"Conall?" Niall asked.

Ailsa started, relieved and worried that he had seen too much.

"Can you help me bring the last of the ale from the car?"

"That I can do. Excuse me for a moment, Ailsa."

She nodded meekly, trying not to draw attention to herself. A pox on the man. Did he not understand his attentions were unwanted?

The other lads from the group sat drinking and talking about philosophers of whom Ailsa had never heard. Unwilling to leave Niall alone with Conall, she remained where she was. She was closer to the car and could overhear any of their conversation. She already suspected what Niall was going to do and knew it was going to fail. *But how badly will Conall react? Will I need to step in and stop him beating Niall into a bloody mess?*

Ailsa could hear the mild banter from where they'd parked the car. Then the atmosphere behind her changed, now heavy with tension. Ailsa held her breath. *Don't do this Niall, don't be a fool.* The strained silence broke. Hushed words met hissed insults and Conall burst from the shadows, a crate of ale in both arms. Ailsa jumped and the trio of lads on the other side of the campfire looked up in surprise.

Conall's face was a shadow of rage, his mouth clamped tight and eyes dark with fury. Conall dropped the crate of ale with the others and the atmosphere around the campsite changed in an instant. Ailsa readied herself to move, to find Niall, but Conall sat heavily beside her, draping one arm around her shoulders, holding her in place.

Frozen in fear, Ailsa didn't move. Her eyes roamed the campsite for any signs of Niall. Conall pressed a jug of ale into her hand and reflexively she sipped at it. *Where is Niall? Is he all right? How can I extricate myself from Conall's arms to go in search of him?*

Niall walked slowly from the shadows behind them, his footsteps unobtrusive on the mossy ground. He looked at Ailsa, caught in Conall's arms, and his eyes darkened. Changing his course, he sat on the opposite side of the campfire.

Ailsa shifted, trying to move away from Conall, but his grip tightened painfully on her arm. He put his mug of ale on the ground, and still holding her, kissed her neck. Ailsa shuddered with revulsion at his hot breath against her skin, his lips pressed to her collarbone.

"Niall," Conall began, sliding his free hand around Ailsa's waist and moving to cup her breast. "A pliant woman gets my cock hard, not a bugger-boy."

Revolted, Ailsa pushed Conall from her, his arms easily letting her go now he'd made his cruelty plain to Niall. But as Ailsa stood, Niall's cheeks blushed with anger and embarrassment.

"Niall, wait," she called.

He shook his head, tears in his eyes. "You betrayed me."

Ailsa watched in horror as Niall fled into the forest beyond the campsite. *The Unseelie already know I'm here. I can feel the frosty touch of Queen Mab. But I can't abandon Niall in those woods either.*

Ailsa sprinted away from the campsite, the noise of drunken laughter following her. *I should never have come here.* The slope was steep, the open moors to her left, the tangle of the woods to her right. Stumbling in the dark, Ailsa heard a faint rustle to her right like boots in leaf litter. She stopped, peering into the shadows.

"Niall?" she hissed.

Eerie silence greeted her, but Ailsa felt the attention of many unseen eyes upon her. Her skin tingled with awareness of the Unseelie. *But what if Niall is in there too? What if they capture him?* Not hesitating lest fear overcome her, Ailsa hurried into the old growth of the forest. The darkness beneath the ancient trees was absolute, the terrain unfamiliar. Twigs and vines slapped against her cheeks, burning tears trickling down her face and stinging the cuts. *Why wouldn't Niall listen to me? Had he not seen my anguish?* This weekend was such a tangled mess.

They'd intended a simple summer weekend with a few friends from Aberdeen. But her infatuation with Conall had made her blind, and it smarted now to think how right Niall had been all along. Conall had brought his three friends, and it had seemed innocent enough to Ailsa. *Because I am a fool,* she reminded herself. Niall wanted to be desired, and it had made him gullible. Now the weekend was nothing more than a cruel joke that Conall could share with his mates as they finished the ale.

"Curse them and curse me," Ailsa muttered. She swiped angrily at the tears spilling stubbornly down her cheeks.

Struggling through the old-growth forest, Ailsa needed to find Niall, and wished she had heeded his advice to stay clear of Conall. Instead, they had argued. She had thrown his wisdom aside and told him to leave. And he had, stalking off into these cursed woods, ignoring the hateful words Conall and his mates shouted after him. Niall had refused to watch her make such a foolish display of herself. He certainly would not tolerate Conall's increasingly open hostility.

"Niall!"

The evening air was chill for all its promise to be summer. Ailsa pushed aside the twisted branches of bramble and hawthorn that tried to block her path. The forest was ancient in here; there was no path to follow, and it seemed to be a vast network made entirely from twisted vines, thorns, and roots. Scrambling over protruding boulders, her shoes sliding on the thick mossy coverings, Ailsa kept steering herself uphill, conscious of the way the forest pulled her deeper into the gloom. Weaving between saplings, Ailsa crested a slight incline and stopped, gripping a slender trunk for support.

"Niall!"

The forest seemed to swallow her cries, smothering them beneath the thick carpet of autumn leaves. Mouldering leaves covered the forest floor. The smell of rotten wood, air heavy with mildew and moss, and beneath that, the odour things best left to decay, assaulted her senses. Gripping another slender trunk, Ailsa pulled herself up a short, treacherous slope. Half-buried stones emerging from the moist soil made treacherous footing, and Ailsa's shoes slid over the moss and rock. Pitching forward, she caught herself in a tangle of branches, hissing in pain as a thorn scratched her palm. Steadying herself, she sucked on the blood that had oozed from her cut palm and squinted up at the sky. She could see neither moonlight nor the hint of stars through the canopy, knowing she needed to get clear of the forest, to the top of a ridge where her calls would carry and she might have some hope of seeing where Niall had gone.

Clambering through the dense forest again, it seemed the trees were intent on keeping her trapped within their boughs. Twisted branches reached for her from the gloom, their twig-like fingers grasping at clothing, tangling in her hair. Alisa's hear raced, memories of her grandma's tales of the cursed lands she walked upon, filled her mind with rising panic. Breathing in shallow gasps, she wrenched the sleeves of her jacket free from a thorny bramble and staggered forward. Tripping, she fell onto her knees, the material of her skirts cut by the stones jutting from the soil. Tears pricked at her eyes. Curse them for coming here. And damn these woods if she was going to cry.

"Curse it all." She wiped at the tears on her face, smearing dirt from her hands onto her cheeks.

Around her, the forest fell silent. The wind that had been idly stirring leafy boughs was eerily still. Ailsa wrapped her arms around her torso, shivering not with the cold, but with sudden fear. She listened, straining to hear. There was nothing—not even the faintest sounds from the distant campsite. She had not run very far uphill from the campsite, not so far that she could no longer hear the drunken laughter of Conall and his friends. She doubted they would stop drinking until the beers ran out and she certainly had provided enough of a spectacle of herself to keep them amused for hours. She hugged her middle tighter, wishing Niall were there. But there was no Niall to comfort her, and not even the scuttle of creatures in the undergrowth, nor the predatory flapping of wings in the night sky. Only an eerie silence, pervasive and chilling, filled the woods.

"Niall?" Ailsa called, her voice barely a whisper in the darkness.

"Niall?" a small voice repeated, child-like but for the haunting chill to the tone.

"Hello?"

"Hello?" the voice echoed in a singsong lilt.

"This isn't funny." Ailsa clenched her fists, perspiration breaking across her skin as she spun on her heel, looking wildly around her. But all was shadows, darkness, and the subtle shifting of trees.

"It is never wise to play games with us, witch of the O'Hanlon line," the voice hissed, all pretence to innocence discarded now and the tone menacing.

Ailsa picked up the edges of her long skirts and ran, half-stumbling over the hems. She felt the soles of her boots catch on the cloth, heard the fabric ripping as she struggled uphill. She did not care. She ran, twigs snagging at her hair, pulling the red locks free from her kerchief. Vines and thorns scratched at her face and hands, the forest reaching for her now, the Unseelie beings that inhabited these ancient woods determined she would pay for her trespass. And trespassing, she was. They had called her a witch of the O'Hanlon line and whether she had ever possessed any drop of cunning talent or magic did not matter to the Unseelie. The women of the O'Hanlon lineage had vowed never to return to these lands, and she had broken that pledge. *Fool that I am*, she thought, scrabbling up the steep slope of rotten leaves.

She heard the silent swoop of powerful wings and ducked. The bird — or whatever it was — circled above, a darkness against the black night. Ailsa stumbled forwards into a deep grove, searching the sky fearfully as she ran half bent through the grasping tree limbs. A savage pain in her scalp jerked her to a halt. She cried out, hands flying to her tangled hair. She scratched and tore, but it was impossibly twisted and knotted around a branch. Screeching in protest, she felt the brush of woody fingers against her own. Ailsa screamed. Heedless of her entangled hair, she yanked her head away from the oak tree, tearing a hunk of curls from her scalp. Gritting her teeth through the pain, she staggered forward, fleeing the oak tree and whatever Unseelie being dwelled within it.

Tears blurred her sight, but Ailsa ran from the grove and, using her hands like claws, she half-ran, half-climbed the slope. Glancing up at the sky, she saw a pale white light ahead of her, its form shifting between tree trunks, moving slowly but parallel to the woods. Hoping that was Niall with a flashlight, certain that he must have finally come in search of her — probably drawn by the commotion she had been making — Ailsa ran towards the circle of light.

Breaking from the cover of the dense forest, the darkness was so absolute Ailsa did not see the hollow ahead. The ground disappeared from under her feet, pitching her momentarily into empty air. She landed hard on her knees, hands slamming into the soft, mossy earth to stop herself from falling face-first. Glancing fearfully behind her, the thick tangle of the woods was like an impenetrable wall. Steadying her breathing, the panic and terror she had felt in the tangle of the trees seemed to have disappeared. But the white light she had been following now bobbed a short distance above the ground directly ahead of her. She frowned, the light suspended in mid-air before it moved, like someone walking with a lantern. But the sphere of light was only knee high, far too small for anyone but a child to carry. Desperate not to be caught in the darkness, nor anywhere near the woods and the reaching trees, Ailsa collected the bedraggled remnants of her long skirts, and hurried after the light.

Searching the darkness of the windswept hills, Ailsa could see no signs of anyone cast against the dark night. Glancing back at the strange light as it moved steadily uphill, Ailsa followed. She watched as the light disappeared momentarily before reappearing further ahead, and in the absolute darkness of the hills, it seemed the light extinguished before re-igniting again in a different place. But as Ailsa walked after it, glancing from the open expanse of the windswept hills to the dense woodland fringe, she found the landscape underfoot was far from smooth hillside. Breathing in ragged mouthfuls of chill air, she scanned the stony terrain, wondering where Niall had gone.

"Niall!"

Ailsa's voice cut through the frigid silence of the moors, startling a few ravens in a nearby tree on the edge of the forest. The birds cawed unhappily, and Ailsa waited, hoping to hear her friend's response.

The light reappeared, this time only a handful of paces ahead, about level with her shoulders. Dashing forward, Ailsa found the windswept ground was stony beneath her boots, the protruding rocks threatening to break her ankles if she was not careful.

"Niall, wait," she called, desperate to reach him.

Ailsa followed carefully over the uneven ground. She stopped suddenly, hands groping in the darkness as her feet touched something hard Groping in the darkness, she traced the edge of a knee-heigh wall. Keeping her gaze on the light, which had remained motionless since she called, Ailsa hitched up her skirts and clambered over the low barrier, finding that the ground sloped steeply on the other side. Realising she was standing on the edge of an earthen mound, Ailsa stopped. She lifted her eyes to the light source, already suspecting what she had found.

It was not Niall. Above her, an old-fashioned lantern rested on the top of the crumbling cairn. The lantern was small and made from wrought-iron that seemed at odds in this abandoned place. Searching the surrounding darkness, Ailsa could see she stood at the edge of a stone cairn, a series of tall, standing stones encircling the inner earthen wall. She was in the middle of a barrow. Lifting the lantern to inspect the mound behind her, she could clearly see the towering stack of large stones. For someone of her lineage, cursed to never return to these lands, this seemed like the place where every Unseelie being that might wish her ill-will would dwell.

"Niall?" Ailsa called, tentatively.

No answer but a mournful breeze that rattled through the forest beyond, tossing leaves and bending boughs in the night. Ailsa shivered.

"Where must it be? Where, O Where?" a croaking voice asked from the shadows.

Ailsa yelped in surprise and grabbed for the little lantern. She spun around, holding the lantern aloft, casting shadows as she peered into the darkness beyond the barrow.

"Who's there?" she asked.

A diminutive figure, grizzled with age, white hair protruding at odd angles from beneath a dirty felt cap, stepped into the light cast by the lantern. He squinted up at Ailsa, his suspicious gaze quickly turning to outrage upon noticing the lantern in her hand. His wild, shaggy eyebrows met in a frown, but then he straightened his disreputable clothing and muttered something inaudible.

"Are you friend or foe?" Ailsa asked.

"I might ask you the same question, lass," he said, indignant.

Ailsa bit her lip in consternation, thinking of all the tales she had ever heard about the malicious Unseelie court.

"I mean no harm to your or yours. I am merely looking for my friend, and mistook you for him."

The little man regarded her with bright eyes. "Your friend chooses a bad night to wander these lands. Only the Unseelie or the mad walk these hills tonight, lass. Which might you be?"

"Probably the latter. Have you seen an angry young man pass this way?"

"I see little without my lantern, you ken?" He inclined his head towards the lantern she still held.

Ailsa paused, thinking. "If I return this to you, will you promise to help me find my friend?"

"Oh, of course, lass." He nodded gleefully, rubbing his grimy hands together.

Ailsa exhaled slowly and warily extended the lantern towards the little man. Quicker than she would have thought possible, dirt-smeared fingers grasped the lantern handle and yanked it possessively away from her. Clutching the lantern to his chest, he smiled widely to reveal sharp teeth. Ailsa drew back her outstretched hand as the eyes of the Unseelie creature shone an iridescent green. Looking at the lantern, Ailsa realised there was no flame flickering within; no candle of any kind that might cause the pale light it cast.

"You promised me your aid," she shouted.

The Unseelie creature holding the lantern paused a moment, his eyes a haunting green like many she had seen on the marshes or heard about in legends of the haunted, ancient barrows. He turned to face her, wrinkled features twisted into a parody of a smile.

"Your friend is at the loch."

Before Ailsa could respond, he vanished from the barrow, lantern light reappearing in the distance. The speed at which he travelled was uncanny, and his movement invisible in the darkness except for the flicking white light. Alone again, Ailsa squinted into the blackness of the night. She remembered they had crossed a ford below where they had camped. *Why did the Unseelie creature think Niall will be at the loch?* She shook her head in frustration. On these lands, nothing good lived near the loch. If he was at the loch, then she must follow the river through these hills until the waterways joined.

Gritting her teeth, Ailsa checked the leather belt at her hip, making certain the blade she carried was still safely within its sheath. There was something comforting about the iron at her side. She inched her way forward into the darkness, the soft-soles of her boots squelching in the mud as she crept from the barrow. The ancient standing stones were like mist-wreathed sentinels, the absence of any wind across the hills making the ancient burial mound feel even more haunted. Not wanting to tarry, Ailsa hastened over the earthen wall and towards the nearest of those solemn stone pillars. Even in the darkness, some inexplicable trick of the Unseelie lands made the engravings in the stone surface faintly visible. Ailsa shivered from the dank air and hurried past the stone circle and back out into the open hills.

The crescent moon shone weakly across the hills, the heather and brambles forming dense thickets of purple flowers and sharp thorns. She followed the troughs of the slope, the glittering body of the loch below, cupped in the hands of the valley. Clouds scudded across the night sky and though she hurried, Alisa kept alert for the wingbeats of the Sluagh, expecting to be attacked by the Otherworld host on such a wild night on Unseelie lands.

The sodden hills hid springs and Alisa tripped more than once on submerged stones, grazing her hands on jagged rock and slipping on the mossy ground. But she kept her gaze firmly on the loch, kept her attention on her goal lest any of the Unseelie try to divert her from reaching the loch. Even as she trudged down the steep hillside, her fears for Niall's safety only increased. These lands were not safe for anyone and Niall would be a tempting plaything for the Unseelie in their efforts to punish an O'Hanlon witch. *Not that I know any magic.* Alisa glared resentfully at the crescent moon as though she might develop some magical means of protecting Niall just by wishing hard enough.

Wingbeats echoed through the night, and Ailsa stopped walking. A chill wind had gusted across the hillside, carrying the raucous cries of birds that were not quite rooks or ravens. *The Host?* Picking up her skirts again, Ailsa ran down the hillside, ignoring the treacherous footing and half-sliding, half-running as she fought to outpace the Sluagh. Wings brushed against her hair and she ducked, twisting away from the reaching talons and snapping beaks. From the periphery of her sight, Ailsa caught glimpses of black plumage and red eyes as the Host assaulted her, hurrying her faster and faster down the slope. Raising her hands into the air, Ailsa beat at the Unseelie birds, knowing the longer the Host pursed her, the closer she would come to madness. Her grandmother had been certain on the lores of the Unseelie, and the Sluagh were not to be trifled with as they were well-known to carry away a wandering traveller or steal his sanity — Ailsa would not fall prey to such a fate, not when Niall depended on her.

The ground beneath her feet grew suddenly very slippery, the stony surface of the hill vanishing as Ailsa stumbled into ankle-deep mud. In her attempts to evade the Host, she'd not noticed the mist thickening around her, and which now clung so closely to the ground that she could scarcely see more than a few paces in front of her. Standing motionless in a hollow, uncertain of whether she was about to stumble into a marshland on the edge of the loch or if she still had some way to travel. Ailsa waited, listening for any clue to where she might be. The sounds of frogs and crickets were discordant around her. Cursing under her breath, Ailsa searched the impenetrable mist for any way out of the marshes. A burbling chuckle from her right startled her, and heart pounding, she swung to face empty air. The same burbling laughter came from her left this time, and repeating the movement, Ailsa followed the noise, spinning on her heel as many Unseelie voices began calling from the mist.

"I want to know where Niall is!"

"Niall, Niall," the Unseelie chanted with malicious joy.

"Tell me where Niall is."

The Unseelie creatures laughed maliciously, the sound surrounding Ailsa in a dizzying cacophony. Clenching her fists in fury, Ailsa tried to gauge direction, testing the squelching ground before her by extending her leg, testing the slope of the land with the tip of the boot. Searching in the mist, near blind as she had been in the forest's darkness, Ailsa found the edge of the hollow she had stumbled into and turned herself around, hoping she now faced the downhill slope where the loch had been visible earlier. And, moving hesitantly forward, she crept through the quagmire. The voices and taunts of the mischievous Unseelie followed her, the sounds of their taunts often blurring with the croaking of toads or the hiss of insects, but Ailsa ignored them.

She did not know how long she crept across the marsh, but slowly the mist lessened and the pale moonlight broke through in occasional silver rays. Hugging her cloak more tightly around herself, Ailsa shivered in the chill of the marshlands, but kept her gaze resolutely on the ground, conscious that the Unseelie were trying to lead her from the path she was following, and would gleefully see her sunk into the marsh, her body preserved in the peat, never able to escape the lands she knowingly trespassed upon.

In the dim light of the crescent moon and with her mind increasingly plagued but gloomy thoughts, Ailsa did not notice the edge of the brook until her boots crunched on pebbles, not mud. Startled, she stopped. A narrow brook meandered from the spring, bubbling from the hillside, the watercourse continuing until it met the loch. Filled with relief at the realisation she had nearly reached the bottom of the valley, she stared at the shining waters of the loch, now only a hundred paces from where she stood.

Carefully, Ailsa withdrew the small iron blade from the sheath at her side. She walked to the edge of the brook. The waters seemed clear and, to Ailsa's considerable surprise, none of the Unseelie had attacked her yet. The thought was not as comforting as one would hope. It made her wary of what was to follow with the loch so close now, and the intentions of the Queen of the Unseelie felt grimmer for the uncertainty.

Ailsa was about to put the toe of her boot into the water when she heard splashing from downstream. Half-turning to regard the source of the noise, she sucked in a breath. An old woman stood on the opposite bank, her face covered by the shawl she had wrapped around her head, but several grey locks of her long hair had worked free and blew outstretched on the wind. Ailsa's heart thudded painfully in the chest as she lowered her eyes to the old woman's task. Between gnarled fingers, the old woman held a bloodstained dress, the clothing tattered almost beyond recognition. But Ailsa would recognise the dress anywhere – but the sight of the dress she was wearing in those gnarled hands was not what sent fear trickling through her veins – it was the scarlet waters flowing downstream from the washerwoman's work. The old woman lifted her gaze from her grisly task and met Ailsa's eyes unflinchingly. There was scarcely a child born in Scotland who did not know the old tales of the Bean-nighe, one of the most powerful beings in the Unseelie court. Ailsa had listened to her grandmother's stories of great warriors and farmers alike who had unwillingly stumbled upon the old washerwoman at a ford, and who met their death within days of seeing her cleaning the garments they would wear when they died. In that moment, Ailsa knew what the price of trespassing on the Unseelie lands would be – she just hoped to rescue Niall before he joined her.

Determined to reach Niall before the curse of her presence lost him any chance of escaping the Unseelie, Ailsa trudged through the frigid waters of the brook, never taking her eyes from the washerwoman. The blood continued to flow from the dress submerged in the water, but the Unseelie woman took no notice of Ailsa, instead continuing to clean the torn and ragged garment.

Once Ailsa reached the opposite bank, her boots soaked and the freezing wind whipping the soggy hems of her dress against her legs, she glanced over her shoulder towards the washerwoman. She was gone. The water of the brook flowing clear in the moonlight, no trace of blood or clothing remained. Shivering in dread as much as the cold, Ailsa followed the curve of the brook as it widened to join the loch.

Pebbles crunched beneath her boots, and Ailsa scanned the empty banks of the loch. Although the Unseelie she had tricked into answering her question at the barrow had been unwilling to reveal Niall's location, the Seelie and Unseelie were both bound by the same rules regarding truth-telling; neither could lie when asked a question directly. The other Unseelie had tried to prevent her from reaching the loch, but now that she had and there was no sign of Niall, doubt wormed its way into Ailsa's heart. *What if the old tales about the Seelie and Unseelie beings unable to lies weren't true? Where is Niall? And how am I going to rescue him before my death already foretold?*

Soft flute music drifted through the night and the wind - which had been a constant across the slopes of the hills - had now fallen still. Scanning the edges of the loch for the source of the music, Ailsa's breathing hitched in momentary panic. Niall was reclining beneath a willow tree, his head tipped up to meet the lips of the young man bending down to kiss him. Despite herself, Ailsa felt a blush creeping along her cheeks. She knew Niall preferred the company of men, had known since noticing how he watched the young men in Aberdeen with the same stirring of desire she felt. They had always been close-friends despite what others such as Conall saw as an affliction, a wrongness about Niall. But she had never shared those views.

"He's happy among us," an icy voice said from behind her.

Ailsa jumped, not hearing anyone approach. She pivoted to face a slender woman, her beauty unsurpassed but a cold thing of starlight and frost.

"I've been looking for him," Ailsa said, glancing warily at Niall.

"Have you found what you were looking for, then?"

"I have found my friend," she agreed.

"And is that what he is to you, witch?"

Cold settled in Ailsa's stomach at the Unseelie woman's words. That terrible suspicion she had been harbouring coalesced. The Unseelie court had paid particular attention to her presence on their lands. *Am I being foolish to think they'd led Niall away from me? Was this an engineered vengeance against my trespass on their lands?* Every story Ailsa knew warned of the Unseelie, their dark intentions and impossible demands.

"Did you take him from me?"

Queen Mab sneered in distaste. "I've no interest in the affairs of mortals. But your friend seems happy with us."

At the Queen's words, Ailsa turned her attention to Niall again. He lounged beside an Unseelie prince on a reclining bed carved from driftwood, overhanging boughs of willows, giving privacy. But the tableau was not what it seemed. Ailsa saw most an empty goblet and food platter on the ground beside the extravagant bed. *Has the prince coerced Niall into drinking and eating what they offered him?* She noticed the fawning way Niall gazed at the prince, showing the unswerving loyalty of those enthralled by the Unseelie.

"What have you done to him, Mab?" Ailsa said. Rage and fear spiked, emboldening her, and she faced the unsmiling Unseelie Queen.

"I've done nothing. Your friend acted on his own violation."

"He's enthralled."

Mab shrugged one bare shoulder in the pale moonlight. "He serves the prince willingly. He has my blessing to remain on my lands. But you and your kin have never been welcome here. What punishment befits such disrespect?"

"I've met with the Bean-nighe. I know I'll never leave these lands."

Mab threw her head back and laughed, the sound brittle like icicles breaking against stone. "Then I need not raise my hand against you, witch. Your fate is sealed."

Outrage and fear boiling over with impotence at her situation, Ailsa turned away from the Queen. She stared through eyes blurred with tears at Niall, who lounged in apparent bliss beside the Unseelie prince, unaware and uncaring that he had cast away any life beyond this enthrallment to a cruel and uncaring being. *If we had never come here, if I'd never set foot on these cursed lands, Niall would be safe.* But she had walked onto the lands of her forbears, and Ailsa knew she'd be a fool if she let herself think she'd not felt the subtle thrill of uncanny magic with Mab's presence. Oh, the Unseelie had known one of the O'Hanlon witches had returned. From that moment onwards, Niall had been as good as damned.

Ailsa ran towards the extravagant bed carved from driftwood

that overhung the water. A willow leaned out across the bed, branches hanging in a swaying curtain, the leaves touching the lake surface like graceful fingers. As she approached, Ailsa could see the Unseelie hadn't carved the driftwood like a ship's prow as she'd initially thought, but like great arching neck of a horse, the mane flowing downward to the water. Without hesitation, she parted the willow curtain, surprising the lovers within.

The Unseelie prince gave a shrieked hiss of outrage, needle teeth bared and his pale, frost-rimed skin glittering in the moonlight. Ailsa ignored him, turning her attention to Niall. Her friend stared at her with dumb confusion, a frown on his face that took far too long to clear.

"Ailsa?" he asked, uncertain.

"Niall. I need you to come with me. You need to get away from here."

"But I just got here," he protested. "I just met this gorgeous man. Why would I leave?"

"That is Robin Goodfellow. A trickster and liar, Niall. Please tell me you ate nothing from this platter. Drank nothing from the goblet."

Niall's frown deepened as he struggled to remember.

"You are too late, witch," Robin hissed, long slender hands pinning Niall's unprotesting chest to the bed. "This one is mine."

"He's my friend. I'll take him home."

"But does he want to leave?" Robin asked, head cocked to the side with a gleeful smile. "Do you think he will choose you, witch? Or will he choose me? Shall we ask him?"

"Stop playing games," Ailsa snarled, anger rising as her blood burned in her veins.

Robin titled his head the other way, watching her with malicious delight and a sliver of fear. "I know you're from the cursed O'Hanlon line. I wasn't told you held such power."

Ailsa clenched her fists, knuckles white and rage flaring words against her lips. She could curse this Unseelie prince, the one that went by many names. She could curse as many of his names as she could remember. True, the curse was less effective if she didn't know his true name, but an uncanny being like Robin Goodfellow had lore enough that most of his names had become like truth.

"Release Niall or I will curse you."

Robin's dark eyes glittered with the challenge. "Will you, witch? Will you try your magic against my blood? I know the Bean-nighe found you, I know—as you do—you won't leave these lands alive tonight. Would you risk the eternity of peace for Niall? Risk the care I might offer or deny him? Would you risk it all by angering me now?"

Ailsa bit her lip, glancing hopelessly to Niall, who only gazed at Robin Goodfellow with unsettling devotion. Enthralled, it didn't matter if Niall couldn't recall drinking or eating anything here. The look on his face was proof enough that memories were already stripped from him and becoming more irretrievable the longer he spent in the presence of the Unseelie Court.

The water of the loch sloshed in the fraught silence. Ailsa dropped her gaze to the support of the massive bed, cold water lapping against the shoulder of the carved horse. Stepping backward, Ailsa shrieked in alarm as a man's dark hair broke the surface of the loch, his broad shoulders emerging as he stood, water streaming down his bare chest.

Staggering away more quickly, trying to escape the uncanny creature, Ailsa's boot slipped on the tacky mud of the shore. Instinctively, she reached her arms outwards, desperate to find purchase on anything to stop her from falling into the frigid waters of the loch. Her scrabbling hands clutched at the slimy grip of the waterhorse, lake weeds still entangled around his fingers. Realising her mistake, Ailsa tried to wrench her hands away, but the waterhorse held firm. His deep black eyes were wide set, his dark hair long and ringleted like the being depicted in the driftwood bed. Steadying Ailsa, he tightened his grip on her hands, the burning pain of winter's bite freezing their skin together, making any separation of the two impossible. The waterhorse smiled, baring the bright white of his too-large horse's teeth, and just visible beyond them, others capable of ripping and shearing flesh.

"Niall!"

Alisa screamed as the waterhorse dragged her into the loch.

She half-turned toward Niall, willing whatever curse Robin Good-fellow had woven around her dearest friend to shatter like ice from a fence railing. But her oldest friend just frowned at her distress, as though struggling to recall why he should care about her fate.

"Niall!"

The waterhorse was immensely strong, and hip-deep in the cold, dark water, Ailsa knew she'd lost Niall, and that she was going to die. Her friend's attention had already returned to the Unseelie prince. How long until she lost her footing on the muddy bottom of the loch? How long until the waterhorse would drag her under the surface? How long until the bite of those razor-like teeth shredded her flesh, her blood blossoming into the loch?

She slipped, the waterhorse tugging her towards him. Ailsa slammed into his broad chest, felt the scrape of those blunt front teeth against her neck. Struggling, she found purchase on the soft, silty floor of the loch once more. Breathing in a lungful of air, knowing somehow this would be her last, Ailsa half-turned away from the waterhorse and looked back at the shore, the Unseelie prince watching with mild amusement, Niall staring blankly from the bed.

"By starlight and frost-rime,
By all the lore, that is true.
By these lands denied me,
By the loch and my blood bound,
I curse you Robin Goodfellow by all the names
you are known."

On the edge of the loch, a howl of rage broke from the Unseelie prince. Ailsa had a moment to smile in satisfaction before the waterhorse wrapped one muscular arm around her waist, pulling her beneath the water. She kicked, fought and scratched, tearing fingernails from her body. Briefly, she broke the surface, looked desperately to the lakeshore. But the Unseelie Court had vanished into the Otherworld that protected them from her curse. Niall sat in numb shock on the carved bed. Ailsa willed him to run, to escape these lands before the waterhorse came for him, too. Guilt drenched her like the waters of the loch. She'd brought Niall here. She knew the lands were cursed. Now Niall was cursed, and Ailsa too. Three curses bound them together. Then the waterhorse's powerful arms tightened around her, squeezing the air from her lungs and plunging her into the loch.

'Three Curses was inspired by Gaelic folklore and legends from Scotland and Wales, and the reimagining of bargains and curses between the Sidhe and mortals and the Gaelic lore about never drinking or eating anything offered by the Fae. I was also interested in representing character diversity within a fantasy context.

The Black Hare

They feared the black hare living in the wild tangle of the woods. Whispers of curses and witchcraft, devilry and forbidden magic swirled about him like a power of its own. In terror of such an uncanny creature in their midst, the community sought to end him. Try as they might, he evaded all their traps, the hunting dogs and men with guns. But they were right to fear him: he was an uncanny being. For when they hunted him, none suspected their quarry walked beside them in human guise, watching and waiting until he could have his revenge.

My inspiration for 'The Black Hare' came from the folklore surrounding hares in British and Celtic folklore. Hares were often shape-shifters, tricksters, and sometimes the Fae or witches took the form of a hare. I was inspired by the hare folklore and especially the darker aspect of Celtic lore was behind my reimagining that delves into these themes.

A Handful of Dead Leaves

The man hurried along the dark road. Oak trees clustered close, overhanging branches trying to block his path. He quickened his pace, casting furtive glances behind him at the shifting shadows. All knew the stories told at hearthside—warnings about the Fair Folk, the dangers of the woods after dark. But the harvests were poor, work not plentiful. He had no choice.

Suddenly, the wind gusted spiralling leaves along the road. He pulled the thin felt coat tighter about his body, stuffing mitten-clad hands deeper into his pockets. Behind him, a twig snapped. He stopped, chest heaving with fearful gasps. Faint laughter echoed through the woods. He crossed himself, whispering a prayer. A fox barked from the nearby meadows. On the horizon, the sun was setting. He scanned the forest with wild eyes, shadows writhing among the oak trees.

He bolted down the road like a spooked horse.

Around him, the woods erupted in a cacophony of squawking, screeching cries. But still he ran, fleeing the wildwoods and that faint, awful laughter of the fae. The oaks above his head shifted and groaned in the wind, branches bending, scratching at him. He darted and twisted, trying to avoid their twiggy grasp. Then he heard the clattering hooves on the road. Fear slid down his spine and settled in his stomach. The headless rider of the Sidhe, the Dullahan, darker than midnight, bringer of destruction and madness. Run, for surely your life depends upon it.

He darted off the road and into the undergrowth. All knew the Dullahan never left the roads. He would be safe here until the spectre passed. He tore his coat free from the clinging branches, staring at the village lights just beyond the hawthorns. A faint track twisted through the bracken, away from the road and reaching oak trees.

He fled along the path, his breath hanging in frozen clouds before him. Leaping over lichen-covered logs and skirting mossy boulders, he focused on the village lights beyond the forest. Branches slapped at his face; fear still curdled in his veins, muddling his wits. He tripped, falling to his knees in a clearing. Sitting on his heels, chest heaving like bellows, he stared around him, noticing the large, irregular stones that marked the circle.

"A fine evening to you, Connor O'Malley."

The man jerked, staring in shock at a diminutive figure on a fallen log — a fae he swore had not been there a moment before.

"How do you know my name?"

"I know many things about you, Connor," he said, lighting his tiny pipe. He stared at the plume of blue smoke drifting upward into the night sky. Finally, he smiled maliciously. "I know you labour long in the fields for others, yet cannot provide for your lovely new wife. I know this winter will be a hard one. And I know you fear for Catherine and your unborn son."

"This is devilry," he protested. "The wee folk are stories to frighten children."

"And yet," the little man said, spreading his hands in a helpless gesture, "here I am. Am I the devil? You're no child and yet you fear me."

"I know better than to treat with your kind."

"I'm sure you do," the fae agreed, bright eyes sharp. "But you wouldn't make a bargain with me, would you?"

He shook his head.

The little man smiled cruelly. "Surely you do not wish your Catherine to suffer in this coming winter? To watch your newborn son starve?"

"No," Connor pleaded.

"I could make certain such a fate does not befall them. I could offer you a way to always protect Catherine from poverty, famine, and the bitter bite of winter."

Connor fidgeted, plucking at the hem of his coat sleeve. The leprechaun—for Connor was certain this hedgerow fae was one of those despised folk—ignored him, and critically inspected a large toadstool.

"The wee folk never offer favours without something in exchange," Connor said. "Tell me what you seek."

The eyes of the leprechaun brightened with malicious glee. "A mortal child for a prosperous future is all I seek from you, Connor O'Malley."

"You want me to steal a child?"

The leprechaun turned a remorseless gaze on him. "Not just any child. I want your first-born son."

Connor's breath caught in his chest. He stared incredulously at the leprechaun. "Why would I accept salvation from famine only to give you my son? What good would riches do me then?"

The little man adjusted his ill-fitting jacket. "If you and Catherine survive and prosper, you'll be blessed with other children. What is one child if you might have more?"

"Such an agreement would be madness."

The leprechaun puffed on his pipe again. "Will your Catherine still care for you when there is no coin to buy food? Or when no fire can ward against the winter chill? When she must watch her son starve? Can you live with the knowledge you could have prevented that?"

"Please don't say such things." Connor looked away from the sprite.

"Then you agree to our bargain?"

"I..." he began, staring in horror at the cruel little fae, "I have no choice but agree."

"Then our pact is made, Connor O'Malley."

The leprechaun's pronouncement echoed in the silence. Connor blinked in shock, staring at the space where the horrid fae had been, where now only the lingering odour of pungent pipe smoke remained. The little man had vanished.

Shivering, Connor turned and saw the cottage lights just beyond the hawthorn trees. He stumbled over the earthen fae mound and hurried for home, the leprechaun's vicious smirk a haunting memory.

The winter famine was as harsh as the leprechaun had promised. Connor watched with haunted eyes as the wintry nights took many lives from the village, the old and very young stolen away on the icy winds. Connor worked the fields as his fellows in the village succumbed to illness and, later, starvation. But Connor and his wife always had baskets of vegetables, bread and cheese long past when others in the village could provide for themselves. Each evening, Connor's eyes strayed to the hawthorn trees around the fae mound on the outskirts of the village, and he feared the birth of his child. But after two turnings of the seasons, Connor forgot his fear and caution of the wee folk, wondering if that night in the woods was nothing but momentary madness.

Catherine and Connor started awake. The wind blew against the house, rattling shutters, whistling through the eaves with an eerie cry. Predawn light, anaemic and grey, filtered through the open window, the lace curtains fluttering in the gusting wind. Catherine's gaze went immediately to the cradle in the room's corner; her hand clutched her breast. Dread lodged in Connor's stomach as he climbed quickly from the bed. He had expected this for so long now, and yet he was unprepared for it. He grabbed a guttering candle from the bedside and hurried to the cradle, already expecting what he would find.

At first, he thought the cradle was empty. The covers appeared undisturbed. There was no sound from his son. *They returned for their promised boon,* he thought wretchedly. Connor lifted the candle higher, revealing on the white blankets a small, knitted toy. But the thing within the cradle was not his son. A cruel mockery had been placed on the smooth white blankets: twiggy limbs bound with vine, the tiny bones of forest animals assembled to form a skeleton, bird beaks and hedgehog spines glittering in the candlelight. The woven head of bone and forest detritus rested upon the lace pillow Catherine had lovingly sewn, the protective charms decorating the hem now askew. Connor wanted to retch. Instead, he reached for the pillow, then stopped, hand shaking.

Behind him, Catherine gasped, grabbing his arm. She stood in shock; a soft keening sound escaped her mouth; her lips were drawn back in a hiss and she suffocated a wail. Carefully, Connor slid the pillow from beneath the awful mockery of a child. A small pouch lay beneath, woven from the finest furs and spiderweb. He picked it up, acorns dangling like strange decorations from the vine-woven ties. It was heavy in his hand, the unmistakable clink of coins within. Catherine gave a shuddering groan, finally collapsing to the floor, strength failing her.

Still not speaking, Connor tipped four gold coins into the palm of his hand. Disgusted, he tossed the fae pouch into the cradle but away from the woven thing within. He stared at the gold in his hand. His heart felt like a dying thing; it flailed in his chest, beat once, then seemed to stop. Had he sold his son to the Fair Folk for four gold coins? That was not enough to keep them from the beggar's hedgerow. Already the villagers suspected some eldritch dealing. How else had he and Catherine survived the winter famines, prospered when so many starved, grown wealthy enough to buy the debts and lands of their fellows? Behind him, Catherine was silently mouthing her son's name, but soon enough her grief would turn to rage. Soon enough, she would direct the blame to him.

He could not let her know the truth of what he had done. And yet, the sacrifice of their son had kept them alive. Surely she would understand that. Without the aid from the wee folk, they would have starved with the rest of the village. He would make sure she understood why he had agreed to the leprechaun's offer.

Connor knelt, grasping Catherine's arms, and lifted her up beside him.

"What have you done?" she cried over and again.

"It was to save us."

Catherine's sobs became wails, and she beat her fists against his chest. He held her, taking the blows of anger and despair. He deserved them, but he knew she would come to accept the loss of her son. Connor understood he had deceived Catherine by not telling her, but she had been complicit in her self-deceit; never once had she wondered about their good fortune and where their prosperity had come from.

Connor put the gold coins into his trouser pocket and waited for Catherine's anger to ease. When at last the pale sunlight of mid-morning streamed through the open shutters, Connor tucked his wife into the bedcovers. He hastened to the window and closed the shutters, glancing down at the cradle as he did. Despite his irrational hope, the cradle was still empty. He picked up the fae pouch, surprised to find the weight and clink of gold returned to it. Frowning, he upended the contents. Another four coins rolled lazily across the floorboards. Connor's hands shook with something akin to excitement as he took the coins in his pocket, stacking them on the floor beside the cradle. He stared at them and then at the other four coins scattered across the floorboards.

"I hope one day you will understand the sacrifice made," Connor said to the unmoving form of his wife huddled in the bed.

When Catherine did not speak, Connor bent to retrieve the eight gold coins, dropping them into his pocket. He glanced at the fae pouch and quickly took it before leaving the room.

"My mother used to say the sea carried away sorrows," Catherine said, looking at the drizzle falling across the mountains behind the house. "I wish we could have left these lands and moved to the seaside."

"She was right about many things." Connor grimaced. "But you know why we can't leave these lands."

Catherine turned, watching her husband frown as the waistcoat buttons strained around his belly when he shifted on the settee.

"The doctor told you to be careful of indulgences lest the gout return," she chided him.

He waved her concerns away, pushing his slightly swollen feet into the long boots and standing up. Like many things about Connor, evidence of his greed and consumption of their fortune became more obvious each day.

"When will you return?" she asked.

"Not until after midnight."

Catherine regarded her husband as he stood with one hand

on the latch of the heavy front door, top hat in his other hand.

"Stay away from the fae mound," he warned and, not waiting for her response, stepped out into the night.

"We always do," she said, the door closing on her words.

Catherine did not watch her husband leave, nor wave him farewell from the cottage steps like she might have done many years ago. She had loved him once, until that night when he returned home from the wood; fearful glances always cast towards the hawthorn trees surrounding the old mound. He had never told her of the bargain he had struck with that wretched hedgerow fae. Not a word until that morning the wee folk took their son. Since then, they'd been blessed with prosperity and wealth. Connor owned more than half the lands around the village and more than half the debts for business within the township itself. Catherine had birthed four healthy children, not a serious injury or fever among them, but the shadow of her husband's betrayal still hung about their marriage. It did not matter what gowns or gifts he showered upon her—she knew they'd bought their fortune with the leprechaun gold Connor carried on his belt, the fae pouch he would never part with. Yet when Connor was not here, Catherine often looked to the fae mound ringed by its hawthorns and felt a longing for the son she had lost.

The sudden laughter of her children drew Catherine outside into the warm night air. Her two eldest chased fireflies about the garden, their whoops of joy echoing in the silence. She sat in the wrought-iron chair, head tilted back to gaze at the night sky— the perfect starry dome above—and she frowned at a strange sensation humming through the garden like a plucked cello string.

Opening her eyes, she looked towards the hunched form of the earthen mound. There was a light moving between the hawthorns. Shepherds searching for lost sheep? She frowned, knowing the local shepherds refused to pasture their flock near the mound. They would not dare walk among the hawthorns on a Midsummer's Eve, not for an entire lost flock.

Catherine watched as a tall youth walked across the fields

towards them, lantern held high in one hand. She could only stare at the boy. He would be nearly twenty years now, but his limbs were lithe like any youth and his curling black hair the same as Connor's, but his eyes were hers.

Catherine met the blue gaze and knew her eldest son. She took the hands of her younger children, entranced by the appearance of her son all these years since the wee folk had stolen him. He did not speak at all but waited with the lantern to illuminate their passage and Catherine followed, her other children trailing behind as they stepped beyond the hawthorn trees, the wooden garden gate sighing in the breeze.

The half-moon hung low above the fields as Connor walked up the estate drive. The servants were long gone to bed and Connor stalked inside to an oddly quiet house. The fireplace had been stoked for the evening, but the rear doors onto the garden patio were wide open. Cursing Catherine's forgetfulness, Connor peered outside, noticing the children's toys discarded around the patio. Annoyance warred with dread as he surveyed the eerily silent garden. No crickets, frogs, nor night birds, only a terrible sense of absence hung about the garden. Suddenly, a breeze blew the wooden gate at the far end of the garden. It squeaked loudly in protest. Connor's heart thudded. They always kept the gate latched.

Beyond the gate were the open fields and the fae mound, hunched and partially hidden amid the hawthorns. Catherine would never go near the mound; she'd never let the children play near it. Connor turned to admire the stone cottage and the extent of his estates. Unconsciously, he reached for the fae pouch on his belt, its presence reassuring the agreement with the leprechaun was unbroken.

Connor's shaking fingers touched the soft fur of the pouch, some of the tension leaving him. He flexed his fingers, wanting to feel the familiar cold touch of gold beyond the fur. The contents of the pouch crackled loudly. He froze. Hurriedly, he pulled the vine-woven threads apart, fingers shaking so badly he fumbled with the opening of the bag.

He stared. The gold coins were gone. Mocking laughter seemed to come from the shadows surrounding the garden. Connor stared wildly around, searching for the source of the torment, but he could see no one. He felt for his pockets, hoping for the familiar touch of cold metal. His fingertips gave rise to another sharp crackle, and he withdrew his hand. The leprechaun's laughter echoed in the garden as Connor stared at his handful of dead oak leaves where once there had been gold.

'A Handful of Dead Leaves' was inspired by my interest in the unique and often jovial representation of the leprechaun in Irish symbolism. A book on the superstitions and history of leprechaun Folklore quickly informed my opinions about these mysterious beings. They were indeed tricksters of the Fae world and considered part of the Sidhe but yet did not disappear under the hills like the others, instead dwelling in hollows and hedges. I was fascinated by the attraction to gold of bargains between leprechauns and those who were misfortunate enough to make deals with them. There were very dark superstitions around leprechauns and stealing children only to replace them with a changeling. This was a delve into the darker side of leprechaun folklore and superstition within the Irish Gaelic realm of Sidhe lore.

The Hobgoblin's Lament

We are the quiet ones, the unseen and unheard guardians of hearth and home. We ask little in return for the labours we perform, the small tasks for many of your folk, but ones we consider of utmost importance. Of what do we whisper in the fading light? We speak of ageless bargains, agreements between our kind and your folk. For these are not your lands and those we once honoured have long since departed for halls beneath the hollow hills. We cannot follow there—those places are beyond this world are not for our kind.

You call us hobgoblins, sprites and many other names that belittle us in your eyes. But your folk still make the bargains with us. For as much as you curse us, there is always milk and a little bread left beside the hearth and front door. None will risk a hobgoblin's wrath. For it is we who keep your rafters *mended, stockings darned, prevent the milk from souring and the bread from burning.*

It's night and all households are abed. Only my gleaming eyes in the darkness betray my presence. Skulking from the shadows, I step into the circle of light cast by the hearth. Someone has stoked the fire low for the night, coals glowing beneath charred logs. I stop, head cocked, to listen. But there is only snoring from the crofter and his wife in the other room. Creeping closer to the fire, I stretch my thin arms towards the warmth, mismatched fingerless gloves not hiding my elongated fingers. I crouch there, enjoying the quiet, my solitude, for the moment. Our kind have always savoured the present.

But what's this? The jug of milk is missing. I glance around the room, search the stonework surrounding the hearth, but there is no offering. *No offering!* I hiss in annoyance, curse the household for its wanton neglect. Our kind ask so little for our ministrations. *No more!* The bargain broken, I'll not tend the hearth nor clean the pots; no mended clothing nor unspoiled milk. We *are* the quiet ones, hobgoblins and mischief makers if it suits us. Let this household rue the night they offended me.

The inspiration for 'The Hobgoblin's Lament' came from the Celtic folklore of the hobgoblins who were Fae beings that were encouraged in households because they maintained the house and the domestic domains providing they were compensated with offerings from the mortals who inhabited the house.

The Bull of Heaven

I woke to the trill of a blackbird. Weak sunlight struggled to push through dense cloud cover and the morning air was crisp. My dog lifted his head from the bed, opening a bleary eye to glare reproachfully toward the window. Lance was a rescue dog, the mystery of his canine parentage reflected in his disproportionately long ears and wiry brindle coat. The blackbird called again, and Lance sighed, jumped from the bed, and trotted purposefully toward the back door. My yard was mostly wild and overgrown except for a small, paved courtyard where Lance and the blackbird had an ongoing war over territory. Sighing with resignation, I climbed from the warm bedcovers.

My bare feet scuffed across the chill slate tiles of the kitchen. Quickly I opened the sliding glass door, letting Lance into the yard before I turned away from the cold morning air, and flicked the switch on the coffee machine. While waiting for the coffee to brew, I twisted my long blond hair into a loose bun. I halted, catching sight of my reflection in the window glass. I barely recognised the thin woman dressed in yesterday's wrinkled clothing. I thought for a moment about how my husband had never understood my obsession with detail, my compulsion for orderliness. *He would not recognise you either*, I thought. The memory of his death hit me again like a blow. Turning away from my reflection and painful memories, I focused on my tasks for the day.

I poured a cup of coffee, inhaling the familiar, inviting aroma. I decided I would try taming part of the overgrown garden, a section extending beyond the confines of the small courtyard. I had recently moved to this small rural Australian village, several hundred kilometres from the nearest major city. This town was old, originally constructed at the crossroads of two intersecting thoroughfares between major capital cities. But with the passage of time, new roads bypassed this once-vital artery and now the hamlet was almost empty. Nature had already reclaimed what humans had constructed. In the decades this house had stood empty, the garden seemed somehow wilder than the surrounding forests, the vines easily consuming garden walls and veranda alike. If I were to make a new life in this place, I needed to tame the garden.

I finished my coffee and rolled up my sleeves, ignoring the pulse of guilt that I had slept in yesterday's clothes. *None of that matters*, I told myself. *None of it matters when he is dead.* Gritting my teeth, I strode into the courtyard, sunlight piercing the morning fog, and started clearing the ground in the garden where I would construct a new stone wall. Sitting on my heels, I manoeuvred the hand-trowel, mechanically scraping away detritus from the long-abandoned garden beds. Beside me, a pile of broken roofing tiles, fragments of charred timber and broken terracotta pots grew. Behind me, Lance bounded around the yard while I wiped the back of my dirt-smeared hand across my forehead. Midday was approaching and already the warmth of the day seemed to leach back into the cold earth.

Winter clouds scudded across the brilliant blue sky, and a breeze rattled bare branches like sabres. Shivering, I scraped away another section of dark soil, revealing a sand-stained shard of pottery. The incongruous light-coloured clay fragment drew my attention, and I peered closer at the shard, amazed at how none of the surrounding moist soil clung to the pottery fragment, none of the surrounding moist soil clung to the uneven texture of the clay surface. I smoothed a finger across the pottery, revealing some carved inscriptions. The palm-sized piece fitted neatly in my hand and was smooth on the sides, as though time had caressed the sharpness from the edges.

I stood up; trowel forgotten beside the garden bed. Walking carefully to the small garden table, I cradled the pottery fragment in my hands. Squinting at the inscriptions, I realised they appeared deliberate, markings covering every available surface. It was not a pattern, or if it was, I did not recognise it. I leaned back on the wrought-iron chair, eyes closed, face tilted up to the midday sky. An inexplicable knowledge coalesced that this pottery was old, and, equally strange was the certainty that if I lifted it closer, I would hear the hissing of desert winds.

A voice whispered close behind me. "Release the bull of heaven."

I stared at the inscription, gaze unfocused, and frowned. I shook my head, half-twisting to stare at the space behind my left shoulder. Did I imagine a voice? Had it been real? I shivered at the implications of hallucinating, but more fearful still was the unwanted intrusion into my usually orderly mind.

Lance whined beside me, breaking the fugue of strangeness that engulfed me. I shook my head, then stood so abruptly I nearly knocked the chair to the paving stones. Without hesitation, I moved inside the house, still holding the odd clay fragment in my hands. Although I walked purposefully, I could not ignore the uncomfortable awareness of a presence behind me.

Once in the kitchen, I placed the pottery fragment on the countertop. The clink of the clay against the hard surface seemed to echo in the quiet house. My hand trembled as I reached for my phone. There was something I could not explain about the pottery, the inscriptions and the texture of the clay itself, that jarred against reality. After uploading the photo I had taken, I searched for similar images online. Although I wanted to justify my instinct that this was some ancient and unusual pottery fragment, I equally wanted the comforting confirmation that my thoughts were ludicrous. Surely, I was just being over-imaginative?

Less than a few brief seconds later, I had the answers I sought. I stared at the screen, the rows of many small images, each showing a pottery piece similar to the one I had found. I scrolled through the images with growing consternation. If I had hoped for clarification and some closure, this did not achieve it. Many of the images contained brief descriptions, with the same word repeated throughout. The pottery pieces were cuneiform tablets, all related to museum collections. *What on earth is cuneiform?* I frowned, reaching across the counter for my laptop. I needed to expand my search and find out what cuneiform was, whether it was as ancient as my instinct warned me it was. Most of all, I wanted to understand how a cuneiform tablet became buried in my garden.

The answers provided by an online search seemed improbable. Every article explained that cuneiform script was an ancient proto-writing system that had developed in the Near East over six thousand years ago. My frown deepened as I considered the implications. How did cuneiform tablets become buried in my garden? Australia was a long way from the ancient empires of Iraq. Was the tablet in my yard evidence from some illegal trading or forgery attempts? I shook my head slowly at my rational attempts to explain an impossible event.

I continued to read, realisation dawning on how unlikely my discovery had been. Cuneiform was the common writing system between the ancient Sumerian kingdoms and Babylon, Assyria and Persia. Again, I felt a keen awareness of a presence behind me. Half-turning from the kitchen counter, I was almost expecting someone to be standing a foot behind me. There was no one. I shivered, returning my attention to the search results. *It's an impossibility*, I reminded myself. *You've never studied ancient texts; you've never even travelled to Iraq. Cuneiform tablets simply don't just appear from thin air. This is madness.*

Although it was ridiculous to think the pottery I had found was a genuine cuneiform tablet, I continued to learn the fascinating history of these small palm-sized records made by ancient cultures several millennia ago and half a world away.

Daylight faded outside and as afternoon stretched into twilight, I continued to read. Even as I considered quitting this strange obsession to learn more, my gaze fell on the title of a poem and it flared in my consciousness as though some brilliant beacon: *The Epic of Gilgamesh*, an ancient poem detailing the struggle between a Sumerian king and the powerful gods. The awareness behind me grew suddenly stronger, transforming from a presence to a prickling on my skin, as though long fingers danced across my back. I slapped at my shoulder, certain it was just a spider or another insect. My hands found no insect, but the prickling worsened, now feeling as if a chill breath touched the back of my neck. I wanted to move, to flee, but I glanced warily behind me, certain someone was leaning close to me, almost touching my left shoulder. Again, there was no one.

"Get a grip," I muttered, trying to enforce calmness and rationality.

I returned my attention to the computer screen. They recorded *The Epic of Gilgamesh* in cuneiform, inscribed on similar palm-sized clay tablets as the one I had found. It told the deeds of the heroic Sumerian king Gilgamesh and how he overcame philosophical dilemmas during his battles against the ancient gods. I paused, suddenly unsure of what had seemed so important to me about *The Epic of Gilgamesh*. I shook my head slightly and refocused on the page. One phrase seemed to illuminate amid the surrounding lines of text: the Bull of Heaven. Perspiration broke out across my skin and my heartbeat quickened. I had heard those words whispered to me in the garden. I had not imagined the hissing voice, and now that same phrase was written here. *What was the Bull of Heaven?* Whatever was happening to me, it didn't seem like some mental breakdown or an odd delusion. This was more than that, a coincidence on a higher level, I could not deny. I inhaled slowly and opened the link to another document, determined to learn whatever I could about the Bull of Heaven.

According to the myth, Gilgamesh angers the goddess Ishtar, who sends the destructive Bull of Heaven to extract her vengeance. Gilgamesh, however, slays the mythical bull and dismembers it, casting the hindquarters into the sky to form the constellation Taurus.

A strong but inexplicable fear and precognition shivered through me. I stopped reading, titling my head and straining my hearing. I thought I had heard a faint chuckle. Now there was only the silence of the evening and the distant ticking of a clock. I shrugged, returning my attention to the screen.

Before long, I discovered another account of the Gilgamesh story, a much older version where Ishtar has another, more ancient name: Inanna. The goddess Inanna is the daughter of the sun and moon deities and, in vengeance for an unknown offence, Inanna sent the Bull of Heaven against Gilgamesh. In this poem, the Bull of Heaven is more than a mythic beast to be slain by a heroic king. Inanna has a much darker nature. The goddess of bounty is also the goddess of famine and when she unleashed the Bull of Heaven upon the world, it wrought her h vengeance in starvation, fire, and destruction., Gilgamesh slays the Bull of Heaven and prevents the destruction Inanna sought.

I finished reading, an icy fear settling over me as I stared at several depictions of the Bull of Heaven, the muscular form carved into stone on temple walls, inscribed into gold and silver, shaped into tiny statues and icons. In every representation, the bull is a formidable beast with horns lowered to charge, one hoof raised in challenge.

After dinner, I walked outside into the shadowed garden, following the meandering step-stone path. I halted and exhaled, my breath an icy cloud in the night. I tilted my face upward, staring at the bare winter branches silhouetted against the night sky. I searched the starry dome, seeking the constellation of Taurus, following the path of the Milky Way, noticing the brighter points of significant stars, which were still nameless and unfamiliar to me. The night sky was as peaceful as always, and that familiar sensation seemed to absorb the dislocation threatening to engulf me. I smiled in the darkness, fascinated by the shimmer of stardust along the Milky Way, and I felt complete again as I had not been since my husband's death.

When the cold became too much for even the most determined stargazer, I hurried back toward the house, hands stuffed into the pockets of my old dressing gown. I paused at the glass door, smiling back at the night, and reached for the door handle. Perhaps it was because I wasn't paying attention, but my fingers slipped on the handle, falling instead to the empty earth of the window-box beside the door. The window-box was devoid of plants this early in winter and yet my fingertips touched a textured surface that was not soil. I held myself still, heart pounding as I moved my fingers along the now familiar clay surface, exploring the inscriptions that covered the uneven shape of the clay tablet.

"Bring forth Inanna's vengeance. Let the world be reborn,"

a voice hissed behind me, tone like shifting sand against stone.

I shivered violently, fear rising and drenching me in sudden perspiration. I fled inside, my traitorous fingers grasping the clay tablet in a reaction I could not explain.

Once inside, I pushed myself back to the kitchen counter, breathing quickly, staring in surprise at the tablet I held. Incomprehension consumed me as I stared from the cuneiform tablet in my hands to the one on the countertop. Wordless sobs tore from me and I slowly sunk to the kitchen floor. I cradled my head in my hands, trying to stifle the sounds breaking unbidden from my throat. Lance whined uncertainly from the doorway and approached, tail wagging as he climbed into my lap. The reality of the madness engulfing me seemed stark, and I could no longer hide from it.

I woke in the early hours, slumped awkwardly on the kitchen floor. Morning was just a blush across the eastern horizon, barely a smudge against the darkness of night. Lance was still curled in my lap, but I was bitterly cold. I uncurled my cramped limbs, urging Lance to get up so I could climb stiffly to my feet. I stole a quick glance at the two cuneiform tablets on the kitchen countertop before hastening toward the bedroom, hoping for the oblivion of sleep.

Chilled and frightened as I stepped into my bedroom, filled with the horrible sensation that someone followed behind me. I halted near my bed, staring at the empty expanse, the space my husband used to occupy that would be vacant forever. I shivered in the cold predawn air and took a desperate step toward the bed.

My bare toes touched an object, half hidden beneath the overhang of my bed covers. I sucked in a breath with a hiss. I wanted to recoil, to flee. This could not be another clay tablet. My world seemed to spin around me, the future balanced precariously on my next action. I slid my foot back and saw the now familiar cuneiform script on the surface of the pottery. I stared in disbelief and felt the future shift toward a decisive moment. The constant presence behind me coalesced.

"With Inanna's vengeance slaked, all will grow anew from ashes and bones," the awful voice whispered, breath tickling my ear.

"Go away," I shouted, slapping ridiculously at my ears as if that could somehow silence the voice.

"You don't truly want me to leave," the voice mocked.

"What are you?" I demanded, aware it lingered behind me and half-expecting if I turned around, it would be visible in the doorway.

"I have many names," it hissed. "We're known as jinn or demons, but we are neither."

"What do you want then?" I pleaded.

"What you desire most of all," the thing crooned.

My anguish was a sound that seemed to shatter the room, slivers of me spinning in every direction, reflecting images of my face contorted with terror, fingers raking at my cheeks.

I ran into the sunroom, knees finally buckling, dropping to the floor. Lance skidded to a halt beside me, hackles raised as he stared at the space near the wall-sized window at the northern end of the room. I looked too, but could discern nothing other than my reflection. I stared at my pale face smeared with tears and gave a sharp cry of frustration, scrubbing roughly at my cheeks, trying to enforce some composure. The awful panic that had taken hold seemed to subside, and I sat back on my heels, looking out the northern window as dawn light broke through the morning clouds. I sensed through some precognitive awareness that this was the last dawn I would ever see. The dense cloud mass was already spreading like a blight across the sky, and soon not even the bright morning sunlight would stop it. Alongside that awful realisation came a sense of claustrophobia, as though the air itself pressed upon me, as if it were a tangible, heavy weight.

"Release the bull of heaven." The jinn urged me again.

"Shut up!" I shouted into the silence, turning to face the empty room behind me.

The jinn only laughed, a deep horrible sound that reverberated through the room and sent tremors shuddering through me. I cried nonsensical objections, promised impossible threats, but that taunting voice continued to ripple with laughter. When finally my terror peaked, I scooted backward across the floor, slamming my right shoulder hard into the window ledge. I cried out in pain, echoed by a sharp clatter from behind me that sent another wave of uncontrollable trembling through my body. I turned my head slowly, expecting to see the jinn from the periphery of my vision. *There will be nothing there*, I told myself. There wasn't—like all the times before. I slumped forward in exhaustion, relief rolling through me as I bent my head to my knees. That's when I noticed the fourth cuneiform tablet. It must have fallen when I hit the window ledge. I watched as though from outside myself as my fingers reached for the clay fragment. I lifted it, turning it over in my hand, marvelling at the unnatural heaviness of the small tablet.

"With Inanna's cry, the bull will stamp the earth to dust and vengeance will be claimed in her name," the jinn pronounced with dreadful certainty.

Time passed, or perhaps it no longer existed. I sat in the shadows of the sunroom, cuneiform tablet gripped in my hands as a storm descended on the afternoon, the last of the sunlight cutting thin slivers through the black clouds. The room was suffocating, the sense of anticipation seeming to crush the oxygen from the air itself. I struggled to breathe, fought to master my panic that an unavoidable calamity was approaching. The rooms seemed too small, the temperature was stifling and outside, the sky was too dark. The storm had not broken but seemed to wait, tense and patient, swollen with unleashed rage. The jinn was a menacing presence filling my small house, taunts and cries flushed with exultation.

"Inanna?" I called, uncertain but pleading into the growing shadow of the storm.

The jinn halted its rapturous cries and listened, silence falling heavily around me.

"Inanna?" I called firmly, heart beating loudly as I lifted my face to the gloom outside my window. "Inanna!" I shouted, calling on the name of the goddess again, this time an invocation.

"Do you know who you seek, mortal child?" the jinn asked in a hushed whisper.

"Please stop this," I begged, burying my face in my hand, leaning heavily against the window frame.

"Ah," the jinn cooed. "Only Inanna can grant you that release you seek."

"Tell me how," I sobbed, clutching at my hair as though pulling it from my scalp would stop this madness.

Across the room, Lance growled and stood, legs apart with short hackles raised, but did not approach, just stared at the emptiness behind me. Again, I desperately wanted to twist away. I felt the icy prickle of fingertips brush on my cheek and I might have frozen beneath that touch.

"Only you hold the power to grant Inanna's wish," the jinn said. "In granting her wish, it will return your desire."

"How?" I sobbed again, wanting to move away from the horrible being that seemed to be lurking behind me. I forced myself to hold firm, to ignore the bitter breath that burned like fire on the back of my neck. I barely repressed a shudder as, around me, the pressure of the storm increased and with it, a throbbing pain blossomed in my skull.

"You know what to do," the jinn said.

My eyes focused on the cuneiform tablet beside my foot. I did not let myself think, but focused my attention on the uneven edges of the pottery shard. Suddenly, I could see where it had broken from a whole, where the other fragments had once fitted around it.

"Does it make a poem?" I asked, picking up the tablet. "Does it tell a story like Gilgamesh?"

The jinn howled in rage, the noise reverberating through the house like metal screeching against stone. I clutched at my ears, trying to lessen the noise, but it seemed to tear the air to shreds around it.

"Not a story of destruction like Gilgamesh," the jinn snarled.

"But it tells a story?" I asked, dizziness engulfing me as my vision spun.

"Yes," the jinn replied. "The false hero Gilgamesh is long buried beneath the sands of time, but these foreign lands have never known the stamp of a Bull. It is Inanna's greatest wish to remind humanity of where their faith belongs."

I tried to consider the jinn's words, but the pain inside my skull climbed to a crescendo, the throbbing of my eardrums nearly deafening. Yet still I heard the rasping voice of the jinn behind me.

"Work quickly, mortal child," it advised.

I moved as swiftly as I could, my legs trembling as I gripped the clay tablet, blood dripping from my nostrils. I ran into the kitchen, quickly rearranging the clay fragments, guided by an unfathomable intuition. When finished, I stared at the arranged fragments, the centre still a dark and yawning void.

Hastily, I wiped away more droplets of blood falling onto the countertop, carefully manoeuvring the last piece of pottery into place. The final fragment was the most recent, the one that had fallen from the window ledge in the sunroom. I stared at it, noticing that, unlike the other tablets, this one contained no cuneiform inscriptions but depicted the Bull of Heaven—horns lowered, muscular body tensed, and one hoof raised to crush an enemy beneath it.

I didn't allow myself time to think. I ignored the pain in my fingers as the sharp edges of the clay sliced my skin. I moved with near reverence, carefully lowering the final fragment into place, the uneven margins smoothing away to reveal the tablet, whole and complete as though it had never broken.

The pressure in the atmosphere dropped, the storm grew quiet and silence descended. I could hear nothing since the jinn screamed at me. Now, in confusion, I turned to survey the windows of the sunroom. I looked down in bewilderment at the stain across my shirt, the blood still trickling from my nose. I lifted my eyes again to the windows and, with a quickening of my heart, I walked towards them.

Outside, the massive storm clouds now swarmed across the sky, turning in a slow spiral, edged with flame.

"What have I done?" I whispered.

"What you desired," the jinn chuckled with apparent glee.

"Just tell me what I did!" I shouted.

The silence crackled, paused, before a roar of thunder split the sky. The wind burst into a gale, hurling debris and leaves across my garden, increasing with a strength that shook the large windows of the sunroom. Cautiously, I stepped back from the glass panes, expecting them to shatter from the onslaught. Lance whined piteously from my bedroom doorway; ears flat as he glared at me. No, I realised: not at me, but behind me.

"Inanna granted you the release you sought," the jinn expl-ained. "And in doing so, you released the Bull of Heaven."

"But what does that mean?" I roared against the tempest outside.

"Didn't you understand the summoning?" the jinn mocked. "The bull will bring these lands into subservience."

I remembered the poem from the cuneiform tablets and all the jinn had instilled to me and the recitation spilled from my lips:

"Bring forth Inanna's vengeance and let the world be reborn. For only when Inanna's vengeance is slaked will all grow anew from ashes and bones. With Inanna's cry, the bull will stamp the earth to dust and vengeance be claimed in her name. Release the bull of heaven."

"Exactly," the jinn said jovially. "The foolish mortals of these lands sought to challenge the might of the gods. Millennia may have passed, child, but this is the briefest of moments for the gods. Inanna now takes her vengeance for the defiance of mortal men."

I blinked in dumb confusion. "Inanna is punishing us now for the actions of Gilgamesh?" I asked. "Those actions committed thousands of years ago?"

"Yes," the jinn snapped with irritation. "Inanna does not discriminate between her children. You may think you acted apart from them but his punishment befalls you all."

"How did I do this?" I asked, gesturing to the flame-touched sky, ash now falling from the clouds like rain.

"How else?" the jinn asked. "If Gilgamesh was only one man who committed an injustice, why would it matter if one mortal restores the balance and delivers justice?"

"Justice?" I croaked, staring in horror at the fiery sky outside.

"To gods like Inanna, this is justice," the jinn explained. "It should not bother you, mortal. For now, you are free."

I stared in bitter wonder at the destruction I had unleashed. "Free from what?"

"From me," the jinn chuckled.

I turned then, noticing a sudden spray of sparks behind me.

Dark tendrils of smoke spiralled upward, evaporating almost as quickly as the half-visible form of the grinning jinn, simply vanished. I felt the sudden departure of the jinn as though oxygen was pulled from the air. I lurched forward, clutching the window frame for support. I pressed my face to the glass, unable to stand as my legs weakened. I leaned on the window frame for support, forcing myself to witness Inanna's merciless vengeance borne from my own actions.

I stood mute, a soundless scream caught in my throat as dark clouds edged with lightning coalesced into the massive form of a bull. I tasted bile as the Bull of Heaven lowered wicked horns crafted from lightning. The beast stamped a hoof, molten rain showering down on the earth below, birthing wildfires and flushing the sky an angry red. Tears left ashen tracks down my face as the Bull of Heaven moved across the sky and, where it briefly touched the earth, decimation lay in its wake. After moments that could have been eons, the Bull of Heaven raised its massive head and bellowed a challenge like thunder, hoof stamping and sending more fiery tornadoes across the barren earth below. A hollow silence echoed from the land around me and with a toss of its muscular head, I watched as Inanna slaked her vengeance and the bull retreated.

For a long time I stood there, clutching the window frame of my small house, the landscape surrounding me now a wasteland of burnt forest and charred rock. Clouds of black smoke blew across the window, hiding the barren lands beyond. I did not think anyone could have survived the devastation I had unwittingly unleashed, but I had to save anyone I could. I staggered to my door and with one glance knew Inanna's vengeance for the destruction it was, for wherever the Bull of Heaven had stood, only ash and embers remained.

'The Bull of Heaven' was inspired by Mesopotamian legends and pre-Islamic lore of the powerful jinn. I was fascinated by a dystopian theme where the protagonist is the unwitting driver behind destruction. The trickster aspects of the jinn, the unlikely discovery of cuneiform tablets with a hidden summoning for the Mesopotamian goddess Inanna and the Bull of Heaven that is fought by Gilgamesh in the legends from *The Epic of Gilgamesh*. The improbable combination of ancient Mesopotamian artefacts, the tormenting Jinn compound the grief and instability of the protagonist which was part of the theme in 'The Bull of Heaven'.

The Selkie Twins

The coast was pebbly, sea-foam thick along the rocky shore. The girl walked with purpose, though she had no true destination. Out to sea, the storm was a grey mass of cloud and flickering lightning. She loved the beach before a storm. The ocean heaved with the oncoming tempest, white-capped waves cresting above the swell. She opened her arms to embrace the wildness of it. There was a freedom here, away from prying eyes and judging minds. She loved her family, but they didn't understand her; could never understand her. Her twin brother Liam had understood, but had left her. Twelve years since the shipwreck and the ocean stole him from her.

Liam had loved the ocean too, and it had taken his life. But she was a girl, unable to join a crew, unable to even work for herself. There might be talk of women's rights, but Seána wouldn't see any of it. She gazed out to the horizon, imaging setting foot aboard a vessel, feeling the waves beneath her feet. Here, she'd get scolded just for lifting her petticoats high enough to walk in the water.

The wind gusted, teasing her hair free from its bonds. She clutched at her kerchief, but the wind was insistent, snarling at her red locks until the kerchief blew free. Seána watched the piece of cloth tossed backward against the cliffs. It caught on a rocky crag, snagged and flapping in the gale like a flag.

Seána turned her attention back to the storm. She barely noticed the seal skin on the shore. Half tripping over it, Seána stumbled and caught herself. Frowning, she turned back to the unusual find.

A selkie? Those were old tales, whispered, half-jokes but still believed.

"Seána?"

She turned at the sound of the voice. A man stood a few paces behind her. She blushed at his nakedness, but then studied his face.

"Liam?"

"It is you," he said, smiling.

"How? I thought we'd lost you. The ship went down with all souls on board, we were told."

He nodded, red curls like her own falling across his eyes. "It did."

"Then…how?"

"There's a secret to our blood, Seána. I know you feel it like I always did. The pull of the ocean."

"The selkie? That's an old wives' tale, more fancy than truth."

Liam held out his hand. "Come with me."

Seána hesitated, looking at the outstretched hand of the brother she had lost. Was this witchery? A cruel joke by Liam? No. He'd never been one for cruelty and there seemed no harm in taking her brother's hand.

"What're you showing me?"

"The freedom you've always wanted."

Liam led her to the water, picking up the discarded seal skin as he did. Seána followed a half-step behind, uncertain and scared. *What is happening? Is this really her brother, or a Fae conjuring? What if I walk into the water and drown? Will that be so terrible? What future did I have but working in the mill, marrying a man I don't care for and bearing children I don't want?* That wasn't the life she'd dreamed of since she was young. Her grip tightened on Liam's hand.

They stepped into the freezing water. Waves lapped at their ankles, the tide strong and current pulling away from the cove.

"Take off some of those garments," Liam said.

Her cheeks reddened, and she spluttered, "What?"

"You'll get tangled up in all those layers. Trust me, Seána."

"Tangled up? What're you trying to say, Liam?"

He sighed, sealskin over one arm. "I can't speak the truth

without breaking the bonds of the magic. I need you to just trust me."

Concerned, but trusting her older brother as she always had, Seána obeyed. She took the shawl from her shoulders and passed it to Liam, then turned to ask him for aid with buttons of her dress. She didn't wear a corset, not like the fine ladies in Aberdeen, thank goodness, and her station in life meant she did more manual labour than a corset could allow. Still, it was difficult to dress herself when the buttons were along her spine. Shaking with uncertainty, she dragged her petticoats free and let her discarded boots drag along the ocean floor.

"Come," Liam said.

And, seeing the determination and the love in his eyes, Seána followed without hesitation. He was her brother again, the roguish smile and dimpled cheeks. All the girls in the village had fawned over him, but he'd chosen the sea instead. And now, Seána would too.

They walked deeper into the swell, Seána struggling for purchase underfoot until finally she clung to Liam's shoulder. But the water was getting deeper, the shoreline dropping away. Liam patted her hand and slid the sealskin from his other arm, draping it about his shoulders.

"You need to do this part alone now."

Liam released her, shaking off her grip as Seána struggled towards him. Her head was barely above the water, the waves dunking her again and again. Gasping for air, Seána watched her brother dive beneath the waves and disappear from her view. The weight of her sodden dress was pulling her down and, glad as she was to have left the petticoats behind, she was still sinking. *Where is Liam? Why has he left me?* Looking around her, Seána saw only sky and ocean. *I'm going to drown. Why would Liam do this to me?*

She felt movement around her in the water. She struggled, searching the water's surface for the source. Nothing. She could see nothing. Then, again, something brushed her legs. A selkie. She thought, forcing her mind to focus. A seal. Liam's seal skin… *Do I understand now? Below: I needed to go below the surface too.*

Seána stopped fighting the ocean. She looked to the storm beyond the headlands, lightning and purple-black clouds. The grey swell of the ocean and the white-capped waves. *Down… Let go. This is where I belong.* And she sank, not struggling, not fighting the need for air in her lungs. Below the surface of the water was a swirling mass of sand and seashells. Grit stung her eyes, and the salt water burned her lungs.

The seal approached her with effortless ease, parting the swell to glide to her side. The liquid brown eyes watched her, and she reached out, touching the whiskered muzzle, running her hands along the smooth flanks. A sharp pain spiked through her like she'd cut her hand on a knife. She looked down, her hand transforming, lengthening, splaying as a delicate membrane filled the space between her fingers. Her body convulsed, the transformation pulling her mind into another place, a realm of murky shadows.

When the pain subsided, Seána was near the ocean floor, her body wrapped in the dress. She felt disoriented and strange, and unable to move within the tight bindings of her dress, she panicked. She thrashed about in the water, turning herself over and again, seeing only ocean floor and water above.

Another approached, cautiously brushing a whiskered muzzle against her own. Liam. That was Liam. And she was… different. *I'd been drowning, but now I'm transformed. Seal. I was now like Liam once I'd stopped fighting the sea. This is where I belong.* Seána stopped struggling and slid free from the dress. All around her was the undulating bottom of the sea floor, the current pulling out toward the headlands and the seashells rolling with the tide. It was beautiful in these watery depths. But Seána swam slowly, her flippers still strange and unwieldy to her. Liam cavorted easily around her, his joy at being reunited with her overwhelming them both.

The pull of the sea was intoxicating, and Seána revelled in it. After a clumsy attempt, she followed Liam from the cove. The longer she was in the water, the less the waves and the current proved a challenge to her. They were the same, she and Liam. They always had been. Their mother had joked about her twins being like two little peas in a pod, but it was more than that. The bond shared between the twins was one of the sea, salt water, and ocean tides. And now Seána would follow Liam into the heritage they shared. The bonds of selkie clans must surely be stronger than what had tied her to the land. For their father had disappeared, left while they were still in swaddling clothes, and never returned. *Will I find him now?* It didn't matter. A father who had never truly held a fascination for Seána. She needed only Liam and the sea. And now she had both again.

The selkie folklore that forms the inspiration for 'The Selkie Twins' is part of the exploration of Scottish lore and the close ties between the landscape and the people. 'The Selkie Twins' reimagined those bonds between sea and land; the conflict between choosing one over the other is a common theme in reimagining of selkie legends.

Them

The detective sipped from a coffee mug, grimacing as he swallowed. He frowned, staring into the cup as though genuinely mystified by the contents within. Shaking his head, he tipped the tepid liquid down his throat in a single gulp as though it were cheap whiskey. The grimace twisted into a rictus and he shuddered. Still frowning at the cup, now fortunately empty of the awful-tasting coffee, he picked up a plain manilla folder from the stained folding table in front of him. A stack of glossy, high-resolution photographs and several handwritten pages of notes protruded from the edge of the folder.

Leaning against the opposite wall, invisible even under the fluorescent lights, a gaunt stranger watched the detective, inhaling the air like a predator. As the stranger pushed off the wall, the detective flinched, aware of his presence, even if the corridor appeared empty. The spectre, dressed in a surcoat encrusted with dried blood, pressed closer to the tall detective, silently enjoying the increasing unease that shifted through the man who, glancing around himself, could see no one. Still, there was an imperceptible step back from the stranger, the man's pupils dilating with fear. Grinning with malicious satisfaction, the gaunt figure was drawn to the manilla folder the detective had abandoned on the faux-wooden table with its coffee mug. Several photographs enticed the long fingers to stroke them, images revealing bright splashes of scarlet and the memory of violence, unrestrained rage.

The detective strode back toward the table and the invisible figure. The grey suit he wore had probably fitted a more muscular frame once, but now hung unevenly on his wasted body. This was a man who knew the cruelties humanity inflicted on its own kind. His features were haggard, bearing razor nicks from too many hurried shaves, and his eyes sunken hollows from too many sleepless hours.

"You ready, Pete?" a voice interrupted.

The detective startled, hand falling to where the weapon on his hip would normally rest. But they'd all securely locked their guns in the firearm safe downstairs. On seeing his partner, Pete immediately relaxed, lifting his hand to his chest, feigning a heart attack and folding forward, the universal gesture of surprise and relief. His partner smiled in greeting, but exhaustion haunted him too. He looked older than his years, and this testified to his habit of, caffeine and. His blue eyes slid to the manilla folder open on the table behind his partner, and his shoulders visibly slumped beneath the weight.

The gaunt figure standing beside the table focused intently on the second detective, but remained invisible to both men.

"Good morning, Jon," Pete said with a weary smile.

"It's never a 'good morning' when that creepy little twerp is here," his partner said.

"There's something wrong with him."

"Astute observation," Jon teased, saluting with his takeaway coffee.

"Was it the eight brutal murders or the insane gibberish that gave you that idea?"

"You know what I mean," Pete insisted.

"Yeah, I reckon I do. You had enough sleep for this?"

"Not since we got this case."

"Me neither."

Both men hesitated, eyes meeting over the manilla folder with its gruesome portfolio of crime scene photographs. Those horrific images haunted both men almost as thoroughly as their suspect, a young man who had inflicted such rage against complete strangers for no reason anyone could fathom.

"Still want to do this?" Pete asked.

Jon grimaced and shuffled the photographs inside the folder, gulped the last of his takeaway coffee and tossed the cup into the garbage bin. The paper cup rattled against the inside of the metal bin. Both men started in surprise, the noise echoing in the quiet police station. Trying to calm their frayed nerves, they straightened their suits and continued down the corridor toward the interrogation room, where their suspect and his attorney were waiting.

Pete and Jon walked past the two-way mirror station, wanting to observe their suspect before entering. The skinny kid sat with bony shoulders slumped, elbows on the table, one foot tapping to an unheard beat. Responsible for a murder spree that had terrified the city for two hours, he looked like any common street junkie: bad teeth, thin, sallow skin and hollow eyes. His attorney sat as far from him as she could get, her body language signalling fear and unease.

"Let's just leave it today. Go to the pub instead?" Jon suggested, grinning but oddly intent.

"Tempting," Pete agreed, but kept watching their suspect. "Thomas is supposed to be heavily medicated. Should I ring the psychiatric facility?"

"Let's just get this done with," Jon sighed. He sounded resigned as he reached for the doorknob.

Pete hesitated in the doorway, watching Jon greet the attorney and settle himself at the interview table. Thomas's attention was on Jon, keenly watching Jon and his lawyer outline the interrogation parameters. Pete wondered how, with the cocktail of anti-psychotics and sedatives Thomas was supposed to be taking for his persistent delusions, he still seemed a threat. He entered the room and shut the door firmly, metal locks snapping into place. It offered no comfort; the danger was in here with them.

"Detective," Thomas greeted, smiling too-widely, pupils so dilated his entire eye seemed black.

Pete grunted in reply. He felt Thomas's gaze roam over him, an oily residue left in its wake. He felt nauseous again, the revolting coffee sloshing in his gut.

"Let's get this done with, Ms Greenberg," Jon said, continuing his conversation with the attorney.

Pete fought to keep his breakfast down, sweat staining his skin with a sour-smelling reek as he stared at Thomas. This kid was the reason he would never sleep soundly again, the reason eight innocents would never return home.

"State your name for the record," Jon requested, glaring at the kid.

"Thomas Matthew Carmichael," he enunciated clearly to the recorder, arms folded neatly on the table.

"Thomas," Jon continued, forcing a smile. "Do you know why you're here?"

He arched an eyebrow in mild annoyance, remaining silent.

Jon glowered, then frowned, a faint ripple in the shadows of the far corner.

"You mean, do I understand I'm accused of killing a bunch of strangers?" Thomas finally asked, languid smile barely concealing his veiled aggression.

Jon stared into the shadowy corner; the darkness seemed to shudder with Thomas's words. Glancing sideways, Jon didn't think Pete had noticed anything, but he could have sworn there was something, *someone*, standing in those shadows.

"You're implying you didn't commit these crimes?" Pete asked, interrupting a hushed monologue from the lawyer.

"I didn't kill anyone. I've told you before. It was *Them*," Thomas said, leaning back in his chair.

"Ah, of course," Pete said, feigning sudden recollection. "Demons haunt you."

"Is this seriously what your client is arguing?" Pete asked incredulously, brows raised as he stared at the lawyer. "The 'devil made me do it' defence?"

"*Devils*," Thomas corrected smugly. "Plural, remember?"

Pete sighed in frustration, running his hand through his hair. He caught movement in the periphery of his vision and froze. Hand still raised to his temples, heart racing, he looked up towards the two-way mirror on the wall opposite. Again, faint movement just behind him. He looked deliberately at his own nervous reflection and then at the space behind him and Jon. It was empty.

"Tell us about these devils then," Pete said, ignoring the rising hairs on the back of his neck. "How're they responsible for your crimes?"

"*Alleged* crimes," Thomas reminded him, grinning.

"Of course," Jon said, unsmiling, rolling his eyes. He shifted forward, elbows on the table, suddenly feeling as though someone was standing just behind him. Rolling his shoulders with exaggerated effort, he glanced behind him. A figure was there, a tall man in a medieval surcoat stained by old blood and gore. As Jon stared, the long pale face twisted with a cruel smile, black eyes fathomless. Jon blinked in panic, but the phantom was gone.

"Do these devils have names?" Pete asked, frowning at his partner.

"Of course they do," Thomas replied, a knowing smile quirking his lips.

"What're these names then?" Jon demanded, conscious of movement on the periphery of his vision.

"Ever heard of *The Lesser Key of Solomon*?"

"Does it have anything to do with why you brutally murdered eight strangers?" Pete asked, sighing. "Ms Greenberg, I suggest you advise your client to stop wasting our time."

"*The Lesser Key of Solomon* was a grimoire written in the seventeenth century," Thomas offered, ignoring his attorney. "Although not written by King Solomon as it purports, it lists the seventy-two of demons King Solomon bound, then imprisoned. Since its discovery by the Babylonians and release of the demons, men have sought to bind them again."

"Let me guess: these seventy-two demons are responsible for the murders, not you?" Pete asked.

"Not all seventy-two, that'd be preposterous," Thomas snorted.

"Obviously. Which of these seventy-two are haunting you?" Jon interrupted.

Pete sat back in his chair; folding his arms over his chest and sighed with satisfaction. Thomas looked uneasy. Whatever Jon had just inadvertently touched on was a chink in the armour, a weakness they could use to prise the truth forth. "You've seen them too?" Thomas whispered, licking his lips.

"The tall one in chain mail," Jon agreed easily.

Pete quickly glanced at his partner, but there was no sign of where this new avenue of enquiry was taking him. Ms Greenberg looked equally surprised, straightening in her chair, a slight frown creasing her tailored eyebrows.

"Abaddon," Thomas clarified. "He's the warmonger, executioner."

Pete glanced again at the two-way mirror, thinking the shadows were too dark there. He shivered despite himself. Movement in that shadow flickered again. Pete noticed Ms Greenberg stiffen in her chair.

Staring directly at the shadows, Pete steadily made out the features of a slender, well-dressed man who surely had not been present moments before. The demon stepped forward, elegant long hands resting on the attorney's shoulders, a teasing smile as if he and Pete had shared a confidence. The demon leaned forward, face just inches from Ms Greenberg's throat. She sat rigidly still, every instinct warning her of danger. Desperately wanting to lunge across the table and push the man away from Ms Greenberg, Pete remained in shocked silence, aware Jon had not reacted to the stranger. The demon leaned closer, inhaled deeply at Ms Greenberg's throat, eyelids fluttering with undisguised lust. Pete ground his teeth, watching the demon sink beside the woman's chair, one arm possessively about her shoulders. Pete struggled to contain his outrage; the intimacy of the display perverted by her unwilling participation.

"Who is the handsome one?" Pete asked.

"Among the demons?" Thomas chuckled. "That's Belial. Be careful tangling with him; he's known for beauty and treachery both; it's Belial that Man invokes when summoning Satan."

Pete watched the handsome demon whispering to Ms Greenberg, whatever he was saying too low to be overheard. The blank, slightly wistful expression on the young woman's face made Pete uneasy. Turning instead to regard Jon, Pete was conscious his partner now watched him with the same intense concern he had shown only moments earlier.

"I'm aware of the irony, Jon," Pete murmured.

Jon nodded, and with unexpected violence, thumped his fist on the table, making Thomas and Pete jerk in surprise. "Tell us about these," he shouted, flipping open the manilla folder, partially revealing the grisly tableau of crime scene photos within.

Thomas stared at those photographs as if caught in a dream. Reverently, he reached out, a fingertip tentatively stroking the surface of one glossy digital print, and smiled. Pete inhaled, and fighting the rising nausea, slid the photographs across the table. As expected, Thomas practically pounced on the offering, sorting through the images which Jon and Pete had deliberately jumbled, changing the sequence of crimes, locations, and victims that had occurred during the several hours-long murder spree. It scarcely took more than a few minutes for Thomas to arrange the photographs into a near-perfect chronology, his memory retaining an unimaginable recollection of the horrors he had inflicted. Ms Greenberg remained motionless and mute beside Thomas, unresisting as the demon Belial whispered in her ear and casually stroked her cheek like a lover.

"Where's the last one?" Thomas demanded, hands spread protectively across the photographs.

Jon repressed a smile, scooping up a handful of crime scene images he had stacked on the grimy floor. From the corner of his eye, he watched the demon, Abaddon, step closer to his chair, now standing between him and Pete. Refusing to be intimidated, Jon tossed the photographs to Thomas, who greedily snatched at them. In seconds, they covered the surface of the large table, high-resolution photographs with every image marred by red stains, smears, splatters, or pools of blood. Thomas exhaled a little shakily and leaned back in his chair like an artist surveying a masterpiece. Pete swallowed roughly and gave a brief nod of acknowledgement to his partner.

"You've got an astonishing memory," Jon said, forcing flattery from his lips when Pete knew how revolted his partner truly felt.

"It's always been my gift," Thomas replied, transfixed by the violent memories preserved before him.

"It's unfortunate you're just like any sadist, though," Pete interrupted.

"If it wasn't for your weakness, the plea for insanity might have been successful. But you're like any addict. You couldn't help yourself. You *needed* to see your complete work."

"It *was* perfect," Thomas hissed. "You can't just show pieces of it or it won't work."

"What won't work?" Pete asked, fear creeping through his veins.

"You don't know, do you?" Thomas asked, smiling slyly. "You knew I wasn't some crazed, rabid killer. But I'm not the only one whose fatal flaw is arrogance."

"Why kill those people?" Pete shouted, stabbing a forefinger at the photographs.

"It was a summoning," Thomas chuckled. "When I started this spree, as you have so delightfully called it, there were only two demons at my side. The third, Aeshma, Lord of Wrath, required a summoning of blood and death in equal measures before he might walk this earth again."

"You evil, crazy little fuck," Jon snarled, standing up so quickly his chair slammed into the wall behind them.

"Aeshma?" Pete asked, dread covering him with clammy sweat as he glanced around the small room.

"You've both seen Belial and Abaddon now. Wherever Aeshma walks, violence spreads like a pestilence."

Suddenly, the overhead lights fizzled, plunging the room into darkness. The only illumination came from the fading afternoon light. Outside the interrogation room, beyond the corridor, security alarms wailed piteously.

"I told you there was something wrong about him," Jon shouted from the doorway.

Pete turned toward the doorway and squinted at the silhouette of his partner standing there, gun drawn. The gun that should have been downstairs with his own in the firearms' safe. Without comment, Pete raised his hands in the air, in a gesture of submission and compliance. Still, Jon took several shaky steps forward, a shadowy bulk lurking behind him. Pete stared beyond his partner to that shadow warrior, the demon, Aeshma, clad in black armour, face hidden by a helm, sickly red glow emanating from the eye slits. Trembling, Pete stared at the bloody mace gripped loosely in the gauntleted fist.

"I told you to leave the creep alone," Jon continued, still advancing stiffly. "Why couldn't you leave well enough alone, Pete?"

Pete stared at his partner, all wild eyes and rictus smile. Slowly, Pete reached toward Jon, hoping to find his partner, his friend, but Aeshma's fist was gripped hard on Jon's shoulder. The gun roared, echoing in the small interrogation room.

Pete fell, gasping, to the ground, blood already pooling around him. He could not move, knew the bullet had gone deep, blood rapidly choking him. Shocked, he stared at the young lawyer, still sitting at the table, his blood splattered across her pale face. But Ms Greenberg seemed completely unaware of anything around her. Jon blocked the doorway, writhing and screaming as the three demons converged on him, insanity finally consuming him. Pete forced himself to look away, unable to watch. Instead, he stared at the skinny kid they had arrested. He should have listened to Jon. God, how he should have listened.

'Them' is a dark reimagining of Demonology and the legendary Book of Solomon, a fraudulent document written in the seventeenth century detailing the names of the demonic lords of Hell. I was inspired by the concept of demonic possession and the lore behind demonic presence influencing behaviour. 'Them' is a modern crime dark fiction exploring the realms of demonic influence and the legends of demonic lords being enslaved and controlled by King Solomon.

Pan's Dance

Music echoed through the thickets, and the youth stopped on the path. He'd walked too late beneath the shady branches. The moon was barely a silvery glow in the night sky, but the shepherds had already settled their flocks for the night. He wouldn't follow the music. He wouldn't leave the track. The music called again, sweet as a lover's kiss and with as much promise. The god Pan danced tonight, skipping through groves beneath the moonlight. The trilling pipes beckoned. He hesitated, his resistance failing.

Overcome with music and madness, he stepped from the path and followed Pan's dance.

'Pan's Dance' was inspired by Ancient Greek mythology and the forest god Pan who was influential in leading mortals astray in the groves and mountains. There is a legend of madness associated with Pan and those who join his dance will follow his music in endless dances through the forests.

The Monsters We Become

I needed to find my daughter. *Just focus on finding Ayla. Nothing else matters*, I thought. The wind howled in a furious voice, cursing me for my foolishness. Cursing me for trying to cross the permafrost. This was *Inuit Nunangat*, the homelands of the Inuit, a world of ice, snow, and frigid water. I was a stranger here. I was not Inuit. *These are not my lands. Who am I to tread here?* I staggered forward, single-minded focus on the horizon. *Just find Ayla.* I could scarcely see through the blizzard. The mountain peaks in the distance resembled broken teeth jutting from the permafrost, and it made me feel more afraid. *How long since she left the house? How long since I last saw her?* Heart pounding in my chest, panic biting at my heels like a wolf, I kept running into the storm.

The storm beat against me, hissed its outrage in any icy voice. *How long until he comes after me?* A quick glance behind me, and fresh fear pumped through my veins. I stumbled, boots sliding on the frozen ground, and nearly fell. Arms wheeling in the air, I found purchase again in the fresh snow. I stopped, heaving in a mouthful of cold air. I was so tired. I felt like the cold would seep into my bones, freeze the marrow into gory crystals. *If I die out here, who will find Ayala?*

"It'll be okay, sweetheart," I said, as though she were beside me, could hear me.

A mother was supposed to protect her children. But I had failed Ayala. I had failed my daughter and now she was alone out here. Alone and in danger. Paul was right. I was not a good mother. He was always quick to remind me, quick with his fists too. I had been angry when he took the job in such remote territory, moving me away from Toronto, from everything I knew, taking me to *Inuit Nunangat,* to these inhospitable lands that did not want me. But then Ayala had been born, and she embodied every hope I had ever had. I hoped too that the Paul I had married might return to me once more. Instead, I'd only felt the sting of his disappointment. His shame at my weakness, my inability to measure up to his expectations of a wife. I longed for the man I had loved, but the Paul who kept me at home with only a small child for company was like a stranger to me. Surrounded by ice and snow, it seemed his heart and mine had frozen as well. Those dark glances he gave me whispered threats to do better today, or he'd take Ayala from me. My daughter, the only light and warmth of bitter days. I promised him I would do better, would be whatever he wanted me to be, if only he would promise not to take Ayala away from me.

The keys to the snowmobile were missing this morning, and I realised Paul had taken them to work with him. *If I had the snowmobile, I could find her.* But it was a useless hope. All I had left of Ayala now were her small footsteps rapidly disappearing beneath falling snow. *You've only yourself to blame.* And that sneering thought in my mind was right: I had not listened to her. She had insisted someone was calling her name, someone outside in the storm. The next thing I knew, she'd gone, just footsteps in a blizzard.

The permafrost surrounding me was a haze of undulating ground and swirling snow. I pushed forward, leaning into the strength of the north wind as it whipped and tore at me. I could not feel my feet inside the boots, my steps becoming more exaggerated as I trudged through ankle-deep snow. I stumbled, numb feet curling beneath me, cold snow soaking my pants. The cold was piercing, jolting my heart into a staccato rhythm. Dully, I realised the blizzard had stopped. The heavy silence snapped me from my fugue, and I listened. The storm seemed to loom, and I huddled against the ground like prey waiting for the jaws of some predator to close about my throat.

Panting with ragged gasps, I hauled myself upright, breath hanging like frozen plumes before me. *Where is the trail I'm following? How have I got so disoriented?* Frantically, I searched the ground, looking for any signs of Ayla's footsteps. Sobs broke from my lips. I could not have lost her. *Where is the trail? Oh God, help me, where is Ayla?* Crawling on my hands and knees, I wiped snow from the icy crust, hoping beyond reason to find small footprints beneath. But there was nothing, just more ice. Only more ice and snow around me for miles.

Sitting on my heels, I turned my face to the grey clouds. An eerie silence stretched around me. I heard the faintest of cries. Soft and pleading. *Ayala.* My heart felt as though it had been torn open with a knife. *Thank you, God, she's alive.* Dizzy with relief, and pulse thready, I staggered forward on my numb feet again, chasing across the permafrost after an echo.

A gust of wind slapped at me, ice crystals peppering the exposed skin of my face and stinging like hundreds of tiny blades. Wincing, I closed my eyelids to slits, squinting through the snowstorm to the ridge ahead of me. *Is someone there? Are they moving towards me?*

"Ayala!" My voice was a raw and broken thing.

Snowflakes swirled haphazardly around me in lazy spirals. In the unexpected calm, I saw a tiny figure ahead of me. Screaming Ayala's name, I ran towards her, but she did not answer, nor even stir. A terrible foreboding slowed my steps. Everything about the kneeling figure was wrong. The Inuit had legends of the *taqriaqsuit,* or "shadow-people", beings who dwelt on lands separated from ours by a thin veil that was jealously guarded.

Voices rose from the surrounding permafrost, some barely audible at first, more like whispers heard from a distance, others were like shouts drifting on the wind. The kneeling person in front of me never moved, though through a white haze of snow, I caught glimpses of other half-seen figures. Despite my thick parka, I felt stripped bare, my skin and nerves exposed to the air. The half-forms of the *taqriaqsuit* circled me, voices echoing from different directions, shouts and laughter, questions and cries. Panicking, I ran from the maddening cacophony and the swirling snow.

Blindly, I stumbled heedless of the snowdrifts, careening down the steep slope, until my boots slapped against solid ground. I stopped, pivoting to survey my surroundings. Back the way I had come, I could see the crest of a rise, the undulating permafrost stretching beyond to be swallowed by the blizzard. Ahead of me were densely forested mountain slopes, pine and spruce dusted in snow. Below me, a wide, flat swathe cut through the valley and, tapping the toe of my boot against the ground, I heard the *click* of solid ice beneath me. A frozen river lay beneath the scant covering of fresh snow. *Where am I? Where is Ayala?*

"Ayala!"

My voice echoed back at me in mocking heartbreak from the mountains. Grief and shame dragged at me like weights threatening to pull me under. I had failed my daughter. I hugged my abdomen, remembering how she had once been a tiny spark of life growing within me. Exhaustion surrounded me, darkness at the periphery of my vision, like a wolf pack circling wounded prey. I could forestall the inevitable no longer. I dropped to my knees, all my strength spent. Hopelessness and despair leeched the life from me as efficiently as the cold. Shivering against the snow and ice, I pulled my knees up to my chest. *I will die out here and never know what becomes of Ayala.* I tried to open my eyes, but icicles had already formed on my eyelashes, a chill weight against my cold skin.

I slept. Or perhaps I only drifted into the depths of unconsciousness, my body refusing to surrender life just yet. The blizzard was a distant howl, a hissing beast of ice and fury. I ignored it, holding to a distant thread of hope that I may still find Ayala. Somewhere in that liminal place between life and death, I heard the plaintive cries of a child. My child. I jerked upright, forcing my eyes open, crusted ice shattering against my cheeks. Looking frantically along the frozen river, I saw a vague shape bobbing against the white. *Is that a child?* The pale pink parka seemed to move closer to me as though following the curve of the riverbank. *Not following the riverbank, she's following the river.*

"No. Don't cross!" I yelled.

But seeing me, she came towards me.

In horror, I watched the sheet-ice break, saw her plummet into the dark water visible through a long crack that ran several hundred metres down the middle of the river. In the eerie silence, I could hear the child's pleas as the current carried her, dragged her beneath, then thrust her to the water's surface again.

I got to my feet. Numbness had crippled me, and I could barely stand, my legs threatening to buckle beneath me. I watched the child a moment longer, then certain this was no trickery by the *taqriaqsuit*, I ran after my daughter. My heart raced in a wild panic as Ayala struggled against the river's current.

"Mommy's coming, sweetheart!"

My feet slid the last few metres to the jagged edge of the ice. Falling to my knees, I thrust my hand towards her. My fingertips brushed against hers. I felt her try to grab hold of me before the current dragged her under the water again. I lurched forward, dunking my arm to the shoulder into the water, and heedless of the frigid cold, felt around for her. *Where has she gone? Why hasn't she surfaced again?* Swirling my hand in the dark depths, I brushed something. *Clothing?* Hands numb with cold; I dug my fingernails into it as hard as I could.

Pain lanced up through my arm. Shock, sharp and terrible, overwhelmed me and I screamed as my blood filled the water, spreading through the ice, turning the riverbank crimson. In reflex, I pulled my hand from the water, a deep cut slicing my flesh from bicep to palm, severing two fingers and cutting the tendons to the bone. My arm hung uselessly from the elbow. I stared uncomprehendingly at the fatal wound.

In the middle of the river, a black head bobbed to the surface. I stared as a woman turned to face me, her skin ice-blue and her black hair slick like waterweed. She opened her mouth and hissed at me, revealing sharp fangs like those of a seal. I stared dumbly, cradling my ruined arm as my lifeblood pumped into the surrounding snow. The woman reached beneath the water's surface and dragged a sodden bundle towards her. My daughter, my Ayala, hung limply in that elongated, webbed hand. Roused to my senses by the sight of my daughter's body, I dragged myself forward using my uninjured arm, leaving a bloody trail behind me. Dizzy with shock and blood loss, I was desperate to reach Ayla. From the water, the woman hissed another warning at me, holding Ayala's corpse to her chest like she was the most precious thing to her and not her victim. Then, without another sound, she dived beneath the ice, taking my daughter's body with her.

I screamed, my voice raw with grief and rage, and bitter with self-hatred. Darkness lurked at the edge of my vision, and shadow-beings clamoured for attention, my sight fading even as I tried to ward them off. Blood spread outward on the ice in an ever-expanding circle around me. Death slunk closer, but I bent all my rage on the woman in the water, one of those creatures the Inuit legends warned against, the *qallupilluit*, monstrous women from the icy depths who stole away unwary children for their own. of those creatures from Inuit legends a *qallupilluit* had taken my daughter.

Consciousness returned in a haze of impossibility and shock. I looked up at the night sky, the aurora borealis shimmering and dancing like a multi-hued ribbon of light. Yet I felt no wonder, only an absence. Smeared blood stretched from the sheet-ice to the riverbank. *What has happened to me? Where is Ayala?* My memory snagged like a fishing line on a submerged tree root, and I frowned. Struggling upright to a seated position; I hunched my shoulders against the frigid wind. And just like that, memories returned with a sudden slap. The sharp-toothed *qallupilluit* in the icy water, the sight of my unmoving daughter, held a like a bundle in those long, webbed hands. My arm, the pain, my blood.

I stared in horror at my right arm where the *qallupilluit* had struck me, remembering those long claws parting flesh to the bone. A thin, silver scar ran the length of my right arm. The flesh had healed, no sign of the fatal wound remained. But that was not what drew my attention and sent fear trickling through my veins. Pale blue scales covered my arm where once there had been skin. Worse horrors revealed themselves as I forced myself to concentrate. My uninjured hands were now elongated, the fingers joined by a sheer, membranous tissue and each finger tipped with a curved, black talon. I looked at my other arm with the same disbelief, inspecting the scales and webbed digits, caught between a mounting terror and certainty in my insanity. *What has happened to me?*

Frantically, I searched around me for anything that might wake me from this nightmare. I recognised only the frozen river. Then I frowned. When I lost consciousness, I had been at the edge of the broken ice. But I had woken on the riverbank, not where the attack had occurred. Focusing on the bloodstained ice, I noticed a darker red had soaked through the fissures in the glacier, rusty with the colour of old blood. My body had made a smear across the surface of the ice, a much brighter shade of red where I had hauled myself from the water's edge to where I now sat. Where had the older blood come from, then? I looked beyond the river to the permafrost as though the answers I sought might appear.

I straightened and rested my back against a half-submerged tree; the solitary willow had been caught mid-fall into the river, the deep freeze of winter trapping it there. Now its bare branches hung down over the ice; the tips crystallised with hoar frost. Scanning the frozen waterway, I could no longer see where the broken ice had been, where I had last seen Ayala in the monster's grip. Hauling myself up onto the bowed trunk of the willow, I surveyed the river and its surrounds. And there, near to where I now stood, the scarred river ice was just visible, its surface thickened into uneven ridges as it had frozen.

Something about the poorly mended river ice reminded me of my own scarred body and I looked at the tough mass of bluish-grey scales that now covered every inch of my skin. Now that I was standing upright, I could see these horrible scales through the tattered remnants of the clothes I still wore. The shreds of my jacket and pants hung from my limbs like the vestiges of who I had been, and now were a reminder of what I had been. Angrily, I tore the fragments of clothing from myself, hissing in voiceless outrage at the monster I had become. I crawled towards the water's edge, determined to look upon the truth of my transformed horror.

Contempt filled me and looking at my feet, the bones so awfully transformed and elongated, the deformation as sickening to see as my hands, I glared with fury at the thick webbing which now stretched between each toe. Stumbling into an awkward gait, I made it to the edge of the river and collapsed to my knees. A weird keening escaped my lips, the sound so foreign to my ears, and at first, I did not recognise it as coming from my throat at all. Haltingly, I leaned across the water, determined to see the truth reflected there with my own eyes, yet frightened of the implications.

The blue-grey scales that covered my limbs and body had replaced my skin entirely, my face covered in smaller, more delicate versions of the same scales. The transformation of my bones was not only in my elongated limbs but the width of my cheekbones— and now wide-set eyes of blackest night stared back at me. Even my once-blonde hair was now dark as waterweed. I parted my thin lips, opening my too-wide mouth and saw the finely pointed, serrated teeth of a predator. There was no trace left of the woman I had been, and this face might have belonged to a stranger; except I remembered a similar face, another who had looked like me—the *qallupilluit* who had stolen my daughter from me. And now, just like Ayala, all that remained of who I had been was a memory.

The transformation to a *qallupilluit* may have saved my life, prevented my body from bleeding out beside the frozen river, but this shift had been more than just one from skin to scales. Again, I looked at those thick, blue-grey scales; like a toughened hide, they covered my breasts and ribs, the muscle and flesh now taunt, no longer feminine, and the once-familiar curves of my hips had narrowed, a shape more suitable for cutting through water than for ever bearing another child. I splayed my webbed fingers over the flat abdomen where once Ayla had been a spark of life, nestled and nurtured within me. But now she was gone. *Is m my daughter now bones cleaned white by fish in a watery grave?*

Immobilised by the horror of these dark thoughts, imagining Ayala's tiny body nothing but bone and empty eye sockets, the orbits staring up at me through thawing water, I crouched on the riverbank, staring into the water as though I could see her skeleton on the stony river bottom. Human voices carried on the wind, so faint that I nearly did not hear them. I jerked my head up, searching the length of the river and the permafrost wastelands beyond. Nothing. But there had been voices, I was nearly certain of it. Doubt niggled at me, certainly with memories returning of shadowy half-forms, the haunting *taqriaqsuit* and my desperate attempts to escape the swirling cacophony of their voices. Those shadows owed love and loyalty to none in this realm; and they had delighted in taunting me, had delayed my efforts to find Ayala. If I had been faster, if the *taqriaqsuit* had not turned me around in my tracks, I might have reached Ayala before the *qallupilluit* could snatch her from me. I glowered at the permafrost, wondering if the cries I had heard were real or just the worrisome wishes of a mother who had lost her only child.

A feeble cry, much softer than the others had been, and so quickly silenced by the icy winds. A child's voice. There was a child out there alone, distressed and calling for help. Had it really been Ayala's body the *qallupilluit* had clutched to her chest? *In the confusion of blood loss, had I been mistaken? Does Ayala still live?* The distraught cry echoed on the fingers of the gale, and I knew it was my daughter. I would recognise her voice anywhere.

Heedless of the cold water, I dived deep. The webbing between my newly elongated hands and feet propelled me quickly through the frigid waters, and the narrower hips of my body allowed me to cut through the water like a blade. Those strange, ebony eyes transformed the ice-blue water and where my sight had been murky before, everything was perfect and clear. Above me on the ice, I could hear a child sobbing, the hiccups of distress. Using the taloned nails in my hands, I punched upwards through the ice sheet, splinters of ice showering towards the leaden sky above me. Startled silence from above. But bobbing in the icy waters, I flipped the webbed feet and, using my powerful arms, hauled myself onto a narrow promontory of ice that I had made.

It was a narrow ice shelf, a segment that had originally torn free from the river and was now sundered anew. A tiny figure stood alone, waiting in stunned silence but balanced safely in the middle of the floating ice sheet, and staring at me with undisguised fear.

"Ayala."

Her name came out as a guttural hiss and I cursed the throat of a *qallupilluit*, the unsuitability and inability of it to form the correct sounds I desperately needed now. Eyeing me with caution, the little girl stepped backwards, perilously close to the edge of the ice. My heart thudded painfully and instinctively I reached for her. She paled, the sight of my taloned hands frightening her further. *Ayala. My miracle of miracles.*

"Ayala." I tried again, more harsh sounds breaking from my lips.

She trembled, staring uncertainty towards the permafrost and the blizzard beyond as though someone might rescue her. I watched her, frightened and unsure. How she must have wandered alone for days out here, how dehydrated she must be, and how it was a miracle she had survived hypothermia at all. Knowing she was just confused, the terror of being lost and alone, the trauma she'd endured and how her health had suffered; I would see her safe now. I reached for her again, hesitating briefly when I looked at the unfamiliar mittens on her hands, the blue parka she wore now instead of her pink one. *Where have these new clothes come from?? Who took such care of her but now let her wander near a river?*

"Ayala," I enunciated, having to pull my lips back from my tiny, pointed teeth to speak her name.

"I'm Ellie."

I stared at the little girl, the quavering note of uncertainty in her voice. I shook my head, dumbfounded. She'd been wandering alone too long, scared and confused. However, she had survived out here; she had made an imaginary world where she was safe.

"You must be so cold."

I had said the words so carefully and now crouched, holding my arms outstretched to embrace her. *My* lost child. She cast several hesitant glances around and then walked to me, and I enfolded her in my arms. Around us, the blizzard fell silent, fresh snow now blanketing the permafrost as the quiet of the winter descended. Gently I stroked her head, kissing her hair and, with soothing assurances, clutched her to my chest.

Still murmuring softly to this child, to *my* child, I walked to the break in the ice, my elongated feet gripping the edge, pale blue water beneath us. The little girl stirred in my arms, mumbled something from where she nestled against my chest, her words lost beneath the sound of my heart. But from the corner of my eye, where my reflection waited on the surface of the water, I nearly glimpsed the monster that she saw, the monster I'd become. I had been a terrible mother once, and I vowed I would not be so again. This time, this child would never leave my side. I would not fail her. And, still whispering softly in my strange new voice, I plunged into the frigid water, the little girl held grimly in my arms.

'The Monsters We Become' is a fictionalised reimagining inspired by Inuit and Aleut legends about the *qallupilluit* – a humanoid female that hunted and stole children to take for her own beneath the ice. This was a legend that resonated deeply with me and the concept of transformation into such a being was a fictionalised exploration of memory loss, abuse, grief and loss.

Bones and Fur

Standing from the firepit, the monster roared, spittle and gore flying.

Coyote glanced to the forest shadows. "Ready, brother?"

Hidden in the foliage, Fox nodded.

Coyote grinned. "Monster, worm-rotten, devourer of humanity."

The cannibal bared teeth sharpened to points. "Trickster."

The monster charged, slashing at Coyote. But Coyote wasn't just Trickster in name. Grabbing a coal from the firepit, he dashed it into the monster's eyes. Blinded, it howled. Coyote attacked, toppling the monster into the fire. A sharpened claw caught Coyote's hind-limb and dragged him into the roaring blaze. Attacking anew, Coyote ripped and tore at the monster, blood and viscera sizzling in the flames.

When the monster was dead, Coyote limped from the fire. Collapsing on the earth, his body was burnt and charred beyond survival.

"Fox?" Coyote whimpered.

"I'm always here, brother."

Appearing from the smoke, Fox sat beside his dying brother. He watched Coyote die, his body collapsing into bones and fur. Then he stood. He stepped over the bones, careful to tread lightly on the blackened fur. His task done, Fox sat, tail curled around his paws, waiting.

A gentle breeze, crisp like autumn air but with the faint memory of summer sunshine, brushed Fox's fur. He watched as Coyote's bones mended, the fur of his coat bronze again. This healing magic that bound the two brothers was swift. In moments, Coyote drew a shaky breath.

Fox exhaled. "Are you well, brother?"

Standing, Coyote shook the ashes from his coat. "Let's find another monster. I enjoyed that fight."

The North American First Nations tales and legends about tricksters Coyote, Fox, Hare and Raven led to my inspiration for 'Bones and Fur', which is a fictionalised reimagining of these legendary figures. I am fascinated by the ideas of transformation and trickster heroes who have very powerful personalities and are held in reverence for the lessons they teach.

Talismans

The standing stones had always terrified me, but now I could not recall why. Two men led me by my bound wrists, yet I followed, docile and unconcerned by the surrounding procession. Above the mountain ridge, the sky arched in a vast black expanse painted with stars, the autumn breeze without chill. I focused on the path ahead; the incline rising toward the mountain peaks. There, the golden moon illuminated a cluster of standing stones on the plateau between rocky crags.

Staring at the moon, the first awareness of fear roused within me. The flaring torches marked the path to where a bonfire waited in the centre of the stone circle. Fear pricked me again., poking suddenly like a needle, prickling along my spine, building with every step until my heart was thudding wildly, like unsynchronised drums, and I wanted to flee, caring nothing for the great hunter, the Horned One. I was not a sacred warrior to this dark god. I tried to turn, my limbs clumsy and slow. A mass of masked dancers pressed me, preventing my escape. Trapped, I clenched my fists, lifting them, preparing to fight. But it was folly. I was scarcely more than a child.

Strong hands caught my shoulders and arms, pinning me. Struggling against my restraints, heart pounding in a staccato rhythm, the animalised figures surrounded me, pressing closer, faces hidden by masks, bodies adorned with antlers, talons, fangs and claws. Panicked, my sight blurred as they dragged me towards the bonfire. There, trembling from exhaustion, I sagged to my knees, head hanging. I let the night air cool my sweaty skin. Desperately, I tried not to hear the invocation to the dark god, nor see the shifting figures silhouetted against the firelight.

A loud drum vibrated through the night. Jolted back to awareness, I searched the dancers in their masks and painted skin, fur capes swaying hypnotically. My chieftain stepped toward the bonfire, the great curved horn raised to his lips and, as he blew, the summons echoed through the mountains like a battle cry.

A female voice answered, clear and unwavering. The drumbeat quickened, writhing silhouettes of dancers parting to reveal the witch. Not the wizened crone they'd taught me to fear since childhood. She was young, her body lithe, movement graceful as she walked between dancers, limbs tattooed with the sigils of her craft. Dressed n a simple skirt made from the same pale buckskin as my own pants, the witch had a pelt from a white arctic fix around her shoulders which was stark in the moonlight.

She raised an ornate bronze bowl to the sky, then knelt before me, a clay bowl of smouldering herbs in her hands. Blue smoke curled around me and I stared into her dark eyes, the heady smoke relaxing. Instinctual fears became whispers as I struggled to keep my eyes open. She moved the large bronze bowl in front of me, handing the clay bowl and its intoxicating mixture to a worshipper.

I watched, mesmerised, as firelight flickered on the bronze bowl, a constellation engraved in its centre, symbolising the most ancient of the gods, the Horned One with power over life and death, over mortals and lesser gods alike. Dully, I thought about how much the sigil looked like antlers cast against a swollen moon. Fear struck me then, cold and certain. And I stared at the witch as though seeing her for the first time, her fingers slick with blood as she lay a long blade to the side. Without any words to me, she withdrew. Fresh gouts of my blood now filled that bowl, covering the sigil of the dark god.

Realisation struck me like a blow. But I was too late. My blood pulsed from my ruptured throat, the sharp pain overwhelming my other senses. I fought the bonds on my wrists, desperate to lift my hands to my throat to stem the fatal flow. *Oh gods, someone stop the bleeding. Someone help me,* I mouthed, voiceless and silent. Strength was leaving me, each furious pump of my heart bringing me closer to death.

The witch walked away, cradling the bronze vessel, its contents sloshing over the rim. Steadying herself, she lifted the bowl in upraised arms, honouring the starry sky and the hunter's moon above. Around her, the dancers parted, horned and antlered beings shifting in the firelight with predatory grace.

The grip of my silent captors weakened. I eased to the ground, my captors let me scrabble weakly against the mossy earth, blood soaking into the grass with the last of my life. The revellers continued to dance. Unheeding of my choked pleas, the shadows drew closer.

The flaring, golden light of the bonfire dimmed as the witch called an invocation. A final drumbeat echoed through the mountains, resolute, as first light pierced the eastern horizon.

In answer, my heart stuttered and stopped.

Every lore I had ever been told assured me that the dead could not linger in daylight. In the final moment of death, when spirit and body separated, I longed to evanesce like morning mist with the first touch of sunlight. But I did not. Instead, I was an incorporeal presence among the standing stones, forced to watch, voiceless and enraged, as the masked worshippers departed. I stared down at my discarded body, the chill autumn air already cooling it.

Ignoring the last of the dancers, the witch continued her whispered prayers before the bonfire, lips repeating invocations to her wretched, antlered god. Rage curdled within me, stirring a desire to punish those from my village who had offered me to the witch's magic. But without body or voice, I could do nothing but observe the witch slowly exhale. She cast furtive glances about the deserted clearing before she walked to my body with a reverence that horrified me. I understood in that moment how her magic had bound my spirit to this world, preventing the evanescence I needed to rescue me from the brutality of my death. Hatred welled within me; an intensity I had never known possible.

The witch lifted the long bronze blade she had used to cut my throat. Whispering a prayer above the blade, she turned to my corpse and her grisly task. I endured the bloody labours of her ritual, refusing to turn aside from the desecration of my flesh, as it was stripped away from my bones. Throughout the daylight hours, I listened to the solemn chanting of her invocations. My anger hardened into a weapon she could never break. She worked without rest, arms bloodied with her efforts, my body reduced to parts, to blood, sinew, muscle, and bone.

Stoking the coals of the bonfire, she encouraged embers to flame and placed the ritualised pieces of my body upon the pyre. Exhausted and dulled with a miserable ache, I watched her purify each item of my body, marking the sigils of her craft with my blood or ash, each rune a burning brand carved into my spirit. When sunset drew close and the last of the light drained from the sky, she lifted a bronze pendant into the air, inspecting her work, imbued with the power of her craft. The sigils of her binding magic were within the burnt bone, scorched hair and preserved muscle that she had fastened to the pendant.

The magic of her bindings was like rope, tying my spirit to this earth through the talisman she now hung around her neck. I stared in horror at those sigils she had carved into my burnt bone, into the talisman itself, and which were now writ across my incorporeal form.

She turned to stare at me and touched her lips to the grisly talisman she wore, before whispering a command: "Anlan."

In that single summons, she named me by my true name, that which I'd been in life, and which had greatest power over me. And I understood with contemptuous outrage the horror she had made of me. Not only had she had stolen the vitality of my life, the promise of youth, and offered it as sacrifice, she had perverted who I had been, maiming my spirit as surely as she had desecrated my body.

Rage swelled within me, awakening another power with its ignition. Something crafted, untested and wild burned within me. The powerlessness I had felt without a physical form, the helplessness and fear at my incorporeal existence, now drained away as sensation returned to me. I felt the brush of my fingertips against the long grasses as I stalked toward the witch. On the horizon, a storm responded to my anger, lightning flickering and the wind lifting in squally gusts. But the witch only smiled, a look of satisfaction and triumph on her face. I realised—too late—that my new strength and anger were something she had intended to awake within me. She intended to use me as a weapon.

"Stop, Anlan." Her command stripped my new strength.

"You made me an abomination," I hissed.

She shrugged, eyeing me critically. "Your clan sacrificed you so they might have successful harvests. But you deserve greater honour than that, Anlan. I have given it to you and the darkest god has made you one of his children. If you are an abomination, then you aren't my first."

I bit back my response, choking on my anger. I longed to strike her down, take the storm rolling toward us and pummel her beneath its fury.

"I promised the chieftain your death would save his lands," she continued.

"Did you lie to him?" I asked, trying to read her impassive face, her tattooed features half-hidden by the twilight.

"I owed a debt to another more powerful than your chieftain," she said. "I might yet pay with my life despite the offering I have given."

"I hope you're hunted until the end of your days for betraying my clan. My life was not yours to offer as a debt to your wretched god," I snarled, thunder echoing my accusation.

She seemed unconcerned, but her gaze shifted to consider the quickening thunderclouds and furious wind. "We walk towards your storm, Anlan, and your master. I would speak with reverence of the Horned God in his presence."

Without further elaboration, she shifted the pack on her back and walked west, striding into the brunt of the gale without a backward glance, my muttered curse swallowed by the storm. The further she walked from me, the more difficult it became to withstand the compulsion to follow. Closing my eyes, I refused to move. It did not help; it was as though her talisman was a lodestone. The need to follow her was a compulsion I could not deny, my resistance inflicting pain the further she was from me.

Finally, I could bear it no longer. My shoulders sagged, my will and pride collapsing, and I followed her. As though my burnt heart could feel, sorrow took me—for as long as the talisman endured, I would remain in this servitude, unable to be free.

The witch continued west. Darkness stole over the land, drowning the hills and valleys beneath the growing shadow of the storm. I did not know what other powers she might possess, but I watched her stalk the forest, her senses alert and predatory. She possessed an affinity for the night, and I wondered if her powers heightened with its touch.

The valley curved toward the south, leaving the mountains and the standing stones behind. Although we walked through dense woods, the wind carried the stench of smoke and burnt vegetation from ahead, the scent dredging up memories of fire and bloodstained blades. There was a horror carried with the smoke, a cloying, putrid scent that was more than burnt crops and razed villages. For as long as I existed, I could never forget the smell of burning human flesh and hair. The terrible scent on the wind was a portent of something far worse than my death. Whatever the witch had done, whoever she had brought into the lands of my clan, they had brought death with sword and flame.

"Who is this master you spoke of?" I demanded.

"He is not my master," she said without looking at me. "He will be yours, for I no longer pledge myself to his kind."

"What are you? Are you a sorceress or trader? You barter your own freedom with the spirits of others?"

"Be wise about how you speak to me," she warned. "I bound your spirit to my will until I give you to another."

Rage threatened to overwhelm me. I wanted vengeance for the wrongs committed against me, for the lies she had told my clan. She was a deceiver and deserved nothing but contempt. Although I now possessed a corporeal form, it was at her behest and I wondered if I could take the bronze blades she wore at her hips and spill her blood before she could speak, stripping me to spirit again. But she watched me, aware of my intent as though I had spoken it aloud. Her dark eyes narrowed, fists clenched and teeth bared in a silent challenge.

"Your clan's dead," she said. "I'm not so terrible a master. The blame for torching your village and people belongs to your new master. Seek your retribution with him, not me."

Abruptly, the surrounding forest stilled. Her words numbed my mind. As though the elements shared my pain, no breeze stirred the branches, and no insects broke the silence. Opposite me, the witch waited, alert and ready. Her eyes roamed the shadowy undergrowth. Her attention shifted from my shock to our surroundings, and she slowly flexed her fingers.

A man dressed in leather armour barrelled from the undergrowth toward her, forcing her back. A low growl broke from my lips as he shouldered his way toward me. The storm answered me, the only weapon I needed as I stalked forward to meet the attack. I had never been a warrior or hungered for violence as some of the young men did in my village. But now I desired nothing more than to obliterate my enemy.

The wind roared as the forest echoed with the groaning of ancient oak trees, bending beneath the fury of the tempest. Sudden quakes shook the ground as those massive oaks snapped, falling like saplings as they crashed to the forest floor. Above us, lightning split the night, thunder rolling in a continuous growl across the angry sky. I moved with the rage of the storm, using the force of the tempest to hurl the man before me across the ground. With a sweep of my hand, his body slammed into a jagged tree trunk, bones breaking on impact. He lay moaning in the leaf litter.

"Enough," the witch commanded.

I followed her to where the man lay. I stared at the unnatural twist of his lower body, broken legs and back, his complexion pale with shock. I hunkered down opposite him, hating his wide, terrified eyes as I leaned closer. Despite the shock, he knew death hung closely around him.

"Where is the rest of your army?" the witch asked.

The man's eyes widened further. "They sent me ahead to scout. But the army is not far behind."

"You don't seem afraid of me," she mused, considering the man.

"Another of your kind travels with us," he rasped. "Another

of his kind," he said, glancing to to me.

"What did you do to the village south of here?" I asked, ignoring everything but my growing rage.

"They refused us fealty," he whispered, paling as he met my gaze.

"And what did you do?" I demanded, biting off each word.

"They said they'd rather burn with their fields."

I stared at the muddy, bloodsoaked man. All dead…rather burn with their fields. The words repeated in my mind. Unlike this soldier, who had the choice to defy his master, I could do no such thing. I moved without warning, my strength heightened to the fury of a winter gale, and snapped the man's neck. The corpse looked like a child's broken toy at my feet. Perhaps I am one of the dark god's children, I mused grimly.

Beside me, the witch was silent, her mouth pursed in distaste for long moments before she turned and walked away. Anger still writhed within me and I walked further from her, my fingers twitching anxiously, the night charged with violence, my hunger for retribution unslaked. Beside me, the witch threw her head back, scenting the air like a wolf. I frowned, wondering what darkness had birthed such a creature.

Without warning, a man materialised from the darkness, blade levelled at the witch's throat. I had not seen him, his very presence cloaked from me. Now I stared at the steel sword held against the witch, the rest of his army advancing through the forest behind us.

Lifting my hands, lightning flickering between them in a contained thunderstorm, I studied the newcomer, who could be none other than the master to whom I was promised. Watching me, he pulled the witch against him, blade cutting lightly into her skin, unperturbed by the hungry growl of a tornado around me.

He was tall, an expensive cloak thrown back from one shoulder, revealing an unfamiliar insignia. Wherever he had travelled from, it was far from these lands. Without speaking, he looped long fingers through the heavy bronze chain around the witch's neck and yanked the talisman from her. She did not struggle, but glared in defiance. There was a subtle shift in the surrounding atmosphere when he grasped the talisman. An exchange of power occurred. *Would there be a moment between this transference when I might truly be free again?*

Before I could act, the blade sliced deeply across her throat. I jerked with surprise, blood trickling down the witch's throat, becoming a torrent. She collapsed to the ground, gasping as he stepped over her, advancing on me.

I forced my panicked mind to concentrate. The bonds of the talisman tightened around me. *Did this stranger have complete control of me yet? Did he understand what I was? Did he know how the witch had controlled me? Or had he opportunistically taken the talisman? Could I overpower him and free myself?* The witch had used her will to smother my own. *Was this man her equal in strength?* I gathered the storm to me, a faint awareness of someone new in the clearing but beyond my sight. *Was there someone behind me?* Glancing around, I could see no one. Shivering slightly with the unwelcome sensation someone was standing close to me, I returned my attention to my new master. There was malice to him, his personality tainted. Unlike the witch, he had no sense of wildness about him, no predatory power of the natural order; there was only the unrelenting cold. The sight of the bronze talisman around his neck only fuelled my rage.

I attacked, arcs of lightning thrusting towards him like extension of my own fingers. . Ignoring the warning that I was not alone in this clearing, I drew my lips in a soundless snarl and flowed towards him like the storm itself. He side-stepped my onslaught, the lighting zig-zagging around him as he moved towards me. Enraged, I relied on speed instead and charged toward him. A wall of flame erupted from nowhere. Shocked, I twisted away, but was caught within the tendrils of fire that moved with me, slashing at me like blades.

"You will always be a slave," he shouted.

Summoning the lightning again, using it to escape the flames encircling me, I doubled my efforts, forming a tornado around my body, and pushed against the fire. Whatever attacked me was equal to my efforts and twisted tendrils of flame into the tornado, stealing the strength of my attack and draining me. I slowed, the power of the storm dwindling before faltering, scattering debris across the clearing. I heaved with exhaustion, shoulders slumped as I knelt on the ground. Where the earth was scorched by lightning bolt and singed by flame, I bowed my head before this man. If I hoped to free myself from bondage, I needed to become a master of my power.

"You are indeed her finest work," he said, inspecting me as though I were a well-crafted sword.

"Why kill her if she was so precious to you?" I snarled.

"Her talents were rare, but we could not risk such gifts in the hands of our enemies."

"Forgive me. I don't find that justifiable"

"I suppose you do not," he agreed. "She promised your power would be exceptional, and it is. Many others have not fared so well, forged from such unbalanced magics."

"She mentioned others," I said, lip curling.

"You find that distasteful?" he asked, glancing at the fiery form, twin blades now discernible. "She has indeed made others over her lifetime. But there was only one other like yourself, Anlan."

"Am I supposed to be thankful?"

"War marches across these wide lands and I have a need for those who can withstand it. My king desires the children of gods to serve him, for he will be the ruler of all."

I did not hear him speak the command that stripped my corporeal form away. The witch had always spoken aloud, perhaps as some respect to her dark god. It did not matter now. The bonds of my new master settled around me like a leaden mantle. Cursing him even as the world around me became muted and grey, I thrashed futilely against his overwhelming power. Then, as the remnants of my physical form dissipated, I finally saw the woman step from the fire, sheathing twin blades at her side.

"Don't fight it," she said, moving to my side.

I jerked in surprise. She stopped, hand outstretched to me like she was trying to calm a frightened but dangerous animal. I regarded her warily. She was tall for a woman, lithe and young.

Her bronze skin was covered in the same tattoos that decorated my own since the witch had enslaved me. A vest of soft hide covered her chest and a pleated skirt fell to her knees. My gaze rested on the twin curved blades at her hips. She dropped to one knee, hand still held out to me.

"How dare he," I hissed.

"We're slaves," she said with a wry smile. "He may dare whatever he likes."

I glared at the man through the twilit shadows. Already he had dismissed me into this incorporeal shadow-world. I regarded the woman, this warrior of flame with whom I had fought.

"Slavery is not my fate."

"Then take the talisman for yourself and your freedom with it," she said.

"Don't mock me."

"I do not," she insisted. "Perhaps the witch never told you of the god to whom she prayed? But I can see she did. We are children of that dark god; to us is the responsibility to restore balance, respond to injustice with swift retribution. We're not intended as slaves to mortal men."

I stared at her a moment, the sincerity of her words striking a deep chord of truth within me. "How do we break our enslavement? Raze the empires of those who oppress us?"

She shrugged. "I have longed for retribution." Her tattooed hand gripped mine. The sigils marking her flesh were the twin of my own. "They took our lives and even our deaths from us, but we can still take our vengeance."

I tightened my grip, meeting her determined gaze. Fire danced in the depths of those eyes and I felt the lightning flicker within my own, power stirring to join hers. I had felt nothing but rage since my enslavement, but with this warrior, I felt a sense of union and, in that moment, I knew the dark god blessed us and retribution would be ours.

The inspiration for 'Talismans' came from the prehistoric sites that I visited while in Sweden and the grave burials and artefacts that were left with the dead. A specific individual caught my attention and became the inspiration behind the story in a prehistoric Iron Age culture where human sacrifice was not uncommon. The transformation of the sacrificed individual into a talisman that could protect a wearer was drawn from Ancient Greek, Roman and Celtic legends of powerful warriors whose strength was sourced from an object like a talisman of protection.

Maidens of the Bloody Brook

The track along the sea cliffs was a winding and precarious one. It skirted the edge so close that Cian had to cling with his fingers to the sharp boulders that tried to force him into the churning waters of the ocean below. There were few handholds, and the rock was covered in bird guano from the hundreds of gulls that roosted on the rocky shoreline. Where there wasn't razor sharp rock and guano, the rock was slippery with sea spray. Curse his foolishness! If he hadn't been too in his cups at the tavern, he wouldn't be here now. The O'Henry twins were nothing but trouble, and he couldn't turn down a bet when he was drunk. The walk out of town, beyond the last farmsteads and to the cliffs beset by blustery gales, had sobered him up. He'd heard nothing good about this cursed place except the brook where water spilled into the ocean and, at sunset, if you were careful, you'd spy the maidens bathing in the water.

It sounded like madness cooked up on too much whiskey and old wives' tales. But Cian had heard many of the men about the town talking with knowing smiles about the maidens that haunted the sea cliffs. So when the O'Henry twins had insulted him, asking if he had the balls to walk the sea cliffs at twilight, he'd done what any man would do: he scuffled with them for the affront to his manhood and accepted their bet. If he'd declined like a sensible man, the O'Henry lads would've never let him forget it.

Cian shoved his hands deeper into the pockets of his wooden jacket and continued on the perilous trek. Inching around another boulder, his back bent sharply, the drop and ocean below, his feet found purchase and he followed the path back towards the safety of land. Exhaling shakily, Cian stood away from the cliff edge, anxiety dropping away instantly. He hated heights. Here he was, miles from the last farmsteads on the sea cliffs at twilight. His chest expanded at the pride that gave him. Oh, his father would give him a bollocking when he returned, no less, but he had bested his own fear.

Now he would see whether James and Joshua O'Henry were liars. He knew they were. There were only old superstitions about the maidens at the brook. Cian would prove his manhood and that the twins were talking shite. He kicked at a pebble made smooth by the wind and time and watched it skip and bounce across the path to hit a large boulder. Cian held his breath as it ricocheted off the boulder and landed in the brook with a plop going straight to the bottom.

Cian stood motionless in the path. But the brook continued to flow, gulls circled, overheard with raucous cries and the waves beat ceaselessly against the cliffs. Nothing had changed. Exhaling slowly, expecting an uncanny attack at any moment, Cian took his hands from his pockets. He tried to ignore how badly they were shaking.

Alone except for the curling gulls, Cian faced the mauve-coloured sky and offered a hasty prayer to the Lord. He laughed nervously at his own anxiety. Had he really expected a maiden to lunge from the brook and drag him into the watery depths? Weather-worn crags on towering sea cliffs overlooked the ocean like forlorn watchers on battlements. These were the same cliffs where women wronged by men would throw themselves into the heaving ocean, where the weaves breaking on the rocks below would finish the job. Cian shivered. It was desolate up here.

There was one more task to complete. Cian turned to the brook, clear waters with lush vegetation on either side. Weeping willows overhung the water, trailing branches downstream. Large stones and small boulders formed a natural edging to the brook and several metres from the cliff face was a pile of smooth stones with holes in their middles. Cian knew the old women of the village who traded in lore and herbs called them *hag stones*. He didn't know the origin of the hag stones, but he knew the lore well enough: women who cast themselves from the cliff took them as a token of safe passage to become the uncanny maidens, forever seeking vengeance against the men who had wronged them. The Church condemned such superstition and belief as heresy, but the folklore persisted.

Cian stepped forward to the pile of uncannily smooth stones and selected one at random. Subconsciously, he rubbed it between his thumb and forefinger, turning back to the towering crags cast against the twilit sky. What a fate to leap from there.

The creeping feeling of eyes upon him made him turn slowly around. A beautiful woman sat on a boulder closest to him, naked except for the red hair falling in a wet tangle down her back but only partially covering her breasts. Cian's blood stirred, and he cursed the awkwardness he felt in being a man in her presence. The maiden's sea-green eyes glittered wickedly and her gaze lingered on the unmistakable bulge in Cian's breeches. She kicked her long legs playfully in the water, toes pointed towards the purple sky.

"Come closer, lad," she said.

Cian's legs finally obeyed him and he moved closer to the Fae woman. Not that he had any wish to walk away from her. The generous curves of her body, the shadowed hollows that promised forbidden pleasures... Cian was so close now he could smell the salt-and-wildflower scent of her perfume. He reached out a hand, the hag stone white against his farmer's tanned skin. The maiden wrapped her long fingers around his own.

He smiled, and the maiden drew him closer. Reaching out his other hand, Cian moved, boldly brushing a stray lock aside. She changed in an instance, fingernails growing longer to form sharp talons, her beguiling smile becoming a leer of menace and sharp teeth, her eyes feral and wild.

Shocked into movement, the bewitchment broken, Cian struggled against the maiden's grip. But she was impossibly strong, long talons gouging flesh from his wrists. Fight as Cian might, the maiden bore him below the water's surface. Her limbs shifted from skin the colour of milk to blueish scales.

Cian broke the surface of the water, writhing as she dragged him under again. Tumbled along the bottom of the brook, his face and limbs bashed against the stony bottom, the maiden's nails gripping the hair at the base of his skull. Screaming against the water, Cian inhaled a lungful as his skull slammed into the stones lining the brook. Blood gushed from the wound, flooding the water with scarlet as the maiden tore fresh gouges from Cian's scalp. She acted with mindless vengeance, slamming his skull again into rocks and tearing at his flesh. Cian's consciousness slipped further from him. He tried to move limbs already weakened by the trauma, his failing sight already useless in the blood-clouded water. He screamed, wordlessly and uselessly, as water filled his lungs.

The maiden broke the surface of the brook, bearing Cian's corpse as an offering of vengeance slaked, towing him towards the sea cliffs. She cried her shrill warning to the twilit night, talons imbedded in Cian's back. No longer struggling against her, Cian's limp body was released to float in the frothy brook, bloodsoaked and broken, carried by the gushing water over the edge of the sea cliff to the ocean below.

'Maidens of the Bloody Brook' is a reimagining of the folklore of the morgens from Brittany and other Celtic legends who use their beauty to entice their victims into the water and within reach of them. The men are often drowned by the morgens and have similarities to ancient Greek river nymphs, sirens, Slavic rusalka but share a sorrowful tale of being wronged and suicide by drowning. From the depth of such a sad ending emerges a dangerous and malevolent river sprite who lures men to their untimely deaths.

The Monster

The cravings began not long after he noticed the approaching *storm. It was hunger at first.* Feeling lethargic, Geoff ravenously consumed the supplies in his backpack, but these failed to satisfy his cramping stomach. He tried to ignore the impossible hunger, focusing on hiking beside Daniel, both men cautiously eyeing the storm brewing on the horizon ahead. Soon, Geoff's pace slowed, clammy sweat trickling down his back, chilling him despite the thick winter parka he wore. Clenching his jaw, Geoff pushed onwards, ignoring the concerned glances Daniel kept giving him, the keen gaze of the medical student undoubtedly noticing the pallor, perspiration, and feverishly bright eyes.

"Are you alright?" Daniel finally asked when they paused at the top of the ridge.

Geoff grimaced, hand to his side, struggling to calm his erratic heartbeat. Gasping for air, he bent double, gaze falling on the triangle of bare skin exposed at Daniel's throat, the artery pulsing beneath. Geoff's teeth clacked together as his jaw shut and he shuddered, an awful hunger roaring inside him. He licked his lips and forced his eyes away from Daniel's throat, horrified at the compulsion to bite and feast. Another shudder gripped him, spasms wrenching through his guts. Geoff screamed, falling to the snow, fingers raking at his abdomen as if possessed.

Shouting for help, Daniel dropped to one knee as the footsteps of the other two hikers hurried closer. But Geoff could see nothing. Blinded by the agony, insensible to everything but rage, Geoff's fingernails clawed against Daniel's hands as they held him through the seizure. Geoff flailed, recalling the four of them in the Clinical and Diagnostic Medicine tutorial the day before, the case studies from Canada of wendigo psychosis, indigenous belief in the cannibalistic wendigo possessing those who had lost reality, hungering for nothing but human flesh.

Geoff's fever rose, uncontrollable shivers shaking him, memories and delusions mixing, curdling as his body arched, rigid in spasm. Daniel jerked backwards, Geoff's jaws snapping together, teeth biting empty air just beside his face. Geoff finally lay still, exhausted, on the snow; his friends huddled protectively around him.

Exhaling, Daniel squinted up at the storm, mentally calculating distances. He glanced back at Geoff, already knowing it was too late to turn back and too far to the next shelter. With no other options, they were forced to make a camp, fretful glances at the storm and towards Geoff. There had been no reports of unexpected blizzards this late in the season for several years, but the mountains were unpredictable.

The storm was wild and unconcerned with human orderliness, raging against the hikers and the Australian Alps alike. Geoff huddled deeper into his sleeping bag, the stiff outer layer of his parka crackling as he moved. He glanced at the woman opposite him in the tiny tent they shared. It was barely large enough for two adults, but he and Jessica were childhood friends. She was as much a sister to him as a friend. He saw her fearful expression, unguarded and exposed when she thought he wasn't watching her. When she noticed, her smile exuded her usual confidence.

"Is it that bad?" Geoff asked, grimacing.

Jessica made a face, tried not to laugh but half-sobbed instead. "You're so sick. You know how bad your fever must be."

"I'll be better in the morning. We can keep walking tomorrow."

"Geoff," she began, but he shook his head sharply, jaw clenched in sudden anger.

Her eyes narrowed, watching him with wary suspicion, but he held her gaze, uncharacteristically aggressive. Saying nothing, she threw her hands melodramatically into the air, capitulating. Still with her back to Geoff, Jessica zipped up her sleeping bag and, closing her eyes, fell asleep in moments, snoring softly.

Geoff stared into the darkness. He'd hidden his trembling hands behind his back. He hadn't told Jessica or Daniel, but the outbursts of rage were increasing and, with them, delusions from his seizure. The storm outside moaned like a ravenous monster. Geoff was certain it was calling to him. The wretched spasms of his empty stomach continued; the small amount of food he had eaten for dinner felt vile in his guts. He was so tired of fighting this hunger. But to surrender to that compulsion… He shuddered, clamping his hands against his ears, trying to muffle the howling wind, but somehow it still whispered, taunted him. The storm called to him, as relentless as his damnable hunger.

Finally, sleep trapped him, or perhaps he only drifted in some liminal space.

He woke quickly, jerking upright, sleep suddenly a distant memory. Feeling fully alert, Geoff was aware of something outside the tent. Glancing quickly at the sallow yellow numbers on his phone, the light proclaiming it fourteen minutes past midnight; he unzipped the tent flap and waited, listening to the raging storm beyond.

"The blizzard finally struck," Jessica mumbled, half-asleep but already pushing herself upright. "Are you going outside? Feeling okay?"

"Peachy," he lied, glancing anxiously at the tent flap. "I've got to piss, though."

"Oh, Geoff," she complained, waving her hands in the air. "Are you sure you need to go out there?"

"Do you want me to piss in here?" he complained.

"Not really, but you shouldn't go alone."

"I said I was fine," he said, stepping through the open tent flap.

"You were lying."

"I was exaggerating," he corrected, already on the other side of the threshold now.

"Well, are you sure?" she called.

"Jess, we're not *that* good friends."

Jess laughed softly, but her shadowed eyes were concerned as he shut himself outside with the storm.

He knelt in the snow outside the tent, the icy wind lashing his face. The storm was a vicious thing, the gale bending the snow gums, gusts of snow and debris careening down the mountain. The hunger within him strengthened, a wretched gnawing of his stomach. If only it would relent. The very thought of yielding to that hideous compulsion bent him near-double with agony. He staggered to the edge of the campsite where the nearest snow gums hugged a rocky promontory. He felt as if liquid fire had poured down his throat, a fire now threatening to destroy him. It would just stop if he gave into the hunger and ate.

Geoff leaned against the rock surface; certain he was going to vomit. Daniel had been reserved since Geoff's seizure and only Jessica seemed willing to care for him. Geoff knew that somehow Daniel and his partner Sofie had seen the creature inside him, but Jessica's closeness to him blinded her to the monster he was becoming. He'd already lied to her. He couldn't eat anything without the torment, the *hunger*, forcing him to disgorge it soon after.

"You all right, mate?" Daniel asked, approaching cautiously.

Geoff hadn't heard his approach over the raging storm. He was still leaning heavily against one of the big granite boulders, full weight balanced on one outstretched hand, the other clutching white-knuckled at his abdomen. Daniel placed his hand on Geoff's shoulder, the frown deepening with increased concern. Even through the layers of thermal clothing and the parka, Geoff knew he burned with a terrible fever. Daniel assessed it all with a doctor's critical eye.

Geoff felt detached as he stared at Daniel, noticing how his friend's throat spasmed when he swallowed, eyes widening, fingertips reflexively tightening on his shoulder. Reflexively, Daniel glanced briefly to the tent he had just left, where Sofie still slept. Geoff inhaled, certain he could smell the heightened fear flooding Daniel's body, Sofie's perfume lingering on his skin. Geoff loosened his stance, preparing for Daniel to shout, and readied himself to lunge.

"Sofie!" Daniel called as Geoff leapt.

A wild madness overcame Geoff as he collided with Daniel. They hit the snowbank together as the storm roared, Geoff's howl of rage and triumph joining the gale. Pinning Daniel beneath him, Geoff slammed the heel of his palm down, silencing Daniel's shout. Blood oozed from Geoff's hand where Daniel's teeth had cut him, a coppery tang scenting the chill air. Again, Geoff shouted with jubilation, the monster roaring forth, driven onwards by the storm. Now Geoff didn't deny the monster. He let it flood his veins, pump wildly with his heart- beat. Kneeling over Daniel's body, he felt the uncontrollable hunger fall upon him. This time, he did not resist it. He lunged forward over the body, teeth ripping at exposed flesh, blood bursting into his mouth and bringing a final, savage release.

The satisfaction won with Daniel's death did not last long. Geoff sat beside the corpse; the absence of hunger had almost been intoxicating with the relief it brought. But now he felt the steady rise again of the compulsion. The monster still hungered.

The sound of hesitant footsteps opposite him returned Geoff to his immediate surroundings. Daniel's body lay beside him still, the bloody traces of his ravenous feast plainly exposed. Geoff could smell Sofie's perfume from where he crouched, the scent of it so much stronger now than the lingering traces that had clung to Daniel's skin.

"Geoff?" Sofie asked, fear draining her voice to a whisper as she beheld the scene.

He stayed half-crouched and unmoving beside Daniel's corpse. Dried blood was smeared across Geoff's lower mouth and chin, the thick weave of his sweater crusted with red gore. Sofie flinched beneath the fever-bright madness in his eyes, and instinctively she understood nothing of Geoff remained. The monster in front of her would not hesitate: he would kill her.

Sofie ran, veering sharply to the right, hoping to evade Geoff's reach. But he was quicker than she expected of such a sick man. His hands grabbed at her clothing, long fingers snagging the hem of her jumper. She spun around, colliding with him as the air was knocked from her lungs with a painful grunt.

Geoff seized the opportunity, tangling Sofie's feet in an awkward manoeuvre that brought them both heavily to the ground. Still clawing at him, Sofie dragged in desperate mouthfuls of air, trying to kick her way free from him. But he was like a possessed man, the *need* still driving him, that unspeakable monster making weapons of hands and teeth. He caught Sofie's thrashing fists, ignoring her scratching fingernails, hissing curses and eventual pleas. But it was too late now; Geoff had fed the monster once, and it demanded more. Fingernails raking at the ground, scratching snow and debris clear, he finally tore a chunk of weathered granite from the frozen earth. Hefting the rock in his left hand, Geoff brought the edge down repeatedly into Sofie's face, her shrieks of pain and fear dissolving into the storm.

When silence descended, it was an awful absence of sound, not a relief. Geoff stared at the bloody destruction he had wrought, sinew and bone stark against the snow, exposing what should never be visible. Geoff hesitated, mouth dry and willing the revulsion he knew he should feel at what he had done. But the monster did not feel remorse or pity, it only craved.

Again the hunger swelled, the torment of the monster never satisfied by the gluttonous carnage. Geoff resisted the growing urge, dropping to his knees in the snow and retching. The corpses before him were only bodies now, no longer recognisable as his friends. He found a sliver of solace in that awareness and in the realisation that his bloodstained hands did not truly look like his own, either. Perhaps this was an awful nightmare? For if not, this surely must be madness. The monster growled and sobbed, the ceaseless *hunger* clawing against his empty insides. Why could it never be satisfied? He'd done what it wanted; he'd eaten the flesh. But it always needed more. It was always hungry, the monster, this wendigo.

Climbing to his feet, Geoff glanced around the eerily quiet campsite. Despite the roaring wind of the winter storm, silence hung over the camp, an emptiness that came only with the absence of people. But there was one more. Geoff closed his eyes, listening intently to the storm, hoping the monster was satisfied and would relent this time.

Geoff heard the gentle click of the emergency beacon in their tent. Jessica was still here, after all. The tent flap was nearly completely zipped closed, but not entirely. Had Jess been watching this whole time? Had she seen what he had done to Daniel? To Sofie? The thought made him incredibly weary and sad that this was his oldest of friends and she was afraid of him; she *hid* from him. Anger sparked within him; those darker emotions allowed to kindle as he stalked towards the tiny tent they had shared.

Not waiting for Jessica to speak or emerge, to try running or fighting, Geoff just ripped at the flimsy tent flap, his long arms reaching for her. He caught her around the knees as she tried to flatten herself into the back corner. Mercilessly, Geoff dragged her, kicking and screaming, into the open clearing. Tears ran down her face and Jessica's voice was an unrecognisable, sobbing plea. The knitted hat that normally covered her short hair was gone, thick red curls escaping their bindings to writhe in the storm. Her blue eyes darted to the bodies of Daniel and Sofie discarded only metres from her.

"Geoff," she pleaded.

"It's so hungry, Jess," he offered in explanation, hoping for her forgiveness.

Quickly, he raised the torch he'd taken from her tent, striking her across the temple. Jessica fell sideways into the snow, the successive blows not stopping until she no longer moved. Now, Geoff forced his eyes from her bright amber hair. Another shade of red now, flowing hot and steaming from the side of her face. An awful, bloody red now stained the snow bloody red. Outrage forsaken momentarily, Geoff found the small camp shovel Daniel had insisted they carry and, deliberately avoiding Jessica's body, dug down into the snow, the storm continuing to howl relentlessly around him.

It was several days before the police found the campsite. They found Geoff sitting in the snow, half-dressed and smeared in dried blood. The paramedics, and then forensics, hurried about him, trying to ignore the eerie way he watched them while they catalogued the ruined campsite.

"Tell us where the others are," the police officer said, shaking Geoff so violently his head snapped back and forth.

"I did nothing," Geoff repeated. "I told you it was so hungry."

"What's he even ranting about?" the senior officer shouted, glaring accusingly at the assembled officers.

A female medic kneeling in the snow near Geoff shuffled to her feet, the crisp crackle of her forensic suit an echo in the silence.

"It wasn't my fault," Geoff repeated.

On the other side of the perimeter, a junior officer stumbled into the bushes and vomited.

"Jesus," the female medic said, casting a reproachful glare at her senior officer. "There are human ribs under him."

"What?" the senior officer demanded.

"I think he's sitting on broken rib cages."

"The monster wasn't satisfied," Geoff continued, clutching at his abdomen. "I tried to resist it."

"Is he saying what I think he is?" the police officer asked, paling at the sight of the bones beneath Geoff.

"Sir, are you Geoff Thompson? Do you know where you are?" the medic asked.

Geoff twisted his head from side to side again. "These are cursed mountains; did you know that?"

The police officer raised his eyebrows, but the medic only gestured for silence. Kneeling, the medic inspected Geoff, looking at the many cuts and abrasions on his body, noticing that the blood did not seem to be his.

"It's okay, Geoff. We'll get you away from here. Just tell us what happened to the others."

He jerked as if struck, looking wildly around the snowy campsite, the bloody gouges in the ground and tattered tents. The medic stepped backward as Geoff shuddered with another spasm of recollection.

"I did what the monster wanted, it wanted to devour them," he said emotionlessly. "If we'd known a wendigo hunted here, we'd never have come."

The medic repeated comforting words of consolation as she removed the pre-loaded sedative syringe from a bag on her hip.

124

Still speaking kindly to Geoff, she swiftly delivered the injection. Geoff did not seem to notice, but continued to stare into the distance, eyelids finally drooping before the medic lowered him to the ground with practised ease.

"What was all that wendigo nonsense?" the police officer hissed, immediately stepping forward.

"There's a case they often mention in Medical School about wendigo psychosis. It's found among the Ojibwa Indians of North America, I believe."

"He doesn't seem Ojibwa to me."

"I don't think he is," the medic said, shrugging. "At any rate, they link the psychosis to wendigo lore in Ojibwa culture: it's not found anywhere else."

"Then what's he talking about? Is he a medical student? Or is he suggesting a Native American cannibal monster made him murder and eat his friends?"

"He's not very lucid right now," the medic said.

"Well, unless there's a wendigo spirit in the Australian Alps, we'll need the truth from him, eventually."

The female medic looked down at the unconscious man, blood crusted on his face, and her hands trembled, not in cold, but in fear. Glancing up at the mountain peaks above, she repressed another shiver of fear.

'The Monster' is a dark reimagining and psychological horror inspired by the North American First Nations legends of the wendigo, a cannibalistic winter monster that develops an insatiable hunger and no matter how much it consumes, it continues to starve. The aspect of whether this tale is about a wendigo transformation or a psychological breakdown is something that I was drawn to explore through the atmosphere of confinement by a blizzard and the unknown madness or monstrous truth within one of the hikers.

A Night on Skye

The moon was hidden by cloud, thick mist on the ground, and Caroline knew she was lost. The moors surrounded her in their cloaks of russet, olive and tawny heather. The Isle of Skye had always been a desired adventure for her, but now it was turning fell. Movement to her right; she focused on a darting form. Was that a child? Out here?

Caroline hurried after the child before the poor thing fell into the bog of the marshes. The child was still ahead of her, disappearing and reappearing through the mist. The ground beneath Caroline's shoes was soft, cold water leeching through the soil.

Rounding a bend in the fox trail they were following, Caroline stopped at a large moss-covered stone. There, the little child had paused. Rushing forward, Caroline grasped her thin, stick-like arm. The girl shrieked and turned. She was all gangly limbs, pot-bellied with wild hair and feral eyes. She hissed, lips curling back to reveal pointed teeth.

"You've caught me then, mortal. But do you know the riddle of my freedom?"

Caroline frowned. "Your freedom?"

"Aye," the Fae creature replied. "You've caught me and now must tell me three truths spoken from your lips. Then I shall have my freedom."

"Your freedom from what?"

The vicious eyes fixed on her. "From you, mortal. Tell me a truth no one else knows but be warned, I'll know if you lie."

127

"I never meant to walk these marshlands tonight. I got lost, and so finding you was chance alone. Whatever you are, I never sought you."

"Truth enough, but barely a morsel for one as ancient as me to survive upon. Tell me something more, child."

Caroline shivered in the frigid marshlands. "I always wanted to come to the Isle of Skye. I am like many Australian tourists, searching for their roots. My ancestors came from here, or so I'm told."

"As your bones and flesh might return to them, child. Truth is nothing but a bitter brew drunk often without finding peace for the soul. Your kinsfolk lie beneath these hills and moors, your blood runs through the fissures of the earth as surely as it flows through the veins in your body."

"A final truth I offer you, Fae. I never loved my parents nor understood their ways of trying to love me. I wish I might have had more time with them, with those who were of my blood and should have understood me most of all. But their passing is many years ago now."

"A solid, tasty truth, mortal. A truth that is full of sorrow and regret. But you never asked for the agreement of this exchange. You've released the shackles with you had set upon me. My turn to deliver unto you the truth you seek most. You may have time with those with whom you share blood."

Caroline frowned. Then the ground shifted underfoot, and she staggered. One foot slipped into growing pools of murky water, skeletal hands reaching up to wrap bony fingers around her ankles. The marshes heaved, a quagmire of muddy soil and deep pools of stinking water, the bones of the dead reaching for Caroline.

A skeleton hand around her ankle pulled with unnatural strength and she hit the ground. She struggled and beat at the bony hands and limbs catching her clothing, but still they pulled her closer to a stagnant pool of water. The Fae creature sat atop of the mossy stone, cackling with vicious glee.

"You should have asked the bindings of our agreement, mortal. But you never do."

Caroline screamed, and dragged into the quagmire, water filling her mouth as the dead pulled her under to rest with her ancestors.

'A Night on Skye' was inspired by the ageless landscape of the Isle of Skye and its archaeological record, which tempted me to explore a reimagining of returning to ancestral land only to be tricked into an early grave by the dark Fae who dwell within the marshes and in liminal spaces of Scottish folklore.

Poisoned Fruit, Poisoned Reign

Beneath the apple tree, the queen knelt in prayer. From behind her, the sharp snap of ice halted the woman's approach, no longer masked by a fresh snowfall. The queen turned, reaching for her blade.

"I wasn't certain you'd come, Muirenn," the queen said, drawing back the cowl of her hood, self-consciously brushing at her increasingly silver hair.

"It's been many seasons since we both stood here, Caitrin," the woman agreed, her own features unnaturally youthful.

"Outright war threatens the western kingdoms, and I'm an ageing woman," the queen said self-mockingly, while gesturing for assistance to stand.

"You're fortunate magic aids you, sister," Muirenn said, offering a supportive arm. "Time is beyond our mastery."

"Yet it scarcely marks you," Caitrin observed. "I prohibit glamours within my kingdoms."

Muirenn met her sister's gaze but did not flinch. Standing motionless, hand trapped by the queen's grip, she waited while Caitrin scrutinised her unblemished skin, raven hair unadulterated by grey.

"You've broken my laws. I can't shield you from punishment," Caitrin finally said.

They were standing beneath an apple tree, and Muirenn stared into its boughs. It symbolised their royal house and its reign.

"I wasn't born the eldest, the Warrior Queen," she replied. I look at my reflection each morning, every polished bronze surface showing my fading worth. When you ride into battle, you're clothed in protective glamours, but you deny me the same magical birthright. You deny all in your kingdom the aid of magic."

"Glamours on a battlefield haven't protected me during decades of fighting," she said, fingers stiffly releasing her sister.

Muirenn bowed her head, and Caitrin gently squeezed her hand, then reached up to pluck an apple from the branch above them.

"Let me this once?" Muirenn pleaded.

Standing up on the toes of her shoes, Muirenn picked the reddest apple either of them had ever seen. The red hue that had attracted her attention was like a ruby in the snowy garden, and its opposite side was coloured the darkest green, both hues impossibly vibrant in the grey and wintry surrounds.

"We seek blessing for our house and its continued reign," Caitrin said, biting into the red skin of the apple, its flesh white beneath.

Savouring the taste, Caitrin offered the apple to Muirenn, who took a bite from the opposite side, dark green skin yielding to crisp flesh.

"Your reign might have continued if you'd listened to me," Muirenn finally said.

Caitrin paled, immediately conscious of the cold and numbness spreading from her lips.

"The poison works quickly," Muirenn continued. "Before you die, first know why your councillors betrayed you. I'd always told you, restricting magic to yourself in defence of the kingdoms never made your people feel equal; it only created greater distinction between them and their queen."

Caitrin shuddered, slumping to the ground, paralysis preventing her from drawing a blade. But Muirenn still did not dare step closer. She never heard the dying queen curse her reign. A reign tainted by an unnatural blight, cursed crops yielding poisoned fruit.

'Poisoned Fruit, Poisoned Reign' was a reimagining of several fairy tales and delving into the darker roots of their origins. The presence of cursed reigns, especially in queens, is present in Grimm brothers and Hans Christian Andersson fairytales and includes Snow White and Sleeping Beauty. Aside from these cursed queens, I desired to explore a stronger female role—the knowledge that the queen was cursing her kingdom and future and doing so because of their betrayal.

The Dark Harpist

In the Autumn, the harvests failed. The most fertile lands in the kingdom were far south of the capital, beneath the towering peaks of Schwarze-Berge and surrounded by the Forest. But in the final year of the old King Dietger's reign, the earth turned sullen, annual rains never came, fields lay barren, and produce withered on the vine. In those hamlets beneath Schwarze-Berge, which ordinarily provided enough produce to support the court and almost the entire kingdom, despair hung over the bleached fields and lingered late into the Autumn. But for Roald, who had just passed his twelfth year, the long summer and autumn only meant longer hours in the pastures tending those livestock which had survived the harsh summer.

It was nearly twilight when Roald sat against the cottage stone wall, enjoying the warm evening, and the stranger walked down the dusty road toward their small hamlet. The man was the tallest Roald had ever seen, surely a giant, but he moved with deliberate care, suggesting every step pained him. Roald stumbled to his feet, staring in disbelief, but he did not notice how his own shadow elongated, stretching along the road as though reaching for the stranger.

The man stopped before Roald, and peering down at the youth, squinted against the setting sun perched above the Schwarze-Berge range beyond the valley.

"Is this Schwarze-Berge?" the giant asked.

"It is, sir," Roald stuttered, cursing himself for sounding like a fool.

The man only grunted in response, his hunched shoulders bowed against the chill wind. He wrapped his cloak more tightly about himself, abnormally long arms hugging his torso.

"We have little to spare for travellers here," Roald finally said.

"They summoned a magician?"

Roald frowned at the odd question. "Ah, yes. Yester-morn, some-one committed a terrible act. But the culprit later confessed, there is no danger here."

"I am not here about such trivial matters," he said gruffly. "I'm here to collect the tribute promised in return for services rendered."

"I know of no such arrangements," Roald confessed, glancing toward the hamlet further down the road.

"King Dietger approaches his final days, and the kingdom now suffers at his demise. For the Schwarze-Berge, I restored the balance with the wild goddess. I now seek what's promised me in return."

"I am only a shepherd, sir. Those at the village Inn might have the answers you seek."

The pale-faced giant nodded grimly, glancing about the lands surrounding him. "Your father owns the lands, does he not? Do the other herdsman, orchardists and fowlers follow him?"

"My father is a leader in our hamlet," the boy answered, susp-icious. "What interest is that of to you?"

"I meant no deception, lad. Tell your father that Isebrand seeks payment from him," he said, one massive hand splayed across his chest in supplication.

"I will tell my father, but I can't be wasting valuable time talking to strangers on the roadside. Best be on your way, sir."

"A fair evening to you, lad," Isebrand the giant said before continuing down the road in his awkward, shuffling gait.

Roald leaned against the fence while the evening star rose higher above Schwarze-Berge. A stem of sun-bleached grass hung from his lips. Occasionally he chewed on it, recalling the once-sweet taste of summer grass. The sound of hurried footsteps on the road behind him startled him from his thoughts.

"Roald," his father shouted, wheezing as he hastened towards his son.

"What's happened, Pappa?" he asked, dropping quickly to the ground from his perch atop the fence.

"Did a stranger pass through here earlier?"

"There was a *very* odd fellow, and I thought he must be a giant, but he claimed to be a magician, told me his name was Isebrand. He made me uncomfortable when he asked after you."

"He asked after me?"

"Well, he asked about these lands and if you were a leader among the landholders. I sent him on his way to the Inn. Are you all right, Pappa?"

"I must call a town meeting. I doubt Isebrand will go to the Inn but if he returns here, come find me without delay."

"Yes, Pappa," Roald said, watching his father walk into the evening gloom, an inexplicable dread lingering long after true dark had fallen.

It was well past midnight when Roald's father returned. Drowsy and propped upright against the solid wooden post, the sound of footsteps roused him, and he squinted down the dusty road lit by the yellow three-quarter moon. His father walked with shoulders slumped, and he looked old and haggard on that golden moonlit road.

"Pappa?" Roald called.

"It's done," his father whispered, wrapping an arm around his son and, without further words, ushered him home.

The following morning dawned brisk and clear. Roald and his father broke their morning fast with his older sister and mother, no words spoken to explain the events of the previous night. Despite this, there was a freshness in the morning, and he raced from the cottage, keen to be about his tasks.

Roald had scarcely gone several paces when he stopped, staring in wonder at the landscape beyond the cottage stone wall. Everywhere he looked, where pastures had been sun-bleached and unploughed fields barren, life blossomed around him, green meadows shining with morning dew and, in the distant fields, ripe crops had sprung from the once-barren fields. He shook his head, certain he must be in some otherworldly dream.

Abandoning his tasks, Roald hurried to the barn. Heaving the rough wooden door aside, he heard the familiar bleating of the lambs. Instead of the sickly creature he had been attending the past month, the young beasts seemed miraculously healed and were playfully gambolling about in the straw.

The day continued in a fantastic haze of warm sunshine and a flower-scented breeze. Although Roald pestered his father about the miracles—what else could explain such otherworldly events?—the older man refused to be drawn on any answers. It was nearly twilight again and Roald had given up the pursuit for answers, resuming his favourite observation point to watch the stars. It was not long after the evening star shone brilliantly above Schwarze-Berge that he heard the now unmistakable shuffle of footsteps along the road.

Yawning, Roald dropped from the fence, eliciting a surprised yelp from a puppy sleeping at the base of the post. Without even looking at the road, Roald walked towards the familiar sound of the awkward gait. Stepping into the middle of the road, Roald finally lifted his gaze to meet the giant, heart squeezing in sudden fear.

"You've returned?" he squeaked.

"I have," Isebrand replied, towering above Roald to reveal the pointed front teeth in his horribly elongated face.

"I'm supposed to tell you, the hamlet does not welcome you within its borders."

"Are these lands not fertile and bountiful once more?"

"Yes, sir," Roald agreed, unable to hide his smile but lowering his gaze.

"Yet your father and the townsfolk refuse to pay the tribute for my services and that is contrary to the agreements made for the transformations."

"That is all I am told," Roald bristled. "Pappa would never be unjust."

"Men are often not as we believe, lad. Perhaps your pappa is a man of noble principles, but it is clear the other townsfolk are not."

Roald wanted to object further, to offer some defence for his pappa and the townsfolk, but as he looked across the moonlit pastures, densely leafed trees and bright stars, the words he had intended dried to dust in his mouth. Finally, he shrugged in defeat and gestured for Isebrand to continue along the road towards the village. But while Roald watched, Isebrand never went into the village. The magician left the road, trekking across lush pastures and through a grazing herd of cattle towards an old ash tree. The stone wall blocked his view and Roald strained up on his toes to see what the magician was doing.

When Isebrand stood beneath the ash, he threw back his cloak to reveal the true source of his disfigurement. Roald had assumed that Isebrand was afflicted like many hunchbacks, expecting a spine so curved to bend his back and hunch his shoulders. But disease did not cause the rounded shape across Isebrand's shoulders. Instead, he carried an enormous bone harp. The instrument was the strangest Roald had ever seen, its shape elegant and intricately carved, the skilled craftsmanship clear even from a distance. Isebrand tuned the white pegs, plucked several strings, coaxing music from the instrument before he readjusted the pegs again. Curious, Roald wondered if the harp were truly from bone or if the moonlight played tricks on him.

Then, without warning, Isebrand played. The music was tentative at first, strings plucked gently, allowing the rhythm to crescendo. The haunting music filled the valley, seeming to silence any birds and the nearby lowing of the cattle herds. Roald felt the music shiver along his spine, compelling him to move, to dance and join the swelling beauty of the sound. Isebrand lifted his voice in harmony to the lilting music, and Roald struggled to withstand the compulsion to follow, the need to visit deep, green groves, fresh water brooks and mossy glens. The music tantalised, begging, pleading for him to follow where it led, and to lose himself to it. Instead, Roald dug his fingernails so deeply into the wood of the post before him, determined not to follow.

It was then he noticed hurrying children, twirling and dancing together along the road as they skipped in a trance, following the thrall of the harp and Isebrand's voice. Still, Roald forced himself to remain still, not to go with the other children, not to follow the music towards the Forest at the base of Schwarze-Berge, those woods where none would willingly return. Still, the music of the harp and Isebrand's song washed over him, bringing haunting imagery of woodland groves, curling vines beneath the moonlight and the freedom of the Forest. Struggling against the compulsion, Roald finally sagged against the fence, near collapsing into the sweet-smelling grass.

A commotion of voices like angry hornets woke him from his daze. Roused and quickly coming back to his wits, Roald stared around him, the townsfolk screaming, weeping, and shouting, all their wrath focused on Pappa, who just stood, wearily shaking his head.

"What happened?" Roald asked, blinking away confusion as Pappa forcefully shook him.

"He's taken them all," his father shouted, shaking Roald again. "All the babes, the children, all the youth from these hamlets gone. They all followed Isebrand into the damnable, cursed Forest. All except you, Roald!"

The words made no sense. Roald frowned, recalling the harp and Isebrand's voice summoning him. But he had not followed. He'd fought the desire to walk among the restful trees of the Forest. Still, he had no answers for the enraged townsfolk, and he remained insensible to their questions, demands, the slaps and blows raining down upon him. Through it all, Roald could only ask himself *why*. Why had he not followed the others and the promise of eternal rest beneath the Forest?

'The Dark Harpist' is a reimagining of several different fairy tales from the collections by the Grimm brothers. The inspiration for a new reimagining came from the two different fairy tales, the 'Piper of Hamlen' and the 'Singing Bone', which include multiple versions of each. The transformation of a community which betrays the ancient trust and the consequences for breaking a pact with those who have provided abundance for the hamlets was something that I wanted to explore.

When Dead Gods Walk

Doctor Dayana Quiroz hurried across the sidewalk in front of the Museo Nacional de Arqueología, Antropología e Historia del Perú. The noise of the Lima streets surrounded her as she took the paved steps two at a time, conscious of being late to work again. From the streets behind her, motorcar horns blared, followed by rapid accusations and arguments. Her heels beat a quickstep across the mosaic tiles of the museum floor, the hubbub receding as she moved deeper into the museum.

As she approached the far end of the foyer, the security guards touched the brims of their hats in welcome. It was a morning tradition they shared. She smiled and bobbed slightly, knowing this little ritual brightened their days, and touched her gloved hands to the hem of her wide swing skirt She nodded to the guards and, reaching the foot of a wide staircase that led to the upper storey of the museum, Dayana turned left and began down the less frequented corridor to where the museum staff had their offices.

The corridor was poorly lit, and shadows clung to its corners, the domed glass of the museum foyer ceiling illuminating the vaulted central space and upper storey, but the light did not carry into the catacomb-like corridors. Dayana checked her watch and quickened her pace, skirt swishing as she hastened towards the open doorway at the end of the corridor. Even as she walked towards the narrow window that framed the end of the corridor, Dayana could tell there were no lamps lit within her mentor's office. Fingers gripping the doorjamb, Dayana swung herself around the doorway and stopped, lips parted with prepared excuses for her lateness dying on her tongue. The room was empty.

Frowning, Dayana stepped cautiously into the office. It was unlike Professor Ignacio Torres to be late to work himself, and the older man seemed to delight in half-teasing, half-reprimanding his protégé for tardiness. Dayana stepped closer to his desk, noticing his notebook was open on the table, Ignacio's spidery handwriting covering a fresh page, his pen placed neatly beside the book. Peering across the desk, Dayana read her mentor's entry with growing curiosity. He had noted the details of a series of newly discovered burials in the remains of mud-brick pyramids somewhere in the Andes, far north of Lima. At the very bottom of the page, Ignacio had scribbled four words that drove all other thoughts from Dayana's mind: *Evidence of human sacrifices?*

Dayana did not recognise the burials Ignacio was referring to in his notes. *Are these so newly discovered he hasn't told me yet, or has he intentionally kept them from me and keeping me in my place?* She did not think Ignacio subscribed to the opinions of a lot of older male scientists who saw no room for women in their disciplines. But now Dayana wondered if he resented having a woman as his successor here, if he was not beyond tactics to block her advancement. Since the end of the Second World War, many things had changed, but some traditions were harder to demolish.

She turned slowly on her heel and, thinking of her options, decided to confront Ignacio in the lower chambers of the museum where they housed the collections of archaeological and skeletal remains. If these new finds weren't in the museum catalogue and weren't yet on display, then her mentor would be in the museum's basement chambers, which were well suited for preserving artefacts and skeletons. Glancing back at the notebook again, Dayana sighed in annoyance and went to challenge Ignacio Torres.

The narrow staircase descended into the labyrinth of passages that ran beneath the museum, and it was as dusty and ill-kept as usual. Dayana took the small stone steps quickly, the echo of her high heels preceding her down the staircase. When she reached the first basement level, Dayana paused in the open doorway, a large workroom beyond.

Professor Ignacio Torres stood beside an anatomy table, a human skeleton laid out before him, several smaller tables arranged to the side covered in the artefacts recovered from the archaeological site.

From where she stood in the doorway, she saw Ignacio glance up to meet Dayana's eyes and, to her satisfaction, she noticed a twinge of guilt twist his smile. She knew from even the briefest glance at these extraordinary finds that this would likely be the greatest discovery of his career, one that would eclipse all others, allow him to retire with esteem from his colleagues. By comparison, Dayana knew he would argue that she was young, talented, and had a bright future ahead of her, one which he'd never doubted for a moment and, surely, she could forgive an old man his pride and this last chance at glory. She rolled her eyes at her internal dialogue, and stepped into the room, taking her white work coat from the wooden peg near the doorway without yet looking at Ignacio.

"Professor Torres," she said, taking her position at the table beside her mentor.

"Doctor Quiroz," he said, stumbling slightly over her professional title, still not meeting her eyes.

Ignacio bent over the skeleton, inspecting a blade mark where deep grooves in the neck bones had severed in the head.

"Decapitation?" Dayana asked in surprise, deftly plucking the bony vertebra from her mentor, turning it over in the light to see for herself.

"Possibly done using this blade," Ignacio replied, unable to hide his excitement at sharing this discovery.

His enthusiasm eroded any resentment she'd felt towards him. He'd turned to pick up a wide crescent-shaped blade from a side table where it had rested with the other artefacts, and she shared at the bronze ceremonial knife as he tiltied it towards her, her gaze following its sharp edge. Could this wicked-looking blade be the very instrument that had caused those deep cut marks to the bone?

Carefully, Ignacio took the piece of spine from Dayana's hands, and turning it over in the light, placed the blade gently into the groove in the bone. Dayana held her breath, imagining, how the blade must have sliced through tissue, tendon, and finally bone, nearly severing the head from the body in a single cut.

"Where did you recover this skeleton and these artefacts?" Dayana asked.

"Looters up in the far northern valleys of the Andes reported them after one of their members in an expedition was injured when a structure collapsed. They'd found these skeletons and the gold artefacts inside what we think was a mud-brick pyramid."

"This certainly looks like a sacrifice," Dayana said, her reflection staring back from the ceremonial blade Ignacio still held.

"I know I did not tell you the importance of this find," he began, turning towards her.

Suddenly, the ground lurched beneath their feet, silencing Ignacio's words. They'd both been so focused on examining the skeleton and the artefacts, neither had noticed the warning tremors through the earth that were so common in Lima. The shuddering of the earth beneath them now was no warning but a portent of the violence to follow.

"Run," he said, gesturing towards the stairwell.

Another jolt shook the earth and Ignacio stumbled, the bony vertebra falling from his grip. Dayana ran, staggering towards the stairwell even as she heard Ignacio's warning. Half-turning from the stairwell, her gaze fell with near-hypnotic intensity to the snarling face of a jaguar-god engraved on the blade's handle that Ignacio held. Staggering as another tremor shook the earth, Dayana watched helplessly as Ignacio stumbled, his arms pinwheeling to steady himself. Dayana shouted a warning she already knew was too late. The ceremonial knife lurched in Ignacio's usually steady grip as he stumbled, curved blade slicing across his forearm as he reached for the table to steady himself. Bright arterial blood spurted across the bones on the table, over the faded feathered headdress and golden armbands.

Dayana was already running towards Ignacio, watching him jerk backwards, dropping the sacrificial blade and clutching at the wound on his arm, trying desperately to staunch the pulsing blood flow. But she knew it was already too late: the artery had been severed and no matter how fast she might administer aid, he'd die from blood loss.

Again, the ground shook beneath them, and Ignacio stumbled as Dayana rushed forward to support him. Her slender hands kept pressure on the wound even as he slid weakly to the floor. His eyelids fluttered and he lay back, head resting on Dayana's wide, colourful skirts, his heart beating the life from him. Dayana smoothed back his greying hair, Ignacio's lifeless eyes staring up at the ceiling.

Another earthquake shook the room, and as if breaking the surface of water, noise penetrated her shocked mind. She heard people screaming in the museum above, the howl of the wind and the earth groaning as it tore apart. Steadily, Dayana noticed her hands, sticky with Ignacio's blood, and the skirts of her dress soaked with it. Shakily, she lowered Ignacio's body to the floor, trying not to notice the blood spray that covered nearly every surface of the room. Another earthquake rocked the floor, sending dust and stone debris cascading from the ceiling in a fine haze.

I need to escape here, or this will become my tomb.

Dayana stumbled to the doorway, tripping in her high heels on the broken flooring. Glaring at her fashionable but impractical shoes, she hooked a finger between the straps and tossed them aside. Movement on the periphery of her sight startled her, and turning, she surveyed the skeleton, the golden artefacts, and Ignacio's body, certain she had seen something. *I'm just being superstitious.* But the reprimand felt hollow, and as Dayana inspected the grisly tableau, she noticed the infinitesimal movement, Ignacio's hand clenching around the ceremonial knife hilt.

Jerking in fear, she watched her mentor stand, limbs moving stiffly as if whatever force had reanimated the corpse wasn't yet in complete control. Fear slid through Dayana's heart and, turning, she fled barefoot up the staircase. She ran, not slowing until she reached the main corridor and then, finally, she looked back the way she had come.

You know what you saw, Dayana. Something is controlling him. It's not Ignacio. Whatever it is, it's not him anymore.

Breathing shallowly in the dust-choked air, she continued along the corridor. Large sections of the stonework had partially collapsed and now jutted precariously into the room. Dayana kept going, never so aware of the bulk of the museum and its weight pressing down on her.

Finally, she reached the main foyer, her gossamer scarf pulled tightly over her mouth so she could breathe despite the clouds of dust and debris. She stopped for a moment, shaking with fear and adrenaline. Glancing quickly behind her again, she could hear the unhurried footsteps of the god that stalked her.

Dayana stared in horror at the tiled floor. The cheerful mosaics that had been the legacy of the museum opening in eighteen twenty-two now shone with glass shards from the great dome above. Standing barefoot at the edge of the ruin, she stared at the shimmering tiled surface, wishing she had not been so foolish as to discard her shoes.

A fierce wind whipped through the broken roof. Dayana started at human screams and the howling of monkeys echoing in the cavernous space. In the streets of Lima outside the museum, Dayana could see people huddled in confused groups, all staring at some horror looming above the forest and the mountains behind the city. Again, the wind screamed, the sound of vengeful ghosts and forest guardians bearing down on Lima.

Dayana shivered in the cold gale and another terrible rumble shook the ground and the sky. More stone and glass shards rained down from the ceiling. She turned, aware of another presence behind her. She had still hoped what she had seen in the lower chambers of the museum had been due to the remnants of shock and concussion, but she could no longer deny the truth of what had chased her from the underground.

Alerted by a sound behind her, she turned to see Ignacio's broken and bloody corpse standing at his full height, in a commanding posture the archaeologist would never have used in life. Now, the plumed headdress adorned his greying hair and a wide golden collar engraved with the snarling jaguar-god covered his chest. Dayana trembled at the sight of this reanimated body. The keen intellect that lit the familiar eyes of her mentor was not kind nor gentle, but possessed a cold, terrible hunger.

"Ignacio?" Dayana whispered, praying for the return of her mentor rather than this perversion.

The being that possessed Ignacio turned his gaze on her, and Dayana felt small and weak beneath the ancient, impossible knowledge in those eyes. She could find no remnant of her mentor in this stranger standing before her. The face she had always found kind, occasionally even proud, was now merciless and remote as he strode towards her, crescent-shaped blade gripped tightly in that same lacerated arm from which Dayana had seen Ignacio's life-force bleed into the stones. Glancing again at the shards of glass littering the foyer floor, she sucked in a breath and ran from the advancing form.

Pain blossomed through the soles of Dayana's feet, the sharp stings she had expected quickly becoming a pulsating, and nearly overwhelming, agony. Gritting her teeth, she focused on the daylight of the Lima streets beyond the museum steps. She refused to let her thoughts dwell on the bloody trail she was undoubtedly leaving in her wake. Panting with the pain, she stumbled to the edge of the steps, all too aware of the crunch of glass beneath boots and the terrible being that now possessed Ignacio behind her.

"I will feast again," the god said from above her, his voice like the roaring of a jaguar, and echoing across the Andes like thunder.

Dayana fell to her knees and, refusing to have her life so cheaply taken, she crawled, tears pouring down her face to mingle with her bloody trail.

"I will have my sacrifice," the god intoned, standing over Dayana as she cowed at the merciless eyes of a stranger looking down at her.

Dayana looked across the ruin of Lima's streets, the oppressive heat banished with the storm clouds gathering above the Andes, the promise of life in return for her own.

"Take my sacrifice, nourish these lands and never walk this earth again."

The god tilted his head as though in consideration of Dayana's offering. She trembled on her knees, clothing stained in Ignacio's blood and her own, staring up at this vengeful god. The jaguar-god nodded solemnly and raised the blade. Dayana closed her eyes, felt the brush of air as the blade swept towards her exposed throat in a graceful arc, then there was only the sharp shock of her blood spilling across the museum steps.

The god roared in triumph, bloodied blade lifted to the sky. Thunder rolled across the Andes and squalling winds stirred the forest. Raindrops, tentative at first, splashed on the stone, mingling with Dayana's blood where it flowed into the street. Standing on the museum steps, the god smiled; face upraised to the storm, and without warning, Ignacio's body crumpled to the ground, discarded beside Dayana's own.

Above Lima, lightning snaked across the sky and those dry, thirty years of El Nino broke with the coming storm.

'When Dead Gods Walk' was inspired by a discovery at a mountainous northern site in Peru during the early 1920s. Evidence suggests the Mochre culture who'd lived there had conducted human sacrifices, believing these would break a drought, likely caused by the El Nino cycle, returning the rains and restoring the fertile land.

A Trail Of Corpselights

The two siblings fled into the forest, leaving the ruins of their village and the corpses of their parents to the Nazi troops. Even as the Allied war machine pressed Berlin, the Nazi troops were hastening what horrors they had begun. Greta and Hans hurried deeper into the woods. They had no idea whether their village had harboured Jews, and it seemed unlikely the ash and ruins would speak the truth now. They were alone in the world for the first time. Alone and desperate to live.

It had grown so dark beneath the trees when they finally stopped that even squinting up through the branches, it was impossible to tell if late afternoon light was failing or the dense tree canopy simply obscured the sky. When they were younger, their parents had forbidden them from playing too close to the forest edge; the stern expressions on their parents' faces never quite masked their fear. *That was then*, Greta thought with a shiver. *That was before the war. Before Hitler.* She glanced at her brother, wondering how long she and Hans might survive alone in the wilderness. He shared her dark, straight hair and sun-bronzed skin, but where Greta's eyes were hazel, Hans had dark blue, just like their father. Life without her twin brother was an impossibility she could not contemplate.

Greta hugged the fur stole tighter about herself, inhaling the scent of her mother's perfume. It had been the warmest thing Greta could quickly take from the wardrobe when they'd heard the Nazi troops marching up the hill. Now, she shivered despite its warmth. They had been trekking ankle-deep in snow all day, their boots soaked with snowmelt and, aside from a kerosene lantern, they had no other supplies. They were that awkward age between childhood and adulthood, recognised as neither by the world and now cast adrift upon it.

"Hans," she called, holding out her hand for him.

He was peering ahead of them into the depths of the forest, fixated on something she hadn't noticed. He half-turned and, smiling, took her proffered hand and, with a reassuring squeeze, entwined their fingers.

"It'll be all right, Greta," he promised, his young features trying for bravery but unable to hide his uncertainly.

"When do you think we can go back to the village?" Greta asked, shivering again.

"You're cold," Hans said with alarm, pulling her into a hug.

Greta could feel the slight tremors that shook him. They had survived so much already: the bombing of their village and the deaths of their parents, and now Nazi troops come to finish any survivors in a town known for its Jewish sympathisers.

"In the morning we can sneak back, see if the soldiers have left," Hans whispered, his chin resting on the top of Greta's head.

"And if there is nothing left?" she asked, hating herself for asking but needing to know they had a plan.

"Then we make our own way in the world, Greta," he promised. "Just you and me, as always."

Satisfied with the answer, *any* answer, Greta relaxed into Hans' arms, enjoying the illusion of safety.

Somewhere out in the snowy forest, a twig snapped. Greta stiffened, instinct demanding she run, but Hans held her still. When she seemed calm enough, Hans gently kissed the top of her head, slowing the fear threatening to pump wildly through her body again.

In the darkness beyond the reach of the lantern, something moved. Greta whimpered, willing herself to stay calm. Glancing at his twin, Hans gave a curt nod, and they both stepped forward, advancing on whatever monstrous being waited beyond the shadows.

One, two, three.

On the fourth step, Greta heard a low rumble in the trees. She hesitated, tightening her grip on Hans, reluctantly keeping pace with him.

Suddenly, the shadows surrounding them erupted in threatening growls. They froze, Greta's fingernails biting into the bare flesh of Hans' wrist. The wolves snarled, guttural and low, echoing from all around them. Greta's gaze followed the darting forms through the trees, but everywhere she looked were flashing eyes, snow-dusted hackles, and snapping jaws. They'd been surrounded.

"Hans," she murmured, desperate to escape.

"Ahead!" he replied, directing the lantern into the dense trees.

Several wolves immediately shied away from the lantern light, which revealed the snow-covered forest floor ahead and countless dark tree trunks. Brandishing the lantern higher, illuminating a wide area of the forest floor, Hans took a hesitant step forward, Greta at his side. Peering into the gloom beyond the light, Greta saw it: a faint phosphorescent glow that wandered through the trees, unlike any lantern either twin had seen before. *What was that?*

"Help us!" Greta shouted, voice shrill above the growling wolves.

"Are you certain?" Hans asked, swinging the lantern at an attacking wolf excited by Greta's cry.

"Friend or foe, I'm not standing here to be eaten by wolves."

The sudden absence of steady lantern light and Greta's cries for help drove the pack of wolves forward. The snarling intensified, several wolves snapping at each other. Hans swung the lantern wildly, fending off several opportunistic wolves, rapidly exchanging shadow for light with each movement.

A terrible, high-pitched wail echoed through the forest, chilling Greta and Hans to the marrow. The wolves seemed to pause mid-attack, ears flicking as if listening to a command. Then, as abruptly as it began, the wail stopped, fading into a silence that smothered the woods. The silence permeating the forest was complete, unbroken by the falling snow and creaking tree branches. Without warning, the wolves abruptly turned and withdrew, dissolving back into the shadowy forest as if they had never been.

Hans turned a frantic circle, swinging the lantern wide, searching for whatever had driven off a pack of starving wolves in the middle of winter. But he could see nothing. The forest seemed as empty as it had before the wolves arrived. Greta's eyes darted nervously about the forest, seeing only snow and advancing ranks of dark tree trunks.

"Where did that strange light go?" Hans asked, trying to hide his concern.

"I don't know," Greta confessed, searching the gloom. "I can't see it anywhere now."

"Would have been nice to share someone's camp tonight," he mumbled, shivering. "Do you think it was a huntsman?"

"If it was, he was equally afraid of whatever made that keening sound as the wolves were."

Half-turning in a circle, Hans lifted the lantern again to illuminate the path they had taken from the village. Their tracks were still visible in the snow. If someone had wanted to hunt them down, they were easy enough to follow. Then he saw it again, the same faint glow as earlier, moving through the forest but back along their tracks toward the village.

"Come on, we need to find out who that is," Hans said, pulling Greta after him.

The sphere of light did not follow a straight path through the trees, meandering without purpose, but continuing to lead Greta and Hans away from the dark heart of the forest and towards the relative safety of their village. The wolves followed, never drawing too close, but occasionally Hans or Greta would spy them on the periphery.

Despite their repeated attempts to get closer to the mysterious lantern-holder, the figure remained beyond the twins' reach. The forest shadows gathered so deeply beneath the trees that neither Hans nor Greta could discern if the light they followed was a lantern or like some strange marsh light.

Dawn was a pale blush on the eastern horizon when they finally stopped. Struggling up the steep slope, tripping on tree roots trying to catch their feet, Hans and Greta halted, staring at the sight before them.

Many white, incandescent spheres formed a faint path leading the last hundred paces from the forest, illuminating the snowy ground with pale, wispy light. Hans and Greta hesitated, recalling stories from childhood and old wives' tales about following fairy paths. But this was not a fairy path. They both knew there was no fairy realm at the other end. The pale lights shone, the invitation to walk the path they marked out plain.

"Did Father ever tell you that story about the witch who lived in the forest?" Hans asked, suddenly.

"He told so many tales," she whispered, shrugging apologetically.

"A terrible witch who cursed anyone who walked this forest alone, stealing away their children for her magic. Other stories tell how the ghosts of those stolen children continued to haunt these woods, and if travellers found themselves in desperate need of aid, the corpselights would manifest and show a clear path home."

"Those lights are the ghosts of murdered children?" Greta asked tremulously. "I don't think so. I don't know why boys get to hear these stories and girls do not," she mumbled. "It seems to me if these are the ghosts of children murdered by a witch, and they have seen fit to offer us aid, I should have liked to know the story."

"You've never been just a girl to me, Greta, you're the other half of my soul."

For a moment they stood in solemn silence, watching the swirling essence within the spheres, brilliant like sunshine through sea fog.

"Do you think the witch still lives out there?" Greta asked with a shiver. "Do you think that wailing sound was her?"

"Best not think about it, Greta. Instead, let's oblige those who've shown us aid tonight," he said, squeezing her hand again.

Gripping Hans' hand more tightly, Greta followed her brother down the slope to the edge of the eerie path. Still hand-in-hand, the siblings hurried along the trail illuminated by the corpselights, each brilliant sphere winking from existence as they passed it. When they reached the edge of the forest, Hans and Greta looked back into the dark shadows of the woods. Not a trace remained of any corpselights. Resolutely, they turned to face the ruins of their village, stark against the muted grey sky of the early dawn.

'A Trail of Corpselights' is a merging of the Grimm brothers' fairy-tales 'Hansel and Gretel' and 'Little Red Cap', set during the Second World War. This particular era of history interests me, as do the two fairytales, which both involve children willingly venturing into the woods. In this reimagining, escape into the woods—a place normally avoided because of wild animals and other dangers— leads the children to safety via a trail of corpselights; they escape, but the corpselights are also evidence of other children who were not lucky enough to leave the woods alive.

The Making of Hel

Odin, the All-Father, scrutinised Loki's witch-born daughter. She was magnificent and dangerous. In her pale, perfect face framed by raven-black hair, Odin saw the terrible legacy from both her parents. She possessed Loki's unrivalled intellect and fury, but the icy determination of her witch-mother strengthened her into steel.

Loki observed the exchange while he leant against a low stone wall. He was a slender man, wiry and blessed with a beguiling charm. The former were gifts of transformations Odin had given him when they were younger men. The latter was his own power.

"She's no threat to you," Loki said.

The two ravens on Odin's shoulder cawed in agitation.

"You believe that? No, Loki. This girl you begot is more dangerous than the serpent *Jörmungand* and ravenous wolf pup Fenrir combined. I'll take no risks from any offspring born from your calamitous affair with Angrboda."

"I'll never leave the Iron Wood," Hel said.

Odin turned towards her, hoping to appease her anger. "But I offer you something I denied your siblings."

Hel met his gaze. "Should I be honoured or hesitant, then?"

"The witch Angrboda was strong, and her legacy continues in you. My rule extends across Asgard; Surt holds fiery Muspelheim, and Thrazi the icy mountains of Jotunheim. I offer you a realm of your own."

"Why would you give your enemy a gift?"

"I need an underworld and a ruler of those dead shades, the

liars and unfortunates."

"And where in the Nine Worlds do you propose such a realm?"

Odin was unsmiling. "A safe distance from me. Let me show you."

Odin advanced, dragging Hel to the stone wall. Gripping a fistful of raven hair, he pushed her off-balance. Even as Loki rushed forward, Hel screamed. But he was already too late. She toppled over the edge, screams echoing from the pit, fingernails scrabbling on the icy cliffs for purchase.

"The touch of Nifhelheim is death," Loki said.

Odin was unmoved. "It is."

It was too late, had always been too late. From below in the abyss, Hel's agonised screams intensified as she clung resolutely to the icy surface. Wherever hoar frost touched her, necrotic tissue turned to white bone, but the other half of her body remaining unblemished.

Hel snarled at Odin, "I accept your offer. But I don't welcome your kin in my Hall. Pray they never find themselves there."

Odin paled at her words, the sting of prophecy clinging to them. He bowed his head in acknowledgement, already thinking how to avoid the future she proclaimed. Hel laughed at him, frost-burnt face twisted in agony before she released her grip on the icy fissure. She fell, screaming, to the bottom of the Nine Worlds where Odin had gifted her a realm: Helheim, an Underworld, where resentment and hatred of Odin's kin would, like half her ruined body, never heal.

"You feared her," Loki said, furious gaze on Odin. "But in failing to destroy her, you've only sharpened a weapon of your own undoing."

'The Making of Hel' is a reimagining of the Norse myth where Odin attempts to destroy Loki's children by Angrboda, who were considered monstrous offspring, and including Hel. Odin gave her the domain of the dead but in trickery, threw her into Nifhelheim where the touch of any surface is death. Hel proves stronger than Odin imagined but is scarred on one side of her body, which is corpse-like from the touch of the deadly ice in Nifhelheim. This particular myth resonated with me in the strong female role played by Hel who, despite Odin's attempt to trick and kill her, becomes a force to be reckoned with.

The Dark Horseman

Rian Donohoe had lived in county Cavan his entire life, and his roots were deep. On blustery autumn evenings, when many took shelter by the hearth at the Stag and Hawthorn Inn, Rian would recite to any who would listen—and many who preferred not to do so—how his grandfather had ended a generational feud with the neighbouring landowners, the O'Reillys. No matter how deep in their cups those sheltering within the Inn might be, none dared enquire precisely how such a long-standing disagreement was settled. Instead, the men—and some women too—shared knowing glances, and made secret wardings against the Fair Folk where Rian would not see them. For all could recognise the dark glimmer in Rian Donohoe's eyes when he spoke contemptuously of superstitious beliefs in the Sidhe. So it was, and had always been, that none dared challenge the will of the Donohoes. None except the O'Reillys, of course.

The publican, Jack O'Reilly, *thunked* another tankard on the table beside Rian Donohoe. The room grew still, tension heightening, but Rian ignored the looming publican. Muttering softly, Jack turned away and strode back towards the bar, bowing his head as the roof beams became lower, the ancient Inn floorboards sloping uphill to meet with them. Finally, Rian reached for the ale and drank. Whispered conversation from those gathered at the hearth began again, and Jack started noisily cleaning the glassware.

Suddenly, the heavy double doors at the end of the room slammed open, a fierce gust of wind showering the floorboards with fallen leaves. Those huddled nearest the hearth peered fearfully at the darkness beyond the open doors. The wind howled a challenge, splattering the threshold of the Inn with icy rain, but still no one approached the doors. Jack barrelled across the room, cursing all the saints as he closed one large hand over the iron door knocker and reached for the second when he saw a shadow fall across the edge of the parking yard.

Jack O'Reilly froze, heart beating wildly. He watched the trees beyond the parking yard rattle bare branches like an advancing army. But still no one moved. Then he saw it on the fringe of the woods. Squinting against the poor light emitted from the lamppost just outside the Inn, he clearly saw a motionless horseman sitting astride a black stallion.

Hurriedly, Jack grabbed at the other door and slammed them closed and throwing the ancient iron bolt for good measure. He leaned wearily back against the oak doors and closed his eyes, willing his fearful body to stop trembling. In a sharp exhale, Jack straightened and opened his eyes again.

Men who had been discussing historic winter storms only moments before now stared at him in stunned silence. Jack considered how peculiar his actions must seem, how uncharacteristic. Only Rian Donohoe watched him with a look of vindication, as though finally proved right about some opinion of him. Sighing again, Jack pushed himself off the doors, checking the solid bolts were thrown, before he walked back towards the bar again.

"Seen a ghost?" Rian snickered.

Jack jerked in shock. He resisted the urge to look behind himself, though he half expected the shadowy horseman to be there. But there was nothing, of course. Not even a faint touch of wintry gale through the room. Clenching his fists, Jack ignored Rian's barely subdued laughter at his expense and gratefully slipped behind the bar, pleased to have the solid counter between himself and the terrors of the night.

Throughout the evening, Rian kept careful watch over Jack O'Reilly. There was something he disliked about the big publican which ran deeper than the historical feud between their families.

"What did you see out there?" Liam Brady asked Jack, leaning on the bar.

Jack only stared at the little man, the village postmaster and hoarder of town gossip. Liam knew the affairs of everyone, and Jack had no desire to add to his knowledge. But Liam only blinked rapidly at Jack, glasses perched precariously on the end of his nose, waiting for a response.

"Liam," Jack began, trying to wipe away invisible stains on the bar counter.

"I want to hear this too," Rian interrupted, putting his tankard down with unnecessary force, ale sloshing onto the tabletop.

"This is ridiculous," Jack warned, glaring at Liam. "I didn't ee anything out there."

"You *were* pale as the dead when you closed those doors, though," Liam mused aloud.

"Are you sure you didn't see the Dullahan?" Rian asked maliciously. "Your family has a history of seeing the dark horseman, don't they?"

"Just as much as your family has cause to pay him tribute," Jack replied, slamming an enormous fist onto the bar.

Sudden silence smothered the room as all eyes focused on Jack and Rian. The little postmaster glanced cautiously at both men before haltingly taking his leave, shuffling out of their reach.

"Well, well," Rian chuckled. "There's that famous O'Reilly temper."

"I think you're done for the evening, Donohoe," Jack replied, tossing the cleaning rag into a bucket on the far side of the bar. "I'll ask respectfully that you leave my establishment now."

"And if I respectfully decline?" Rian challenged, dark brows raised.

Tension in the room tightened, as if an unseen force had withdrawn all the air, and even those gathered at the hearthside felt suffocated by it. Around the Inn, tankards were hurriedly drained and glasses of whiskey tossed back as chairs scraped across floorboards and people got to their feet. At the bar, Jack O'Reilly and Rian Donohoe did not stir.

Abruptly, the iron bolts on the Inn doors screeched as the

evening's patrons hurried into the night. Jack's large hands shook where they rested on the countertop, but his gaze did not waver from Rian Donohoe. The double doors to the Inn slammed closed with a thunderous noise, the wind outside rattling the iron bolts before silence fell again. Jack winced as a fleeting image of the horseman on the edge of the woods came unbidden to his mind again. Rian Donohoe watched him with undisguised curiosity.

"You saw something, didn't you?" Rian hissed.

Jack eyed him suspiciously; then, temper rising again, he looked at his own scarred hands on the bar. "So, what if I did? Many of those bastards who just left claim they've seen Fae things in the woods."

"True," Rian agreed, reasonably. "But none of those men would dare tell me about it either, no matter how closely we're tied. I know what they all say about me, Jack."

"Do you?" he scoffed.

"They think not acknowledging the Sidhe is foolish, but it's the superstitious belief in a vengeful horseman that's insane, O'Reilly."

"Why should it bother you if others believe in the Dullahan?" Jack demanded, temper finally fraying.

"What bothers me, O'Reilly, is accusations made by your family for countless decades have tainted mine for generations. My grandfather was right, making certain no O'Reilly would ever own land in this village again. For just as Patrick drove the snakes from these fair shores, if I had my way, I'd drive the O'Reillys from County Cavan."

"Fortunate you're not a saint and just delusional then, ain't we?" Jack mumbled, fists clenched tightly on the countertop. "How did your grandfather obtain such certainty, Rian? Perhaps my grandmother was right when she said he paid tribute to the Dullahan."

"The Donohoes are a great family, O'Reilly, but not so esteemed as to claim the crooked god among our service."

"Get out of here, Donohoe," Jack growled. "Best I not see your face here again this week, or help me God, I'll bring the Dullahan down upon you myself."

Rian glared, but Jack was purposefully ignoring him, already locking cabinets and extinguishing lamps around the bar. Growling an inaudible insult, Rian Donohoe turned away and, collecting his leather satchel from his table, he strode from the Inn without a backward glance.

From the shadowy depths of the Inn, Jack O'Reilly considered himself blessed, as though a tremendous weight lifted from him. Sighing, he glanced at deep shadows shifting in the woods beyond the doorway and continued his preparations to lock up for the night.

Rian Donohoe strode from the Inn and across the parking yard. The only car remaining was his silver BMW parked beneath the lamppost. It wasn't until he was within a few paces of his car that he realised why his vehicle hadn't automatically unlocked with his approach. The key fob was still inside the Inn. Because of the policy to discourage drunk driving in Ireland, patrons deposited their keys with the publicans before admittance. It was a policy Jack O'Reilly seemed enthusiastic to enforce, especially on Rian. Cursing softly, Rian glanced back at the Inn, but the shutters were all secured, the double doors bolted against his return. Already a heavy mist had descended from the craggy mountains beyond the village, shrouding a nearby church and everything else beyond the Inn from view. Considering Jack had evicted him, there was very little chance he'd open the doors to him now. Sighing in frustration, Rian looked about the deserted parking yard one last time, reluctant to leave the circle of light the lamppost provided, the darkness beyond menacing. It was not a long walk back to his farmstead, a walk he often did at the height of midsummer. *But never in late autumn*, he thought, the shadows waiting for him to leave the protective light.

"Ridiculous," he spat, zipping up his leather jacket and stepping into the darkness.

Immediately, the chill wind strengthened, blowing directly from the mountains crags and carrying the frigid memory of snow. Shivering, Rian walked faster, following the verge of the road now, its form shrouded in darkness and so horribly narrow it forced him to walk in the traffic lane. The bitter cold was unrelenting, but determined to keep his mind active, Rian considered his recent conversation with Jack O'Reilly. It surprised him that Jack O'Reilly knew anything of the history behind the feud. Rian had learned the secret of the feud only when his own father was on his deathbed, the secret passed to the eldest Donohoe son well before the times of Rian's grandfather and the evictions of the O'Reillys from their lands. But Jack O'Reilly was not as dim-witted as he'd seemed either. There was a darker secret behind the methods Rian's grandfather had used to dispel the O'Reillys, but the truth of that secret was unknown to even Rian.

Thunder rolled across the distant mountains, and Rian squinted up at the darkening sky and grimaced. Ahead, the road continued across a narrow bridge before continuing through the foothills on the outskirts of the village. The thought of being caught outside in an autumn storm was unwelcome, but Rian knew only one path that would see him safely home before the storm broke. The shorter path he took frequently in midsummer wound through the meadows and into a small woodland copse on the boundary of his lands. But he'd always refused to let anyone know how much the stories of the Sidhe and the hollow hills terrified him. The legends of the Fair Folk stealing Christian people away to become enslaved within the hills, only to release them as bent old men and women, was a fate that haunted him. Far easier to mock others for their fears than admit the truth of his own. Above him, the sky growled in restless frustration, the valley heavy with the anticipation of a storm. Rian shoved his hands deeper into his pockets, glared reproachfully at the clouds, and walked off the edge of the road and onto a barely discernible path through the tangle of the overgrown meadow.

The moment he left the road, Rian was certain he'd made the wrong decision, but refusing to admit to such superstition as a premonition, Rian kept his boots firmly on the path through the long grass, focusing instead on the chorus of frogs and night insects that abruptly fell silent as he passed, only to continue moments later. Walking up the slope towards the dark copse of woods that bordered his lands, Rian recalled that when he was only nine years old, his grandfather had taken him to visit the neighbouring small township of Killycluggin set at the base of a craggy peak. The highlight of the adventure had been an enormous stone in the Killycluggin museum. Carved by unknown hands, the stone was thought by many to depict Crom Cruach, one of the Old Gods, worshipped once for fertility and known by many names that few now remembered. Rian's grandfather had been among those few, telling his grandson how one of the mightiest Sidhe was in servitude to the Donohoe family. It had seemed unlikely to Rian that his grandfather spoke the truth, or that the earnestness with which he spoke of entrapping one of the Fair Folk—especially the Sidhe, a race never known for a forgiving nature —had been anything but delusion. Now, walking a path through the overgrown meadows in the darkness, the thought of his grandfather incurring a debt to one of the Sidhe filled Rian with dread.

The storm growled anew as it approached the village sheltered beneath the mountains, and beyond the fields and meadows, the distant silvery lakes of County Cavan waited. Rian shivered as another gust of icy wind hit him, bending the long grasses of the meadows as if brushed by giant, unseen hands. *If only I'd not left the road*, Rian thought grimly.

Abruptly, Rian stopped, glancing quickly to the woods ahead of him. All around him, every living creature had fallen silent. The sudden absence of frogs or night insects was deafening. Heart pounding and sweat breaking across his skin, Rian shivered in the chill air. A terrible sense overwhelmed him that all the creatures of these fields had curled up tightly in their burrows, seeking protection from whatever now stalked the night, and that he should do likewise. Frantically, Rian looked around the empty meadows for anywhere to hide, or a disused den to shelter within until the threat from the Sidhe had passed. But there was nothing. Exposed on the hillside, framed against the darkness of the woods behind him, Rian was as visible as if he stood in the noonday sun.

Rian heard it then: the jangle of a horse's harness behind him in the darkness. Terror overwhelmed him, and he sprinted for the gnarled branches of the woodland copse. The legends of the Sidhe who claimed the territory of these foothills and mountains in County Cavan for their own, the memories of his grandfather and the Killycluggin Stone, and damned Jack O'Reilly's accusations earlier that evening now coalesced in Rian's mind. Surely his grandfather had never meant it. Surely he had made no deal with the Dullahan.

Even as he fled for the forest, Rian heard the jangle of bit and spur, the sharp sound of horseshoe striking stone and the snorting charge of the stallion behind him. He didn't turn to check, didn't want to see that dark mount and its doomed rider descending on him. Instead, he ran, desperate to reach the forest edge and his own lands. Behind him, the hoofbeats cut deep into the earth, spraying clods of soil across the meadow as the stallion charged him. Breathless, Rian reached the copse, and slinging an arm about a birch sapling, pulled himself in a circle, not losing any momentum, and stood to face whatever followed him.

The mounted horseman crossed the last paces of the meadow, reining in his stallion inches from Rian, who stood paralysed with fear. The horse reared, front hooves striking the air, its rider's black cloak falling away to reveal gauntleted fists on the reins. But the other arm cradled a decaying, severed head, grin stretched wide across its mouldering face.

Rian screamed, and the storm answered, his voice buried by the thunder rolling across bruise-coloured clouds, lightning reaching for earth like skeletal hands. The Dullahan drew his broadsword, stormy sky and Rian's pale face reflected on its surface. Mind panicked with terror, Rian begged incoherently, words tumbling from his lips in sobs. The stories everyone had ever told about his grandfather were true and now he must pay the debt owed. But the Dullahan did not respond, remaining impassive astride his mount until Rian's whispered pleas. Impatiently, the black stallion stamped the ground and tossed its fierce head, eager to be away into the night.

"Donohoe," the Dullahan called, voice as chilling as the empty moors.

Rian swallowed, conscious that the Dullahan knew exactly

who he was, had sought him out specifically on this night. Were all legends of the Dullahan true? Did the horseman expect him to answer for his grandfather's dealings with the Sidhe? Unable to find his voice amid his fear, Rian nodded, waiting for this harbinger to pronounce his doom.

"Do you have the sacrifice?" The Dullahan requested.

"The sacrifice?" Rian stuttered, alarmed and confused.

The black-cloaked rider steadied his restless stallion, the beast snorting, wild eyes watching Rian. But Rian could only stare with slowly creeping horror at this manifestation of the dark god. Suddenly, he jerked with alarm, his mind dredging forth the knowledge and bitter understanding of what the Dullahan requested. Wetting his lip and tasting salt, Rian realised he'd been sobbing uncontrollably for some time now. Fear took hold, and he tried desperately to dart to the side. The Dullahan spun his mount easily, blocking the attempted escape, the stallion's massive shoulders as immovable as the mountains surrounding them.

Rian started stepping backward, hearing his own voice begging and pleading again. He sounded like a petrified nine-year-old again. But surely the Dullahan must be able to tell he knew nothing of his grandfather's debts. He couldn't be responsible for any bargains made generations ago. *Surely the Dullahan would spare me?*

"Have you a sacrifice worthy of my aid?" The Dullahan asked again, merciless as the grave.

"I don't have your head!" Rian finally shouted.

The Dullahan did not move. The storm growled above, lightning reflecting along the naked blade in his gauntleted fist. Then the black stallion paced eagerly forward, sending Rian scuttling backward into the undergrowth. He tripped on a hidden oak root and careened awkwardly into the tree trunk behind. Unable to escape, Rian watched the Dullahan raise his sword, the decayed head from some previous sacrifice still held under one arm.

"If you do not have a sacrifice to offer, I shall take what I am owed."

Rian screamed, voice echoing through the woods as the sword

fell. Thunder split the night, fresh blood splattering the autumn leaves beneath the oak. The Dullahan tossed the fetid, decapitated head of Jack O'Reilly's ancestor to the ground. Then, stooping beside Rian's now headless corpse, he lifted the new sacrifice in his gauntleted hands. An awful grin of terror stretched wide across Rian's bloodless face, and the Dullahan cradled it protectively beneath one arm. The Dullahan sheathed his bloodied sword and spurred his stallion forward, hooves and jangling harness echoing throughout the stormy night.

The reimagining of the legend of the Irish headless horsemen in 'The Dark Horseman' is inspired by the Irish legends of the Crooked God Crom Cruach, an ancient pre-Christian God whose significance is reflected in the Killycluggin Stone in County Cavan believed to be an ancient representation of Crom Cruach discovered at a cross-roads with a nearby Bronze Age stone circle. The sacrifices to Crom Cruach were in to continue the fertility of the land.

Second Chances

Rapid gunfire echoed across the battlefield, thick mist ringing the hill, obscuring trenches and coils of razor wire. Struggling up the steep slope, I clawed at the bloodsoaked earth, hauling myself nearer the top. A machine gun barked, spraying mud and gore in a wide arc.

Terrified, I huddled into the churned earth, hoping they'd think me just another casualty of this Great War. There, amid decay, tears slid silently down my cheeks. I held my breath until the enemy soldiers were past me, conversing in quiet German, scanning the battleground.

I needed to get to the plateau above. I needed to escape. I had lived in this valley my entire life; my village had been where the internment camp now was beside the river. But years of constant battle had stripped the valley of any resemblance to the one from my childhood. I hadn't even been sure where my group of ragged prisoners had been when fighting broke out today. I needed to get to the plateau, where there was an unobstructed view of the valley.

Scrambling up the rest of the slope, I carefully stepped out onto the open ground of the plateau. Apart from a single oak tree, the surrounding forest had never encroached on the natural promontory. It suddenly seemed very strange to me. Standing in that exposed space, I stared in horror. Nothing of the oak tree remained but a splintered stump. Instead, the invading army had constructed a communications tower here, but it had drawn mortar attack, leaving only the twisted metal wreckage of the tower in its place. I looked across the valley, the landscape destroyed and unrecognisable to me.

I felt hostile eyes on me and turned. The two enemy soldiers walked the last steps up the slope, boots sucking against the mud as though the battlefield hungered for more victims. Staring at the guns, terror drained my strength and my legs buckled. I closed my eyes, digging my fingers into the earth for some comfort. I found a chunk of stone and clutched at it protectively as the guns fired.

Distantly, I heard the soldiers shouting. I smiled at the stone still held in my hand and traced the faint runes on it with bloody fingertips. Improbably, I felt no pain, but the heavy silence around me seemed impossible.

Cautiously, I moved, finding only shallow grazes where there should be fatal wounds, as though the bullets had passed through me. Looking around me, I realised the soldiers and battlefield had vanished. The oak tree stood undamaged on the plateau, six stone pillars now marking the perimeter of the clearing. Rising uninjured to my feet, I stared at the nearest monolith, recognising the carved runes on its surface. I lifted the chunk of stone in my hand; the same worn runes as those on the pillar were yet to be marked by the weather or the passage of time. Not tempting Fate lest my second chance be revoked, I fled into the dappled forest.

'Second chances' is a fictionalised reimagining of World War II and the transformation of areas in Germany into a battleground, and the persecution and imprisonment of the Jewish community and any supporters. The folklore surrounding standing stones as portals into other worlds or times follows the grim reality that for many during World War II there was no second chance to escape, which resonated very strongly with me.

The Order Sagittarius

I first heard about the Order Sagittarius when I was only a child. My aunt told me in my tenth year about the Twelve Orders that governed the Empire and of the Order Sagittarius and its priestesses, who foretold prophecies. In the innocence of childhood, the idea of prophetic priestesses immediately took root, blossoming in my imagination until the Order Sagittarius was an obsession. It mortified my Familia that their only child, their eldest daughter, was interested in the Orders. *What will become of their legacy if I entered an Order?* If I did, wealth, status and title would be consigned to the Empire. For my Familia, the approach of my sixteenth year and my independence was a time of trepidation. But like an ordained miracle, on the eve of my sixteenth birthday, my mother was due to give birth to another child. My story began that fateful midsummer day.

"**H**elena!"

I started awake from where I had been dozing in the afternoon sunlight. Tucking the small book I'd been reading beneath a cushion, I hastened to sit up. Looking anxiously along the marble corridors of our house, I checked to see if any of the servants were about. My name still echoed through the upper storey of our house, but from my sheltered position on the balcony window seat, I couldn't see any servants hurrying to find me. I sighed and settled back comfortably against the cushions, knowing they disregarded my presence in the household as willingly as my parents.

These last few weeks had seen me studiously ignored by Familia and servants alike, my mother confined to her rooms as the pregnancy lengthened beyond her expected delivery. The anxious faces of the few servants I encountered showed their unspoken fears. To the household, I was an impending doom. My obsession with the Order Sagittarius had never wavered, but developed into a determination to join the Order once I gained my independence at sixteen. When the familia announced the birth of another daughter, the relief was palpable. In the Empire, wealth and Familia were inherited through the female line. Although my decision to join the Order Sagittarius hadn't been announced to society, I had assumed a non-inheritable role within the Familia. Without another daughter to inherit once I joined the priestesses in the Order Sagittarius, the familia and its fortune would have no future beyond the death of my parents.

Even with my decision known to the familia, they'd still paraded me in society each evening, my parents hoping some dashing young man of an equal or better household would change my stubborn faith. The evening promenades became more tiresome and, fortunately, less frequent with the advancing of my mother's pregnancy. The Familia silently committed themselves to a solemn period of mourning, as though I had died with the future they had envisioned for me. I existed like a spectre in the household, as though without the future they'd originally imagined, I'd already gone from their world.

"Helena!" My father called again.

"Only remembered when needed," I muttered and stood, smoothing down the layers of my ruffled skirts.

I glanced longingly back at the gilt-edged book I'd concealed beneath the cushions. The volume contained the collective wisdom of the Order Sagittarius and was necessary reading for all noviciates. I intended to take my Vows as soon after my birthday as possible. Sighing, I turned away from the book, adopted a polite and dutiful expression, and hastened down the corridor toward the rooms at the far end.

"Coming, Father," I called in what I hoped was an agreeable tone.

I followed the curve of the corridor walls, built from the Empire's famous white marble quarried in our nearby hills, slowing as I neared Father's library. The door was open, revealing the vast room beyond lined with bookshelves. I paused in the doorway, seeing my father stooped over his writing desk. Enormous leather-bound volumes covered the desk, with quills and inkpots occupying precarious positions on what minimal surface remained. I hesitated, hand raised to knock, but took the moment to observe my father, a man whose motivations I understood so poorly but who had complete control over my life.

He was bent over the desk, heavy eyebrow furrowed, thinning hair hidden beneath a fashionable hairpiece that could not ease the press of years revealed in the lines at the corners of his eyes and mouth. I stared in silent fascination, wondering for the first time at the significant age difference between my father and mother. I had never asked her about being married to a wealthy older man, how she had felt being exchanged as a bartering piece between business partners. In the Empire, the oldest households controlled much of the wealth and they only conducted marriages with the Familia in mind, forging alliances to better the prospects of one household and see the decline in others. Marriage was a game of risk that had stakes as high as any merchant's dealings. I hadn't considered the disdain I'd treated my mother with for accepting the role her Familia had expected her to fulfil.

"Father?" I asked from the doorway, hands laced demurely in front of me, eyes on the floor.

He glanced up at me and even though I didn't take my eyes from the floorboards, I felt his gaze sweep over me.

"Helena," he said, exhaling with the snap of his spectacle lenses clicking together as he positioned them on the bridge of his nose. "I received news at mid-morn your mother has birthed a strong daughter."

I gave a polite bob of a curtsy, a small smile curling the corners of my lips, but tried not to fidget.

"Last Festival of the Hunter, your mother paid homage to the Order Sagittarius."

Shocked, I looked up to meet my father's eyes. I imagined my expression was unreadable or quizzical at best. "What? Why?"

"Your mother went to the priestesses seeking a prophecy," he said, wetting his lips and swallowing with difficulty. "You of all will be familiar with the Order Sagittarius, daughter. Your mother sought answer to a question she wouldn't tell me. I only know the answer given in reply."

What knowledge could my mother have sought that would be worth the associated risk? The priestesses of the Order Sagittarius were not the kindly fortune tellers I had imagined from my childhood. The powers of their prophecy were more dangerous to the one seeking it than any could truly realise. The prophecy spoken from the Sagittarius would be either of fortune or ill-fate, but whichever it was, the truth would be unavoidable. It was a risk servants of the Empire took only in absolute need, for once the truth of the future was revealed, it could damage to the one who sought it.

"What truth did she receive?" I whispered.

"She would give life to another but lose her first to the Twelve."

I closed my eyes, hand on the doorframe for support. To many others, those words might not seem unexpected; for my mother, it offered hope but also required a sacrifice. My mother would have a second child, but only if she renounced her eldest daughter, exchanged my life of noble extravagance for the barren cloisters of the Orders. It might seem a grievous cost to some, but I would willingly pay it. I wondered if Sagittarius had granted my mother a boon of Fortune in exchange for her simple offering paid at the Order's gates.

We considered the prophecy foretold to my mother fortunate. So that she might show proper gratitude, she arranged for me to depart from our household estate only two days after the birth of my younger sister. As with any noviciate in the Twelve Orders, I renounced all allegiances, inheritance and fealty to my household and Familia. In the sixteen years since taking my Vows as a priestess to the Order Sagittarius, I have come to understand the perils in having ties to Familia, as prophetic knowledge of the fates for any citizen in the metropolis is accessible to me. One

176

of the responsibilities of priestesses in the Order Sagittarius is to avoid any corruption from the powerful Familia and so I never met my sister nor saw my Familia again.

Instead, I found a new home in the sprawling stone ruins of the cloister, perched on the cliffs overlooking the metropolis. The solace of meditation and prayer with other priestesses offered some respite from our shared burden, the prophetic knowledge foretelling successes: marriages and alliances, harvest boons and safe harbours, or the grim foretelling of death, illness, business collapses or crippling drought. Like many of the priestesses, I took comfort in the strength of the Twelve Orders and our burdens seemed lighter in the knowledge that we enacted the will of the deities we served. This did not prevent me from seeking morning meditation to ease my troubled mind, and I spent part of each week taking the Offerings.

I rose before dawn, slipping on the red robes of the Order and painting my face with the thick white paint, obscuring any identifying features. As a priestess of the Order Sagittarius, I was one of many whose lips spoke prophecies for Offerings to the Order.

With a practised and steady hand, I placed the large brush back into a bowl beside the thick white clay we painted upon our faces and dipped the tip of another, more delicate, into the well of black ink. Closing one eye, I traced the familiar symbol across my eyelid, marking me as a priestess ordained in the Order Sagittarius. It was a simple hand-drawn arrow, symbolic of the Order Sagittarius and used as a seal of exchange in the prophecies I would conduct today.

I didn't inspect myself in the bronze surface of the mirror but slipped my bare feet into the plain clogs, tightened the plaited leather belt around my waist, holding the golden timepiece and arrow reverently in my hand a moment before letting them hang from the tassel on my belt. Without another glance at my sparse room, I slipped out my door and into the narrow, circular corridors of the tower beyond. Moving silently through the narrow passages, I nodded acknowledgements to the youngest noviciates already beginning their daily tasks.

When I finally emerged from the crumbling stone tower, I

headed along the narrow path, following the craggy clifftops where the cloisters and ruined towers of the Order Sagittarius perched as though ready to take flight into storms brewing out at sea. The stepping stone pathway I followed slowly transformed beneath my feet, becoming a narrow cobblestone lane that swept down the rugged hillside to an inner courtyard of a much larger tower, boasting signs of recent repair and a small kitchen garden.

I continued my brisk pace toward a single wooden gate that barred entrance to the cloisters of the Order Sagittarius, its gnarled wooden surface carved with runes and symbols. Most prominent of all was the massive sigil of the Arrow, scorched into the wood as though branded by a giant. My hand pushed flat against the wooden gate and it swung effortlessly on its bronze hinges. Even as I passed beneath the stone archway, I drew in my breath, always conscious of the inexplicable dread that enveloped me as I walked beneath the ancient granite. They'd constructed all the Empire buildings from marble, the metropolis a gleaming contrast to the ashen grey of the ancient cloisters. But like the other Twelve Orders, the Order Sagittarius predated the Empire, had crushed the false deities of the nameless religion before and obliterated all traces of them from the Empire. Everything forgotten and nothing remained except these ancient grey buildings which the Twelve Orders now filled like some parasite inside its host's shell.

Shivering, I pulled my woollen red cloak about my shoulders as I stepped from beneath the archway and into the bright sunlight of the cobblestone street beyond. I followed the twisting lane that meandered down toward the pale, sprawled city on the edge of the water. Listening to the familiar rhythm of my simple clogs upon the cobblestones, I gaze at the metropolis where it slumbered by the glittering bay, waiting like a gluttonous beast beneath the shade of the cliffs. Already tiny boats were visible on the canals branching away from the river, away from the bay and its merchant ships, the cargo and passengers arriving into the harbour for business in the metropolis. The heart of the Empire was a slow-beating thing, languidly stirring in the morning heat.

The sharp clang of morning bells rang across the metropolis, the Twelve Orders calling the faithful to worship. I hastened my step, knowing at even this early in the morning before market, the poorer inhabitants of the metropolis made their Offerings before conducting business of the day, seeking the guidance of the Twelve Orders. It was unlikely that many would visit the temple of Sagittarius this morning. The poorer of the metropolis often saw no need to risk the knowledge of a foretold future when they had so little reason to find hope in it. The wealthy Familia of the Empire frequented the Order Sagittarius when it needed those households with influence and the ability to shift the course of the future.

I hurried through an empty marketplace; the crossroads was scarcely occupied by other travellers this morning. I took the more heavily worn road that led deeper into the labyrinthine metropolis. The complex streets and lanes soon became a confusion of noise and bustling servants hurrying to attend to the tasks of their households. After a brief navigation of the twisting lanes, I came to a large stone temple in the centre of a market square; the building carved from ancient granite and looking out of place among the surrounding marble buildings.

There was a small room at the rear of the temple where I would take the Offerings in return for the words of prophecy. I hurried through the well-lit antechamber, ignoring the splash of the central fountain that chimed like laughter in the bright courtyard tiled with white marble. Beyond the antechamber was a corridor of espalier fruit trees and stone benches occupied by a few of the faithful already waiting with heads bowed as I passed them.

Exhaling a long breath, I finally entered a tiny room at the rear of the temple. I exhaled again, releasing the nervous energy of my hurried pace, then carefully walked into the square room, lighting candles in each corner as I moved. The scent from perfumed candles immediately banished the scent of dusty streets beyond. Moving with quiet efficiency, I positioned a small brazier onto a low table in the middle of the room, placing several more scented candles beside it to aid in purifying the space before I sat back on the large cushion and took a moment to relax, closing my eyes.

Outside the temple, the vibrations thrummed across the

metropolis, followed by the distant metallic echo of a great bell signalling mid-morning worship. I inhaled, waiting a heartbeat until the smaller replica bronze bell on the belt at my waist chimed a response to the larger timepiece. The quiet temple atmosphere seemed to shiver with vibrations. The alchemy synchronising the bells stirred the surrounding air. In the flickering light from the lit brazier, dust motes swirled, then abruptly settled with the final tremble of that strange alchemy. Footsteps hesitated in the passage outside the temple, then continued with renewed determination toward my shadowy enclave.

I rearranged the long red robes and kept my gaze on the brazier as the young woman hesitated again outside the room. A whispered chastisement for lack of courage. Then she bustled into the small room. I kept my eyes on the brazier and the two bronze bowls inscribed with the symbolic arrow of Sagittarius. She seated herself without comment. The confidence she exuded was false, and from beneath my lowered eyelids I saw her hand shake as she dropped a handful of coins into one of the bronze bowls before me. I bowed my head in silent acknowledgement of her Offering but waited, body subtly inclined toward the second empty bowl before me.

Heavy silence hung about the small room while I waited. It was already stiflingly warm in here despite the early hour of the day, the scent of herbs cloying and thick in the air. There was an uneasy pause before another, heavier clink echoed in the room and the young woman sat back on her cushion, her Offering to me finally made. I bowed my head in gratitude, slowly lifting my eyes but never as high as the young woman's face. I could tell from the rich scents that perfumed her body, the rustle of heavy cloth gown as it swept the floor, that this woman belonged to one of the oldest and wealthiest Familia in the metropolis. I hid my surprise that she had travelled across the metropolis and floating markets to attend this temple to the Order Sagittarius and not one closer to the wealthy household estates. Above all, the coin she carried in her purse proclaimed her status. Only the wealthy Familia had access to coin that heavy, where the purest metals weren't diluted. Street beggars and religious temples alike all over the Empire knew such things. The irony wasn't lost on me.

I finally looked at the young woman opposite me, meeting the pale hazel eyes opposite the low table. In the flickering light, I could see how young she was, barely into womanhood, but the earnest expression that met mine was both startling and pleasant.

"How does this usually work?" she asked, gesturing nervously to the low table before us. "My mother made an Offering once, but that was many years before my birth. She never spoke of the details."

"The rites of the Order Sagittarius aren't well known beyond the members of the Order itself."

"My older sister became a priestess. But I never knew her."

Her words struck me like a blow, and I sat, unable to speak in stunned silence that stretched around us. I just stared in disbelief at the young woman sitting before me, fidgeting awkwardly, an anxious smile on her lips. Was this really my sister? I shook my head, breaking the awkward stillness. This was ridiculous. There were surely many young women in the metropolis. I was being foolish to imagine this one was my sister.

"You've made the Offering to the Order," I said, briefly gesturing to the heavy coins in the bronze bowls before us. "Once I light these candles, I'll invoke a wisdom privy only to the priestesses of Sagittarius. You may ask a question of Sagittarius, and in return, a prophecy will be granted. Only the priestesses of Sagittarius can divine whether they foretell a fortunate or cursed fate."

"I understand," she said, twisting her hands in her lap.

I nodded briskly and moved forward an inch to the small table before us, lifting the lid from the brazier to reveal the hungry coals glowing within. Without glancing to my left, I picked up the tall, scented candle I had placed there, practised movements allowing me to bring the taper to the nearest ember while lowering the brazier lid to the floor with my other hand. I kept my gaze on the candle, watching flame lick along the beeswax wick before I carefully positioned it on the table. Deftly, I lit another tall, scented candle and offered a whispered prayer before dashing a handful of dried herbs into the brazier. A dense cloud of scented smoke ballooned into the room, sending the girl opposite me into coughing fits. Unperturbed, I closed my eyes and inhaled deeply of the pungent mixture, waiting for the medicinal herbs to take effect.

"Ask what you would of the Sagittarius," I said, voice flat, the powerful herbs already working.

"I seek guidance on my upcoming marriage. I want to know if the union of our Familia will benefit the Empire."

I felt my eyelids open, my gaze sharpened and focused on the girl before me. But I did not truly see her. In my mind, I saw the infinite number of scenarios that spun outward from her as though she were the epicentre of a bright spiral. Still not fully conscious of my body, I was dimly aware my hand reached for a quill to my far right, dipped the nib into the inkwell. My other hand drew the rough piece of parchment close to me and I wrote.

Normally, my hand was delicate. A lifetime of expensive tutoring from a wealthy Familia had schooled me with good penmanship. But the writing I produced while in the depths of the prophecy surpassed anything to which my former tutors might have laid claim. This script was elegant and flowing. Whatever power guided the prophecy also worked through me in the simplest of ways.

The priestesses of the Order did not understand Sagittarius, nor how those were chosen to be ordained. But now, as that greater power controlled my body, I stared at the girl opposite me. My first instinct had been right: impossibly, this girl truly was my sister. It was for her I wrote the prophecy, allowing the power of Sagittarius to flow through me and whether I penned Fortune or Curse, I would not know until the quill returned to rest.

Time passed, unmeasured by me as I stayed in the depths of the prophecy. I did not know how long I wrote. I knew only when the prophecy was complete. The hissing of herbs upon the brazier had stopped, and the vellum was covered in writing, but the meaning yet to be revealed.

"Take this," I said hoarsely, exhaustion leaving me drained of strength.

She leaned forward and took the prophecy from across the lacquered surface of the low wooden table between us. I noticed her hands shook worse than mine.

I forced myself rigidly straight despite the overwhelming exhaustion and watched my sister. We shared the same recognisable features of our Familia, but she had my mother's wavy locks; I had the severely straight hair of our father. The frown that knit her brows as she read the prophecy could have reflected my own. She was everything my Familia had wished for me to be, everything that I was not. Her name was Sofia, the name of our father's mother, a namesake for her golden hair, which I could see my sister Sofia also shared, a few wavy strands escaping her ornate headdress.

"Praise the Twelve," she said.

Before I could stop her, she leapt to her feet in a swirl of petticoats, skirts and a cloak that threatened to topple the small table and brazier between us. I caught the table and steadied the brazier, preventing the candles from setting fire to anything around me.

"Sofia, wait!" I cried, struggling to my own feet but hampered by the scattered floor cushions.

"Send greetings to my sister Helena if you ever meet her!" she called from the outer room with a quick wave before dashing into the corridor beyond.

I hurried after her, fatigue and the ridiculous length of my robe tangling between my legs. I rushed to the temple doorway and stopped, searching the crowded market square beyond, but I could see no sign of the dark blue cloak Sofia had been wearing. She had vanished among the crowd, swallowed by the sprawling metropolis.

It was important that I find Sofia and fulfil my vows as a priestess to the Order Sagittarius. She had made the Offering; I'd spoken the prophecy, but I'd not fulfilled the last part of our solemn exchange. The knowledge that Sofia was of my own Familia only made my distress deeper. Her eagerness to know what guidance the Sagittarius might offer, to know if her marriage was the right one, she'd read the parchment but not waited for me to determine the most crucial part of the prophecy: whether it was Fortune or Curse. The words written on parchment were only a formal record, lacking all the intuitive insight the priestesses gained when delivering the prophecy. Sofia could not know the hundreds of different outcomes Sagittarius had shown me, the balancing and shuffling of her fate from Fortune to Curse. I needed to tell her the last part of the prophecy.

I summoned a shabbily dressed messenger boy as he darted past the temple. He paused, frowning, then hurried over as I beckoned to him again, recoiling deeper into a shadowed alcove. As a priestess, I had forsaken all allegiances to my own family, severed all ties to the noble households and that ruled the Empire. It allowed me a sense of indifference to the rise and fall of great Familia. Part of living in a cloister and being beholden to the Order Sagittarius was that all correspondence normally went through the Twelve Orders. This provided a layer of separation between priestesses and those who might dislike the Cursed Fate proclaimed for their Familia. Here, that security was now a liability for me. I needed to get a message to Sofia, to my Familia with whom they'd forbidden me contact. I knew I was breaking my Vows even as the messenger boy pulled his homespun cap from his dishevelled hair and gave me an awkward bow.

"Priestess?" he asked uncertainly, eyes on the cobblestones.

"I need you to take a message for me. Will you do that?"

He hesitated, scuffing a worn boot across the ground.

"I'll pay you in coin," I said, already taking a few pieces from the small leather purse at my belt.

He peered up at me, probably uncertain if I was trying to lure him into acting against the commands laid out by the Twelve Orders.

"I don't want no trouble," he began, eyes on the temple behind me. "We've been told we shouldn't take messages for anyone in the Twelve Orders, priestess."

"I know," I confessed, smiling sadly. "I promise no trouble will find you for this act," I continued, reaching into a small leather satchel on my left hip.

He said nothing as I withdrew a shortened quill, inkpot, and scrap of parchment. I leant on the small wooden board I carried for such purposes and scribbled a quick note in my hand, hoping

Sofia wouldn't question the difference between the prophecy and this missive. I requested her return to the temple without delay; the Fate foretold in the prophecy may not be what she assumed. I sucked in my breath and signed it as a High Priestess of the Order Sagittarius and the name of my Familia.

I stared at the finished message a long time, the rattle of cartwheel and the clang of oxen bells a constant noise in the background as the market square filled with traffic before midday.

"Priestess?" the boy prompted, squinting up at me with profound fascination.

I nodded to myself, tore a piece of frayed cloth from my robe and tied it around the message.

"Can you find your way to this address?" I asked, handing him the poorly folded parchment bound by the ragged hem of the robe. It looked so pitiful a missive. I passed him a few extra coins to compensate for any anxiety he might have.

"This is one of those rich Familia," the boy said in wonder.

"You needn't wait for a response. I've asked for a reply to be sent here. Please hurry now. Deliver this before darkness falls if you can?"

"Of course, priestess," the boy scoffed as though I'd offended him.

He gave another awkward bow and turned, running across the marketplace. I lost sight of him momentarily in the crowd, then saw him reappear on the opposite side, already descending the hill and racing over the cobblestones at a reckless pace. I prayed for his swiftness as I thought again of the Fate I'd foreseen for Sofia and the tragedy that awaited her new husband and both Familia if they should marry.

Sunset fell upon the metropolis and still I had received no response from Sofia or my Familia. My afternoon had been busy with Offerings and prophecies. I had scarcely noticed the passage of time outside until the great bell chimed for the last hour of daylight. I felt the keen vibrations through the small temple room and the accompanying chime of the bell at my waist. Sighing, I sat back against the stone wall, its surface warmed through from the heat of the day.

When I left the temple, I searched the dim market square for any sign of the messenger boy. I had told him not to wait, but I had expected an answer from my Familia. The market was already growing noisy with twilight festivities as new traders arrived to sell wares only offered in the evening. Young men already leaned casually outside taverns, tankards of ale and cider gripped loosely in their hands. Voices and shouts were loud and echoed in the evening night.

I turned away from the market, beginning the steep walk along the lanes that rose into the poorer areas of the metropolis. I never understood why the higher elevations were so ill-favoured by the wealthy Familia or aspiring merchants when the fish-markets, butchers, tanners and sewers generated an accumulated stench that hung around the harbour each evening.

Continuing my slow pace up the last of the cobbled laneway, I inhaled deeply from the sea breeze rolling over the cliffs as I finally stood within sight of the cloister ruins. Gulls and sea birds called their evening challenges before settling into rocky crevices for the night. I couldn't help but think priestesses of the Order Sagittarius were not dissimilar.

Closing the solid and scarred wooden gate to the cloisters and the solid tower behind me, needing seclusion within the Order Sagittarius, I went straight to solitary evening meditation and prayer late into the night. I did not venture down for the late evening meal. Instead, I hoped clarity would return and shake away the lingering sense of dread.

The morning dawned cold and grey. I woke on the stone floor, stiff and momentarily confused. A slipper-clad foot nudged me again, and I realised why I had woken. I groaned, uncurling stiff limbs from around the leather tome I'd cradled to my chest. Blinking in the muted light, I stared in confusion at the Abbess, the highest rank in the Order of Sagittarius. She was neither tall nor short but always seemed imposing, her steel grey hair immaculately pinned.

"Come, Helena," she said and left the room, not waiting to see if I followed.

Grimacing, I lurched to my feet, body aching with protest at the cold flagstones beneath bare feet. I hastily pulled my red robe from yesterday more firmly about myself and hurried after the Abbess. As I followed the older woman through the cloister, memories of the hours before my night-long vigil returned. I'd received no response from the message I'd sent to Sofia. Had she sent communication to me here instead?

The Abbess led me into a large, round room in the tower, the space comfortably decorated with chairs and plumped cushions beside a warm fire. Despite the early hour, evidence of the burnt logs and ash within the hearth suggested the fire had been burning a long time already. I frowned as I stared out at the pale sky turning to a lavender hue, the sea an endless stretch of silver beneath.

"Correspondence arrived for you," the Abbess said, her face unreadable as she handed me a thick scroll.

I stared at it, unwilling to close my fingers on the expensive parchment, eyes focused on the gold-leaf stamp pressed deeply into the upper surface. My traitorous fingers finally closed on the papers, but my hands trembled too fiercely for me to untie the gold tassels that bound it. I half-collapsed into a chair beside the fire, my knees refusing to hold me upright any longer. Bitterness welled in me, threatening to crush the air from my lungs. The golden seal of the Emperor glittered mockingly in the morning light.

"You already know what this is, don't you?" the Abbess asked me, glancing from my shaking hands to my teary eyes.

"I provided a prophecy yesterday," I said, stripping the golden ties to unfold the lavish parchment. "I foretold a prophecy for a young woman from my former Familia. Her Fate was a Curse."

"I know you sent a message to your sister, Helena," the Abbess said without reproach, concern reflected openly on her face. "We all have our own troubles relinquishing ties to Familia, to who we are. The boy you entrusted your message returned here this morning with a message for you. He was frantic and explained to me, even though you'd told him not to wait, that the staff at the estate refused him entrance. He eventually got your message into the estate in the early hours this morning, but he was told the Familia had already left the metropolis yesterday for the wedding. He carried the news back here for you, but it troubled him. He told me both the Familia were dead from treachery."

I nodded, staring but not reading the official parchment from the Emperor in my hands. "It was poisoning. Suspected vengeance against Sofia's new husband."

"That boy deserves more than our gratitude and some coin for his loyalty to you. He would not give up your message lightly."

I smiled sadly, dashing tears from my eyes. I waved the thick parchment from the Emperor in one hand as I paced to the window overlooking the sea. Quickly, I read the contents, my emotional smile fading into a severe line.

"The Empire informs me of the recent regretful passing of my Familia. I am reminded as a priestess of the Order Sagittarius, when I took my Vows before the Twelve Orders, I relinquished all claims to property, possessions, and titles of the Familia. The Emperor appreciates the sanctity and honour of the Order Sagittarius and the service we provide the faithful of the Empire."

"I'm sure he appreciates the wealth plundered from the Familia he assassinated in our name much more," the Abbess growled.

I half-turned, brows lifted, and stared at her.

"The enemy of true faith has always been corruption. Unfortunately, in the duration of my lifetime, I have watched the Twelve Orders rot from within, the taint from the Emperor reaching deeper into each Order. To the Empire, the power of the prophecy foretold by a god was an ordained way to strip title, possessions and property from Familia who refused to bend beneath the Emperor's demands."

"I was blind to such manipulation," I whispered, staring at the flames before tossing the Emperor's missive onto the fire. I watched the parchment curl, then catch with flame. "And now my blindness means I'll never know my sister."

"There is a way for the Emperor's corruption to be curbed," the Abbess said, rising quietly to her feet to stand beside me at the window. We watched several noviciates tend to vegetable plots in the courtyard.

"How?" I finally asked.

"We need a new cloister in the northern limits of the Empire. Somewhere beyond easy reach of the Twelve Orders," she began. "In such a scheme, for us to strengthen the power of those resisting within each of the Twelve Orders, I'd need an abbess able to defy the Emperor."

I watched the noviciates and thought of my younger sister, who would never grow old, her life and all those around her simply extinguished to gain coin and property.

"I want vengeance for my Familia. Tell me where to begin."

'The Order Sagittarius' is a historical fantasy inspired by the Venetian city-state after the Middle Ages. In my fictionalised historical fantasy, I explored the dominance hierarchies in of the Twelve Houses or religious orders and the long-established wealthy households who both fought for control of the city-state. 'The Order Sagittarius' is set during the unravelling of the domination of the Twelve Houses and their manipulation over the city-state which is the beginning of the end for the established hierarchy. I have an interest in the machinations of historical establishments which dominated the political, military and domestic landscape and the slow implosion from forces within working against the inequality such establishments had created to benefit the upper echelon of society.

Black Wings At Samhain

At Samhain beneath a golden Hunter's Moon, none dared walk the roads alone. A chill wind rattled forest branches, cascading autumn leaves. I hunched beneath my cloak, hastening my steps. *Beware the Sluagh.* Those hearthside warnings still echoed in my mind. And glancing at the harvested fields, a scarecrow danced in the growing gale.

"There are *no* Sluagh."

Wingbeats stirred the air, and with heart pounding in terror, I ran. But the Sluagh pursued, talons raking my skin. The black birds of the Sluagh tore at my sanity, leaving me to madness and the wildness of a Samhain night.

'Black wings at Samhain' was inspired by the Irish and Scottish folklore of the Sluagh, a dark Fae host of the dead that would drive many into madnesses and leave them fools if caught within their grasp, and the folklore of Halloween—a liminal time when the borders between life and death are thin and the Sluagh could cross the into the mortal realm.

The Grave Robber and the Church-Grim

We all grew up with fireside stories of the church-grim. Our elders and their elders schooled us in stories of ghosts, making us fearful of the restless souls that might haunt our nights if we were unwary. But I grew into a sullen lad, disbelieving in the old folklores, scoffing at tales of the church-grim. It must certainly be an invention of wealthy churchmen to keep their precious gold and silver safe from prying eyes and nimble fingers.

"You've lost your wits," my sister said.

"I told you already, Marta. I'm not afraid of any children's tale."

She pointed the soup ladle at me. "Perhaps you should be."

I snorted. "Keep those old tales close to your heart, little sister. But they'll do you no good as you starve."

"So, you're going to rob a church? A holy, sanctified place?"

I screwed up my face. "No. Someone always bars the church doors despite talk of the church-grim guarding the house of God."

She returned to stirring the soup. "So, what *are* you planning to rob?"

"The graves."

"You're robbing the dead? Oh Pytor, that's worse!"

I shook my head. "Not the poor graves, Marta. Think what precious items they interred in the tombs."

"I'd rather not," she said, ladling weak soup into two bowls and passing me one with an apologetic half-smile.

"Think what meals we can have when we have money, Marta."

She crossed herself and sat down opposite me. We made a hasty grace above our meal and ate. I felt her gaze on me, but refused to look at her.

When I had finished the soup and used the hard brown bread to soak up any residue, I stood up from the table.

"Pytor?"

I put on my boots before responding. "Yes?"

"Please reconsider."

Stopping, I looked at my younger sister. She was not classically beautiful, nor even could be considered pretty, but she had a fierce spirit none could deny. "I'll be back before dawn. You'll not even have time to miss me."

"Be careful."

I nodded once, shaking away the sense of foreboding at her words, and left the house.

Outside, I pulled on my heavy coat and twisted the wooden closures tight. Stamping my boots on the stoop, I trudged into the snow. The constant swirl of snowflakes quickly obscured any light from the house, and I soon found myself alone in the gloom. Fortunately, I knew the way to the church as well as I knew my way home. I might not be a regular parishioner anymore since the death of Papa and Mam in the coldest winter just past, but I had attended regularly enough before then.

Pulling my scarf around my face against the cold, I continued head down into the storm. Walking across the town Square I could just see the church spire in the near distance. My boots hit an icy patch of cobblestones and I fell loudly to one knee, cursing. I paused, waiting for someone to raise an alarm at my outcry or an inquisitive neighbour to come outside. But nothing happened. Was my shout lost to the fury of the storm?

Hauling myself upright, I continued across the square without further incident. The only indicators of my passage were my heavy bootprints, already filling with fresh snow.

I stopped at the iron gates to the churchyard. The church was a dark, imposing shape in the swirling snow. There were no lights on within; the house of God was closed for the night. Glancing around me, I hooked one foot onto the iron railing of the fence. Testing my weight, I leapt the fence, landing easily on the opposite side. My breath was visible as ragged puffs in the frigid air. I waited until my heartbeat steadied, then turned to survey the graveyard. I could see no signs of any guards, priests, or mourners. But considering how foul the weather had become, it was likely none would be around to witness my exploits tonight.

Despite my earlier assurances to Marta that I no longer believed in superstitious tales like the church-grim, I still looked to the church for its guardian. Marta and I had grown up listening to the old folklore, the church-grim monstrously sized, fierce animals buried alive within the church walls and reawakened as revenants to protect the Church and its boundaries. It always seemed like such a nonsense to me. But now, alone in the graveyard at night with ill intent, I could almost believe in the church-grim.

Skulking through the graveyard, I dodged headstones and iron fences around the graves, both part-buried in the ankle-deep snow. The winter trees rattled their branches together like sabres and I shivered, but not from the cold. *Was Marta right?* I shook my head. We needed the money and, with few workers being hired, we would starve before I got enough labour to keep us fed and clothed. The country had become a bitter place these last years.

So, moving as quietly as I could towards the graves, my gaze flicked between shadowed headstones and the old oak tree growing in the middle of the churchyard. The legends of our town said the oak used to be a gallows tree, a place to hang guilty men witnessed by the community they'd wronged. It was an ancient, gnarled, and towering tree that dwarfed the church beside it. And on this night, the wind howled eerily through its branches.

Pulling my coat tighter about myself, I hurried towards the cluster of tombs at the far end of the graveyard. I stopped, sure I was being observed. Exposed as I was in the middle of the graveyard and no longer hidden by shadows, I looked to the church. The windows were still dark, the massive front doors locked and barred.

But I could still feel a gaze upon me. I was certain someone or something watched me. *The priest? Another graverobber? The church-grim? Don't be so foolish. It's just an old superstition, nothing more.*

And yet I felt a presence in the churchyard with me. It was a cold, oppositional force that wanted me gone. Hunching my shoulders, I hurried towards the stone tombs.

I stopped outside one of the more modest of the tombs, deciding to begin my burglaries on a less obvious target. The wind was picking up strength, sending flurries of snowflakes across the town. My hands were almost numb, but I took the iron bar from inside my belt. Then I felt, rather than saw, a quick movement behind me.

I grasped the iron bar in my hands and turned around to face my attacker. No one. The ground showed no boot prints except my own trailing back through the snow. Nothing. Slowly, I turned back to the tomb and hefted the iron bar once more. Wedging it between the slightly rusted lock and the door, I heaved with all my strength, shoulders and forearms straining with the effort. I pulled back against the lock, and it moved, flecks of rust drifting to the snow. Then suddenly it gave way. I staggered backwards, arm swinging to prevent myself from falling, but dropped the bar in the effort.

The double doors swung open with a screech of hinges long since used. Quickly, I looked around the graveyard and again to the church, but all remained still. I took hold of the iron doors before the storm blew them open and provoked another shrill alarm. Warily, I stepped forward to the edge of the tomb and peered inside.

Its cramped space was dank and dark. Snowdrift had thawed and frozen enough times to form an icy crust at the entrance. Leaves from the Fall had turned into frozen detritus on the floor of the tomb. But my prize lay in the centre and along the rear wall. I glanced briefly at the family name and crest carved into the stonework across the back wall of the tomb before entering. A spiral stone staircase led down to the crypt beneath, but I ignored this, not wanting to touch the corpses or steal from them just yet. If I could take enough from the trinkets lining the back wall of the tomb, Marta and I might never again need to steal from corpses to survive.

Reaching the stone shelf, I stared in amazement at the silver goblet, blade, and a sword on open display. Why had no one else considered taking these already? Surely I was not the first to decide grave robbing would make ends meet where honest work would not. I picked up the silver goblet and tested its weight in my palm. It was heavy. The same family crest I'd seen on the tomb was inscribed on the goblet. I could find a buyer unlikely to care about whether it was actually mine to sell. One look at my thin clothes from last season and anyone would know the items I possessed weren't rightfully mine.

I pulled a cloth bag from my jacket pocket and put the goblet and a silver candelabrum inside. I then carefully picked up the steel dagger. I had never seen such craftsmanship before, nor such finely inlaid jewels that glittered even in the dim tomb. I slipped the dagger into the bag to turned to leave. Glancing back briefly at the ornamental sword, I reminded myself I had more than enough.

Leaving the tomb, I was careful to keep the items in the bag quiet. The heavy cloth helped to muffle any noise of them clinking together as I walked. Hastily, I closed the iron gates to the tomb, willing them to shut quietly. The metal still protested, but luck was on my side and the screech of wrenching hinges didn't break the quiet night. I flipped the lock back onto the latch, but knew it couldn't be properly secured. The next wild storm would blow the doors wide open, and my thievery would be discovered.

But for now, I had no other care except escaping the churchyard before someone noticed me here. Turning to leave, I felt a prickle of unease again, the same sensation of being observed. My gaze roamed the headstones, but I couldn't see signs of anyone else. *And why wait until after I robbed the tomb to stop me?* No, I was being ridiculous. There was no one else here. Shouldering the bag of stolen items, I started walking back through the graveyard.

The snow fell in lazy spirals around me, and the night had become eerily calm. I heard the light patter of footsteps behind me and spun around. A cockerel, the size of a man, ran towards me, beak open and taloned feet moving with deadly speed across the snow. It was a monstrous creature of black and blood-red plumage, its eyes like abysses. Choking back a scream, I dropped the bag of stolen goods. I reached for my dagger but had no time. The church-grim's beak closed around my wrist, opening flesh to the bone. Hot blood spurted onto the snow, and I howled with agony.

The cockerel was terrifying. A terrifying rage urged it onwards, its wings kept tight to its body, the feathers around its neck raised. It skipped behind me, and I turned too slowly as the spurs on its legs came at me like twin razors, first one, then the other, striking my lower abdomen, opening my skin and parting muscle. Blood poured down my trousers, my intestines exposed and steaming in the frigid air. Clutching at my ruptured guts, I dropped to my knees as the church-grim charged forward to attack again.

The beak pecked hard and sharp at my face, blinding me in one eye. Blood poured from the socket as I screamed in pain and I tried to fend off the creature. But I couldn't dissuade it from its task. I was the trespasser here; I'd wronged the church and I would pay the cost. The church-grim rushed me again and again. Blood coated my face, hands, and body, and I collapsed to the earth, knowing I was dying here in the snow, the surrounding ground splattered with gore and soaked with my blood.

In my last moments, I wondered if Marta would ever be free from the shame and destitution my actions had caused tonight. I wished I had believed the old lore and prayed God would forgive my trespass. I watched the church-grim's bloodsoaked spurs descend, knowing they were the last thing I'd ever see.

The inspiration for my reimagining of Swedish folklore and legend in 'The Grave Robber and the Church-Grim' came from archaeology, historical accounts and folklore of entombing an animal like a rooster or cat inside the walls of the church where, according to the lore, it would be reanimated as a force capable of protecting the churchyard from robbers.

The Eldritch Wood

"You're a weakling," the boy sneered.

"Am not," I said, clenching my fists.

"Nah, you're just a girl. Go through the woods then, prove it."

I shifted uncomfortably. I might be a girl, but I wasn't a weakling. "Meet me on the other side."

My words rang like a challenge. The boys stared, dumbstruck, then shrugged. My gaze strayed to the ancient woodland behind us, seeming to hunch against the evening. It was only a small, fenced parkland outside town. I could cross it in half the time it'd take the others to walk around. But no one ever went through there. Everyone knew it was cursed. That was even before the missing children. The townsfolk spoke in terrible whispers of the eldritch monsters that had slaughtered their youngsters, laid them near the cathedral with eyeless orbits staring back at the forest. They'd all been children much younger than me.

The wrought-iron gate screamed in protest as I entered. Standing still, I sensed the preternatural menace of the forest, as though it were aware of me too, waiting and watching. Glancing back at the others, they urged me onwards with encouraging shouts and scornful jeers. Beneath the gnarled branches, it was impossibly dark, and the forest swallowed all awareness of the world beyond. Peering into the twilit gloom, I could faintly see a path snaking ahead, between alder and clambering ash.

"Don't leave the path," I whispered, arms hugged tightly about myself.

Above me, a branch creaked. Clammy sweat chilled my skin as

I squinted up into the canopy. Nothing but shadow and darkness, twisted tree limbs, and silvery spiderwebs. I shivered, inexplicably aware of being watched. I could almost sense them drawing closer to me—those eldritch nightmares crafted from hearthside tales.

Stay on the path, leave the path. We do not care. We hunt as we please.

The words came from above me. Rigid with terror, I could not move. Were those silver eyes or reflected moonlight? Sharpened teeth or light and shadow? Were those long, twiggy fingers reaching for me? I ran, feet carrying me nimbly over the uneven ground. Were those things truly in the trees above? Were they watching me now? Were they following?

A breeze brushed my face. The faint and feral touch of bat-wing against my skin. I screamed. Running beneath low-hanging branches of an ancient oak, I focused on the spire of the cathedral ahead, a silhouette against the golden moon.

Something tangled in my hair. I screamed, stopped, and struggled wildly, tearing loose a handful of hair. Fearing the strong twig-like fingers reaching for me and the gossamer wings beating the air above, I escaped the woods.

Still screaming, I vaulted the wrought-iron fence surrounding the park. Stumbling up the cathedral steps, I realised my friends were nowhere in sight. Sobbing, I hid in a shadowed alcove, conscious of the forest, the gaze of many eldritch hunters still upon me, and the memory of those twiggy fingers scratching at my eyes.

The inspiration for "The Eldritch Wood" was the notion of woods as places that are haunted or inhabited by dark entities. Children were told to avoid these places, which were often associated with death or child-stealing Fae.

Loki's Choices

Threatened by the giant Thrazi, Loki had a choice to make. "I've found a tree growing golden apples just like the one you tend!"

Idunn stared, disbelieving. "Impossible! Show me."

And Loki lured her to Thrazi as promised. But without Idunn, the apple tree sickened, fruit withering, and the gods aging.

Odín grasped his shoulder. "You've not seen Idunn?"

"What's happening?"

"Without Idunn's care, the tree is dying."

Ah! Loki had another choice to make. *Return Idunn and restore the gods? Or leave them to rot with time?* Loki grinned at the chaos he had wrought and made his choice.

'Loki's Choices' is a reimagining of the Norse mythology where Loki makes a decision to save himself at the expense of the Norse gods. Loki is an intriguing trickster figure in Norse myth and he was often used by Odin to make decisions that the respectable leader of the gods could not make or fulfil. Even so, Loki's own choices are often questionable, and trying to unravel some of the mystery surrounding him is part of what I enjoy most about Norse mythology.

The Bones of a Dead God

Crouched before the brazier, the priest stared at the painted figures on the chamber wall, the battling gods of life and death. He regarded the various obsidian blades arranged on a stone slab before him. In a handful of heartbeats, the ritual would begin. Once the moon reached its zenith above the mountain, when pale light bathed the pyramids clustered along its ridge, the Aztec Empire would turn to the temple of Tlalxicco, and on this night in the month of Tititl, the powers of the death-god Mictlāntēcuhtli would be replenished.

Below the temple, chanting echoed through the night, seeking to appease the demanding might of Mictlāntēcuhtli. From the passage beyond the chamber, scuffed footsteps and grunts of exertion preceded two muscular guards, a bound slave between them. Forced to his knees on the carved black steps, the slave's eyes were wide with fright, pupils so dilated they seemed entirely black.

Knowing his part in the ritual could risk no error, the priest reached for a wide obsidian blade, moonlight reflecting on its surface. In this precise moment, this chamber beneath the temple became the cavernous Underworld of Mictlān, and tonight, he must invite the death-god to feast. Offering a prayer to the depiction of battling gods—Mictlāntēcuhtli and Quetzalcoatl, the bones of mankind held between them—the priest slashed forward with the blade, severing living flesh and spilling lifeblood onto the temple stones.

Tonight, he must traverse the Underworld, and Mictlāntēcuhtli would be within him. This sacrifice was the god's feast. He inhaled deeply from the smoke rising in the braziers, its cloying fumes drawing him further into the trance. He no longer heard the muffled, agonised groans from the slave lying helpless on the stones. The power of the ritual consumed him as surely as the death-god. He selected a fine, thin blade, and the guards turned away with twin expressions of unease. Then, kneeling in a congealing pool of blood, the priest stripped tendons from joints, served limbs from body. He worked through the hours of darkness, the blood-leached face of the slave frozen in a rictus scream.

Time fled swiftly towards dawn, and wearily, the priest studied the corpse before him, marked so inexorably by a violent death that Mictlāntēcuhtli could not deny the slave entrance to the most honoured level of the Underworld. Throughout the Aztec Empire, all knew Mictlāntēcuhtli's preference was for those with the greatest endurance in their final moments. Satisfied this sacrifice would receive the death-god's honour, the priest studied the stars, assessing the hours until dawn. He must finish the ritual soon or risk Mictlāntēcuhtli's wrath.

In the grey pre-dawn light, the priest sliced away flesh from the body, deft fingers skilfully carving the bones for Mictlāntēcuhtli. The guards shifted anxiously, glancing fearfully at the faint glow on the horizon. Then, as the light blossomed, sunlight filling the temple chamber, the priest sat back, head bowed and exhausted beside the re-assembled skeleton—the bones of a dead god towering above him.

'The Bones of a Dead God' is a reimagining inspired by the Aztec mythology surrounding the death-god Mictlāntēcuhtli. The archaeological and historical material provided a rich resource for my fictionalised account of the sacrifice and resurrection of a Mictlāntēcuhtli from the bones of a sacrificial victim.

Hildur the Cursed Queen

Mortals have always told stories of the hidden people, the elves that dwell beneath the mountains. All the stories are more warning than magic because the elves can be wrathful. To Hildur, born a commoner among the elves, mortals were as much a mystery as she was to them. She'd never met a mortal, never ventured beyond the safety and splendour of the underground kingdom. Being born to the common folk, she possessed no powerful magic, nor was there anything remarkable about her. She argued her moderate height, black hair and dark eyes were no startling beauty compared to the ladies of the court. But there was something that set Hildur apart: there was a spark in her eyes, as unflinching as the basalt chambers and as bright as the diamond fissures. Despite Hildur's protestations of commonness, she didn't go unnoticed. Her dark beauty and strength captivated Einar, King of the Elves. Their courtship didn't go unnoticed either, and Hildur felt the malevolent gaze of Einar's mother on her always.

"I've spent my days among the court and its simpering ladies, Hildur. Compared to you, they're all pale shadows in the dark, you burn so bright."

"My king, I'm a commoner; you can't take me as your queen."

Einar's black eyes met hers, and he smiled ruefully. "I'm the King, Hildur. I may take whomever I wish as my wife."

Hildur relaxed into his embrace. "You know I love you deeper than the night and will do as long as the moon follows the sun."

"Then what causes your hesitancy?"

"Your mother."

He laughed, rumbling like thunder. "My *mother*?"

"She's voiced her disapproval of our union. I fear her retribution."

Einar held Hildur tighter. "My mother is *my* concern."

She looked up and kissed him lightly. "You know my heart is yours forever. I'll be your queen."

The night they married, and Hildur stood dressed in the white furs of the arctic fox, bejewelled in the diamonds and lava stones hewed from the mountains, Einar's mother stood to make a toast at their wedding feast.

"To the King of the Elves, son of my blood, and to his queen, I offer these words and magic: Hildur, I curse you, banish you from these halls. You will be as common in the mortal world as you were once here. But I am not merciless. You may return to these halls and my son once a year when winter is at its darkest. Let's see if you sway mortal commoners as easily as you did my son."

Einar stood, outraged. "Mother, take back your curse! You can't do this to our people. These people who have taken Hildur as their queen as surely as I have. You can't do this to Hildur, who has shown you nothing but care and honour."

"She's the ruin of our line, you fool! It would appal your father to see you marry the common folk. I tried to steer you honourably, make a just ruler of you. But you wouldn't see reason and so you've forced me to act. Let's see how long you last without Hildur beside you, bewitching your heart and urging your lust. You'll see sense soon enough and cast her aside as you should have done long before now."

Hildur sat beside her groom, silent and pale. Mortals have no love for elves. *How am I to live beyond the mountains and among humans? How am I going to survive this curse?*

"Hildur," Einar said, "I'll make her revoke her words."

"You look so pale, my love. Are you alright?"

"I'll never be all right if I am to leave your side."

He exhaled, wounded, as though Hiludr's words c had struck him a physical blow. She would never be the same once cast from the mountain hall at dawn and into the world of mortals. This was their first and last night together for a full turning of the seasons.

"I'm sorry, my love," she choked, tears welling in her eyes. "I don't know how I will cope without you."

"You're strong, my Hildur. You'll find a way and return to me next season and we'll dance again in this hall. By then my mother will revoke her curse. Have no fear, my love."

Hildur believed him. He was King of the Elves, after all. This was his domain and his people that she and he now ruled together. None would stand against the love they bore each other, nor that the people bore them both. His mother would recant her curse by the next time Hildur walked into these halls. She need only wait and survive the mortal world to return to him.

The curse was true. In the morning, Hildur resisted its power as long as she could. She dragged her feet and scraped her fingernails against the black stone of the tunnels, but it did no good. The halls of the elves rejected her and forced her from them. Beyond the dark caverns of the realm she had always known, the twisting spine of the hills and valleys disappeared to the ocean's shores. Hildur stood and watched the curling smoke from several farmsteads in the valley below and fixed the glamour about herself that would allow her to pass for a mortal woman. She looked behind her at the dark crevice in the black stone that led to the underground chambers of the Elves, and her heart grew heavy. *A year away from her beloved!* Dressed only in the common clothing of the elves, Hildur shouldered her small pack of provisions and walked away from the mountains towards the nearest farmstead.

The farmer eyed her curiously. "Hildur, is it? One of the old names, aye? Well, if you work honestly and fairly, I could do with a housekeeper. You've no husband or children?"

Hildur lowered her gaze. "No. It's just me."

209

"Sorry to hear that, lass. Life is hard on us. My wife and I would gladly accept you. Keep yourself out of trouble and you'll be more than welcome here."

"Thank you, Joe."

"We're a long way from the nearest villages here, so I know it's a hard life. I've a few shepherds who tend the flocks but we're a small household."

"I promise to work hard and repay your confidence in me."

"All will be well, Hildur. Go see my good wife and she'll show you what needs attending."

The household was small and only a handful of men and women gathered that night for supper. Hildur glanced around the table, her heart beating fiercely with the absence of her husband. She knew the magic to return her to him each year. These were not her people and would never be.

After the meal and into the darkness of the evening, they gathered beside the hearth to tell tales of the trolls, witches and elves. In those stories, Hildur heard the distaste and fear mortals felt for her kind. She bore them no love; they had no kindness for her. It made what must come easier.

Among the magic of the elves, there was a powerful tool to force another to her will. She was Queen now and the magic of her people flowed strongly in her veins. She would see her beloved again at the turning of the year. But she must fashion the tool necessary to make her journey home. If Einar's mother thought her nothing but a commoner and the mortals treated her the same, she'd make an example. She missed Einar with all her heart, longed for the touch of his hands and the sweet kisses he gifted her.

In the days that passed in the drudgery of being a housekeeper to a mortal family, Hildur's heart grew as cold as the mountains of her home. She owed the family nothing, owed the shepherds who treated her as a servant even less. Who were these men who tended flocks in the meadows all day? What gave them the right to make crude jests and ask her if she had a lover waiting somewhere for her? She was a queen, and these men were less than sheep to her.

The night was bitter and snow already falling, winter fast approaching as Hildur stole across the garden to the brook behind the cottage. Fearful of discovery, she glanced back at the farmstead. No lanterns had been lit. She'd not been discovered. Whispering in the ancient tongue of elves, Hildur curled her hand into a fist and thrust it into the frozen water. Ice shattered, and she reached deeper, heedless of the shards of ice. Fingernails sharpened to points, Hildur found what she needed and tore a lava stone from the frozen bottom of the brook.

Lifting the dull-looking rock closer, Hildur examined it beneath the glow of the northern lights. There, as the sky shifted green and blue, she saw the magic buried deep within the stone and smiled. Still kneeling in the snow and ice, she keened softly to the stone, speaking in the language of the hidden people, the elves beneath the mountains. She spoke of the separation from her king, the curse that hardened her heart to the mortals she shared the drudgery of her days, and how she must act to see her king once more.

"What are these mortals compared to my people, these farmers and shepherds who speak of my kin like we were cold and cruel? Let me show them what it means to be cruel, little stone. I ask you to take a new form. I am Queen of the Elves, and there is a strong bond between our people and the underground. Cursed from my home and people, help me return there once more."

The stone grew warm in Hildur's hand, and beneath the shifting light of the winter sky, it answered the summons of the queen. Smiling, Hildur whispered in the ancient tongue again. The lava stone grew hot in her hand, but Hildur held it, recalling the lava that flowed from the peaks of the mountains. The black surface of the stone became red with heat and like the lava it had once been, it transformed, lengthening into the shape of a bit Hildur had seen the farmstead horses endure.

When the stone had transformed and grown cool in Hildur's hand, she stood and walked calmly back to the farmer's cottage. Tomorrow she would see Einar again and greet his mother with cold fury because beneath the curse, Hildur had the endurance of glaciers and the harshness of winter blizzards.

Hildur bided her time in the coming days as winter grew deeper, the days and nights eternally dark. The household gathered before the hearth every evening and told morality tales of young gentlemen and goodly wives. Hildur listened to them all, noticing where elves and trolls attacked or challenged mortal heroes, her people always depicted with ill intent. She would show these simple mortals what wrath truly looked like.

The housewife looked curiously at Hildur. "Will you come with us to Church on Christmas morn?"

Startled from her revery, Hildur met her gaze. "Forgive me, no. I would visit a family that day."

The farmer raised his brows. "Your family?"

"Yes," she said. "I had to seek work against my wishes. I would spend that hallowed day with my husband."

"Of course. We did not know of your husband, Hildur."

She nodded demurely, adopting the habits of the women she'd heard described in so many tales over the course of these winter months. Mortals seemed obsessed with women who behaved in gentleness and humility. Hildur recalled that there had been other legends of warrior women, but these had long faded from mortal memory, it seemed.

She needed to act now if her chance to visit Einar was to happen. Waiting until the homestead was abed and sleeping, Hildur slipped from her servant's chamber, the lava stone in one hand. It was warm, the magic potent still, a glamour concealing it as a mere stone. When Hildur released her will, the stone would resume whatever form she wanted.

One shepherd had spoken desire to travel with the farmer's family to Church in the morning. Hildur knew her chance had come at last. The homestead was small; the shepherds housed where they tended their flocks. Tonight she must act.

She paused in the corridor, feet bare on the frigid floorboards, and glanced both ways. No sign of light beneath the doors, no wandering servants. Inhaling, Hildur slipped into the shepherd's chamber. Standing on the other side, she gently closed the door behind her. She could see the shepherd sleeping on the bed, the rise and fall of the bedcovers as he breathed. He hadn't stirred.

Moving forward on silent feet, Hildur bent over his bed. He woke with a start and she acted fast, shoving the lava stone into his mouth and whispering quick words to drop the glamour. The stone transformed immediately. Although the shepherd struggled, the lava stone lengthened over his tongue. Murmuring wordlessly, Hildur dropped the bridle she had woven of twigs and rushes over his head. The magic tightened, fastening the bridle and bit into place. Wild-eyed and panicked, the shepherd looked at Hildur.

She shook her head and soothingly brushed his cheek. Not caring who discovered her now, she dropped her glamour. It replaced the unappealing brown hair with her midnight locks, the mud-brown of her eyes turning black as basalt and the pale perfection of her skin shining against the northern lights. Looping a long fingernail around the bridle, Hildur led the shepherd from his room. Compelled by her magic and forced against his will, he followed as though he were as docile as any work horse.

Outside the cottage, Hildur forced the man to stoop as she climbed upon his back. Holding the reins of the woven bridle in one hand, she took a whip made of reeds and with a powerful slap against the man's rump like he was a horse, she forced him towards the looming mountains.

The night was silent around them except for the sound of Hildur's whip tearing fresh wounds from the man's body. Blood ran freely down his legs and arms, but he found no sympathy from Hildur. When he stumbled in the snow, the whip was a quick a reminder of her will over his own. Bit tight in his mouth and maddened with pain, the shepherd was forced up the steep slopes of the mountain passes, ignoring his faltering gait as he trudged forwards on numb feet. Let mortals understand the pain she endured for her truest love.

Climbing higher into the peaks and crags of the mountains, Hildur reined in the shepherd. Ahead of them, a glacier had carved the side of the mountain open, revealing a drop into a dark crevice. Despite the magic binding the shepherd to Hildur's will, the man paled at the sight of the underground entrance to the kingdom of the elves. But Hildur paid him no heed, securing the reins of the bridle to the basalt cliff with a binding magic.

"If you try to break this bridle in my absence, you'll die before you can stumble a few bloody paces."

The shepherd nodded, fearful of Hildur's wrath and the whip she still carried at her side, its tip dark with his blood.

Turning back to the crevice in the mountain, Hildur strode forward and disappeared into the darkness of the underground kingdom.

The kingdom of the elves rang with the sounds of celebration and merriment. Hildur hesitated, hand to her heart. *Have I replaced her own heart with a stone by the cruel actions required of me?* She would know, the moment she saw Einar again, if her heart was stone or not. Standing taller in the homespun mortal garb of a servant, Hildur walked proudly into the chamber of the royal court.

Silence fell as the elves turned to their queen. The music ceased to play, and the children halted in their dances. Hildur stood poised between fear and malice, fearful of not being accepted but determined she could bend these people to her will if required. But one by one, the elves bowed and curtsied to her, the court uncaring of her mortal attire and how she had debased herself as a servant.

"Hildur!"

She turned at the sound of Einar's voice, tears running down her cheeks as he ran to her. They embraced, and he pulled her fiercely to him, his arm strong about her waist.

"Oh my Hildur, how I have missed you. Every night apart has been a torture."

"Every day and night has been mine."

Einar pulled back slightly, meeting her gaze. There was something darker in the depths of her eyes now, a harshness he hadn't seen before.

"Tonight is ours. Let's banish all others from our minds."

She half-smiled, still affected by the darkness of her past. But she squeezed her husband's hand and let him lead her to the banquet table.

Einar was true to his word, keeping Hildur's mind from darkness. With the table covered in all finest dishes she'd longed for in her banishment, and for the magic of those hours, she forgot the torment of the past year. But her husband saw the change in her and he maintained a white-knuckle grip upon the silver goblet throughout the supper.

Hildur rose and left the royal table, speaking with the ladies of the court, who brightened immediately at her presence. But Einar turned to his mother and met the outrage in her gaze.

"Revoke the curse, Mother," he said.

The old woman looked at her son and wordlessly shook her head.

"You don't do yourself, me or this court any honours. Instead, you are a bitter old woman to the people."

"I'll never accept one such as she," she spat.

Hildur had drawn nearer and laid a hand upon the back of Einar's carved chair. "This punishment you force me to endure for him, I'll meet. This curse you've laid upon me breaks your son, the king, more than me. I was born to common folk, as you remind me, and I'm a servant to mortals now. But know this: I'm Einar's queen, and mortal pain, blood and death is nothing if I spend just one night a year with him."

Einar listened to Hildur's words, and the fury and coldness in them stilled him. This wasn't the woman he'd married, and yet he'd seen that diamond-bright spark in her eyes like hardest and the most beautiful of gems.

"Your curse has failed, mother."

Einar took Hildur's hand and led her towards the centre of the chamber. Despite the hasty appearance of the king and queen, the musicians were already playing. But even as Hildur and Einar stepped onto the dance floor, Einar's mother spoke again.

"Ask her the true cost of tonight."

Holding Hildur's hand in his own, Einar ignored his mother's words, allowing the music to flow around him. But even as he held Hildur close, felt long-denied desire stirring within him. His mother's words were like a weight around his neck.

"You want to know the answer, don't you?" Hildur asked.

"How did you know?"

"I can feel your unease, my love. I'll answer true, for we promised never to hide anything from one another. The cost of my passage here each year is a mortal life. The magic needed to travel swiftly is a price paid in blood. In the morning, just before dawn, I must leave you and take the man I've left outside and return him to his bed where he will die from his efforts. You know these ancient magics as well as I do."

Einar was silent, but they continued to dance, moving around the hall with all the eyes of the Elven kingdom upon them.

"This is a terrible price to pay, Hildur. You must know how it's already changed you."

"I may be a cursed queen. But *my* curse lies on those who treat me unjustly. None shall break me."

'Hildur the Cursed Queen' is a reimagining of an Icelandic legend of the elves, with elves often known as the Hidden Folk. My 2019 visit to Iceland inspired a lot of my writing of Icelandic, Viking and Norse legends, myths and folklore. The unique landscape plays such a pivotal role in all Icelandic legends and folklore, including modern-day involvement with the land. The legend of Hildur and the elves is an intriguing one where real love can triumph but at a very high cost even for the Hidden Folk.

Selene and Endymion

She saw him on the mountainside of Latmos, a shepherd guiding his flock to shelter for the coming night. The sky was fading towards night, but pale Selene cared only for the beautiful youth. Drawing nearer, she bespelled him with a touch.

"What is your name?"

He stirred, not waking. "Endymion."

"You're mine now, sweet Endymion. None shall take you from me. You'll never know fear or regret, hatred or sorrow, old age or death."

And with a sigh, Selene stretched languidly beside him. Whisper soft, she kissed his eyelids, and though they fluttered at her touch, Endymion never woke.

My reimagining 'Selene and Endymion' was inspired by Ancient Greek mythology and history. The moon goddess Selene can only love Endymion while he's sleeping. The reality that keeping Endymion asleep so that only Selene may love him but never truly know him is an intriguing dark aspect of this Greek myth.

The Bargain

The night was cold, autumn already entering its final throes
and winter looming closer. Frost was settling on the supple
forest branches, and mortals clustered about hearths in the
evening, sharing tales of the gods and the Folk. Our lives may be
much longer than those of mortals, but their collective memories
spanned generations, and this lore taught them to fear us. As one
of the oldest of the Folk, I am part of those who maintain harmony
with the lands. More than the embodiment of these lands, more
than the tales in mortal lore, I am part of a host of beings who
preserve an eternal bargain with these lands, allowing the energy
to flow, renewing life from winter into spring, an ancient balance.
It is an exchange of energy, able to be withheld in times of great
need, but never destroyed, not even in the deepest winter, when
the lands lie dormant before the release of flooding spring rains.

I moved to the edge of the forest, the fields beyond mottled
shadow beneath the weak light of the quarter moon. They had
not yet brought in the harvest, and the tall grain crops shivered
as I walked through them. Tonight, I was not here to warn of
winter's approach. Instead, the rasping breath of the dying man
drew me.

The squat house lay in a hollow below the last of the fields,
separate from the other houses that tried to distance themselves
from the influence of the forest beyond. The house was modest
for the times and not as large as those of surrounding estates.
Unlike the lands beyond this humble farmstead, these fields
had been prosperous for generations, the family blessed by the

fortune our bargain provided. Such pacts are rare these days, with many mortals drawn to a religion promoting the One God and his churches of wood and stone. We endure the fading worship of the older gods and the once-common offerings that encouraged us to dwell on these lands. The Folk are timeless, born from rivers, starlight, forest, and hewn from the stone hills; it is upon us that the guardianship of these lands rightfully rests. Tonight, I would bear witness to the end of one generation and the beginning of another. On the morrow, I must strike a new bargain, to maintain the balance and ensure a continued renewal of these lands.

I stepped closer to the wooden house, the windows still lit even in these dark hours before dawn. Such was the mortal fear of darkness and death that they kept away all shadows this night. In the wake of my own steps along the invisible boundary that marked the threshold of the house, hoar frost laced across the frozen ground. I peered inside the dwelling, hearing the nervous whine of the hound nearest the door as it cringed closer to the hearth, away from the frosty windows. Even from where I stood on the shortened grass of the dooryard, I could clearly hear the raised voices chanting in prayer from the rooms in the upper storey.

Inside the house, I saw the crouched forms of house sprites, the diminutive Folk who provide similar protection and care for the dwelling as my kin provide for the lands beyond. I caught sight of my reflection in the leadlight glass pane. This night, I had glamoured my form to resemble the monster mortals expect. The Folk have no true form and no need for one, but tonight I had chosen the long, sinuous limbs of aspen bark, silver eyes glittering like starlight and a headdress of curling frost. This had been the glamour I used when the now-dying man had sworn an oath to me. I threw back my head and called into the night, the sound unmistakably eldritch and signalling the end of our bargain.

I felt the dying man's breath hitch in his failing lungs and his realisation that his last moments had come. To mortals, the cry of the Folk was told in their lore as the keening of a banshee. I was not a harbinger of death, but I was the embodiment of these lands and I felt the passing of the old man as he stepped between the veils. Although I had already turned away from the house, striding toward the forest, I heard a brief pause in the prayers from the house before the wail of mourners cut through the predawn calm.

In the moments after dawn, when the forest was a realm made entirely from shifting shadow and mist, I moved through the branches, formless except for subtle, dappled light. I had observed the funerary customs practised by the mortals, listened as they whispered last words to the dead man and offered my own, unheard by mortals except as the sighing breeze. I was immediately aware when the familiar boot tread reverberated across the forest floor. As the embodiment of these lands, my awareness extended into these woods. The tree roots were my veins and nerves, the breeze was my breath. I was unsurprised when the old woman's familiar voice called through the forest. I knew mortals had such little understanding of our ways, and I tolerated her misguided attempts to draw my attention through a spoken summoning.

"Wood witch," the widow called. "We make this offering so you might bestow your blessings on these lands."

Her words may be unnecessary to gain my attention, but the pact of which she spoke demanded my response. I let my presence be known, filling the forest with a subtle shiver, leaves trembling in an unseen breeze. Before the old widow could speak again, her son interrupted from where he crouched beside the deep pond. I saw the shimmer of scaly limbs beneath the murky surface, and autumn leaves quickly tumbled from the surrounding oaks as if they had been physically shaken. The being in the water dived deeper, away from my disapproving gaze and from the possibility the young man might spy it there.

"This is ridiculous," he now said to his mother. "Father was a madman and I won't be talked into wasting even the smallest of our hard-earned produce on such heresy."

"The bargain between our family and the Folk has existed

for generations," the widow continued, as though this were a familiar argument. "Our family has always prospered from it. Do not anger the Ash Wife."

"Madness. There'll be no more spoken of this." He picked up a hunk of burnt bread and one of the shrunken apples. "I'll waste no more of our scraps on this wood."

"Charles," the widow pleaded, hand reaching for her son. "Your father was a good man."

"These lands are mine now," he said, already turning away. "The harvest needs bringing in."

The old woman watched her son walk away, then bowed her head, the weight of his decision settling over her.

I hissed my anger at this arrogant young man defying his mother with such insolence. The wind responded, blowing sharply through the canopy, swaying treetops before an eerie silence descended. The widow looked beseechingly at the gnarled ash tree where her family had placed offerings for generations, the site of an exchange of energies between what the lands gave and what the mortals returned. I watched as the young man stalked back, striking the remaining fruit from his mother's hands. I followed her gaze as she watched the withered apples bounce once before rolling to a halt against the root of the tree.

"The harvest?" the son snapped. "Unless you want to starve?"

The widow bowed her head and turned, following her son. I waited in the preternatural calm of the forest. Mortals told stories about the Ash Wife, a malevolent being seeking vengeance. I watched the old widow glance fearfully back at the ancient ash and whisper a voiceless prayer. I was one of the Folk and we had obligations deeper than the ties to this family. I would try to make the young man understand the necessity of the bargain his ancestors had made and, if he would not keep it, then these lands had no obligations to him or his kin.

I summoned the Folk of these lands at twilight. I waited in front of the ash tree, staring at the deep pool in the centre of the clearing, its spring-fed water reflecting starlit sky, broken only by the willow branches that bent to touch its surface. In this place our powers were strongest, flowing through the veins of the woodland, the fissures of the earth, and the meadow grasses. These forests were my domain, but tonight I invited the more powerful and lesser beings into my woods, where we could decide our course of action.

I felt the quiver of energy pass through the forest as each of those I had invited entered the woodland. We did not need physical forms, and many of us did not use them. Tonight, though, certain magic required a physical form and my glamour embodied these woods with a robe woven from cobweb, draped over skeletal limbs, stretching to cloven hooves and hand-like talons. I adorned the equine skull with lichen, and a mane of raven feathers formed a headdress.

The energy in the clearing increased, many other Folk pressing into my domain. An unseen wind stirred the canopy and the roosting black carrion birds squawked in raucous alarm. A cascade of autumn leaves spiralled to the ground, then tumbled and gathered into a glamour. The forest troll stood, its bulky form squat and long-snouted, boar tusks protruding upward. It waited, improbably dark eyes like lava pebbles reflecting an ancient cunning and intelligence. I bowed in acknowledgement to the forest troll, then turned my attention to the lesser beings who had gathered in the shadows: those of the forest, meadow, waterways, and the hollow places. I focused on those surrounding me, summoning the deep bonds between us, addressing them in the oldest of languages shared by us, our conversation expressed only by thought and emotion.

We are the Folk, guardians and protectors of the harmony between the lands and the races reliant on them. We have kept the bargains struck between the mortals and these lands, ensured the renewal of life-force continues. All of you assembled here will recall we are guardians of these lands and cannot endure alone. There may come a day when mortals will no longer recognise our power as necessary and we may fade beyond this veil and into the next.

When my silent communication stopped, the Folk surrounding me in the clearing ventured closer, perched in the tree branches, on stones, or peered up at me from the waterweed. They passed to me their feelings of sorrow, acceptance, reverence and acknowledgement of the past.

"What of the bargain with these mortals?" the troll rumbled aloud from the shadows, its voice like grating stone.

"We must first determine if we can persuade the young man from his current path and agree to the bargain of his ancestors," I said.

"If we can't deter him?" a hoarse whisper came from beneath the waterweed, two large, amphibian-like eyes regarding me with feral interest.

"Then the bargain is betrayed, and protection revoked," I answered with a curt nod, the skeletal jawbone snapping sharply.

The water sprite lifted her head above the pond's surface and smiled, revealing too many pointed teeth in an overly large mouth. In a ripple of scaly limbs, she vanished beneath the dark water again. The troll lifted his long snout to snuffle at the air, black eyes meeting mine before he, too, grinned his satisfaction, lips curling around massive tusks.

"We must make our actions as one," I said, raising my skeletal arms to encompass the gathered host.

The Folk followed me to the forest fringe. Beyond the reach of the trees, the fields lay empty and fallow; the harvest taken in for the season. Without hesitation, I stepped across the boundary between forest and meadow, my cloven hooves sinking into freshly ploughed soil as I moved across the fields laid bare to prepare for the coming rains. I lifted my skeletal muzzle to the night sky, the air already heavy with the scent of approaching rain and the thunderstorms that lingered on the horizon, swallowing the starlight.

"My kin," I called across the silent land. The Folk gathered opposite me, a host of beings, clothed from shadow, leaf and rock, all murmuring their agreement with voices like shifting branches, rustling leaves, raindrops and breaking bone. I nodded to acknowledge the forest troll, his lava-pebble eyes glittering darker than the night shadows. I met the unblinking gaze of the scaly water sprite who had curled like pond fronds around the troll's massive neck. "Our actions will renounce the bargain once struck over these lands."

"You have not consulted all of us," a tiny voice interrupted from near the ground.

I tilted my head to regard the diminutive Folk now gathered around my hooves.

"You did not speak against me earlier," I replied, displeasure clear in my tone.

"We were on our way," the leader said, gesturing to the tiny mount he rode, a field mouse that cleaned its whiskers without fear of my towering presence.

"House sprites are beings of the household," I noted. "You have worked tirelessly to ensure harmony between the mortals and these lands. It would be folly to exclude you in any debate on our course of action."

The little sprites regarded me, their glamour made from bundled sticks stitched together with roughly spun yarn. Each wore unique clothing made from discarded cloth decorated with broken buttons and other household items carefully carved with tiny runes. I looked at them, their smooth upturned faces shaped from clay and odd arrangements of hair sprouting from their scalps. I had never truly understood those among us who dwelt beside mortals, and it made negotiation with them difficult.

"Without the aid from those of you with power over the household, our protection, once removed, is not so easily felt by the mortals," I said. "Do you share our abhorrence at how the mortals refuse to make offerings and meet the obligations of our bargain?"

The smooth features broke into wrinkles and a grin. "We do," he said merrily, patting the field mouse he rode, then looking at the others accompanying him. "Our offerings have been restricted far too long," he said with a nod, pale hair like dandelion-fluff waving with the movement.

"Then we're agreed," I said, jawbone clattering as I thrust my muzzle toward the sky in triumph.

I stepped away from the house sprites, moving further into the open expanse of the empty field. Moonlight pooled about me as I walked, the raven-feathered headdress darker than the sky above. When I stood in the centre of the fallow field, I turned my face again to the starlight. The scent of rain and ozone saturated the atmosphere in anticipation of the autumn rains, these life-giving storms before winter. I lifted the oak staff in my talons, the burgeoning power and steady thrum of energy shifting beneath the lands. But there would be no rain this autumn, only an early winter. I held the staff toward the half-moon and spoke the curse into the night.

The invocation echoed through the lands like the whisper of dry leaves, the steady gathering of mist and the gentle wash of water upon a riverbank. I slammed the tip of the staff into the ploughed soil, the echo of the invocation reverberating. Nothing stirred in the night. Instead, an absolute and uncanny silence filled the lands. The house sprites held their mounts in place, the little creatures wanting to move, uneasy amid the suffocating hold on the landscape.

Finally, I let my breath escape, air whistling through the teeth in the skeletal jaw. I bowed my head, summoning winter and pulled my staff from the ground, a clod of earth lifting free with it. I stared with regret at the husks of seedlings planted earlier that day.

"Let our task begin," I said to the Folk as I drew nearer to them, stalking across the fields with renewed determination. "If we cannot pull the mortal man from his path, we shall take the path from him."

I led the host across the empty fields, the half-light from the moon already consumed by the approaching winter storm. Thick clouds swirled above, swallowing the stars as the snowflakes drifted downward, spiralling toward the ground. Within moments, the ploughed fields that had been awaiting rain were layered in snow, buried beneath a preternatural winter.

I continued toward the shadowed bulk of the house, conscious of the distant groaning of the wood as it shuddered with the weight of ice-encrusted branches. Focusing on the task before me, I skirted the dooryard and fences surrounding the house entrance. It was a modest building, belying its prosperity.

Windows shuttered, doors barred against the night. But not even locks could keep us out.

Inside, I could hear the quiet cries and moans of its inhabitants, already assailed by the Folk. No longer bound to the obligation of the bargain, the household sprites had turned their guardianship into malicious pranks. The house no longer carefully protected, the winter chill crept through window shutters, extinguishing hearth fires, spoiling the milk and ruining foodstuffs. Pausing outside, hoar frost preceded me, lacing the windows and reaching up the sides of the house as I stepped across the threshold and into the young man's room.

Once inside the shadowy room, I stared down at the Master of this household. Youth marked him pitifully, bedclothes tossed amid his nightmare, feather-pillows thrown haphazardly about him. I changed my glamour, limbs elongating, clothed myself in forest hues and snowflakes, long white antlers reaching above me into the shadows.

"Wake," I said into the darkness.

He started upright, opening his eyes, and stared. He met my gaze, focusing on the skull's empty eye sockets. He leaned on his elbows, motionless in panic, chest quickly rising. I tilted my head in silent question, watching him flinch, enjoying the considerable height the antlers provided.

"Do you know me?" I asked, voice hollow in the night.

He opened his mouth to reply, faltered, wet his lips, then tried again. "You are the being my mother calls the Ash Wife."

"I have many names, but that is one."

"You're a demon."

"I am the embodiment of these lands. My bones are the earth you toil, my blood the water quenching your thirst. My pleasure is your fortune. My displeasure can be your ruin."

"You're unholy," he snarled. "I'll have no dealings with such evil."

"Then ignorance will be your downfall," I said. "A bargain was struck and continues through the generations of your family. In return, we bestow prosperity, but we can find other mortals to make allegiances. We need not continue our bargain with you.

Understand, though, if you do not honour it you discard any blessings and protection we might offer."

The young man lifted his gaze to the crucifix above the doorway. I was silent, unaffected by his actions as he whispered a prayer. His features were rigid, and he continued to stare fixedly at the talisman above the door.

"Demon," he hissed.

I withdrew from the house. The frozen stillness of the winter hung heavily around the lands. On the eastern horizon, the dull light of morning touched the sky, promising a brittle warmth. I waited in the dooryard, solemn and motionless but conscious of the pleas and muttered curses coming from inside the house.

I heard the widow calling to her son, voice quavering. "The Ash Wife came to you and you denied the bargain she offered?" she asked, incredulous. "Charles, you've doomed us all. There are no eggs this morning, no milk. Three of the goats died in the snow. The crops will be ruined, and we haven't any dry wood even if flames would kindle in the hearth."

"This is all superstitious nonsense," he fumed; his words were followed by the sharp noise of flint being struck. The repetitive sound continued without success, then abruptly ended in a muttered curse. I heard him stalk upstairs, then I moved closer to the thick glass, frost and shadow shifting around me.

The widow stood facing the window, unable to perceive me even though I stood only paces from her, our fingertips nearly touching against the glass pane. I understood this woman was one of the few who honoured the old ways and traditions, a believer in the Folk. I watched as she sadly bowed her head, acknowledging defeat in that her son was not the man she had hoped he would become. I felt the tinge of sorrow, knowing that my actions would take her life and these lands without another bargain made for her kin. I bowed my head in acknowledgement of the old woman and stepped away from the house, my anger lashing forth in the furious winter wind that rattled and tore relentlessly at the window shutters.

The winter months were harsh, and I held the lands in its bitter grasp as heavier snow fell and temperatures plummeted. Throughout the days and endless nights, I roamed the frozen woods or perched amid the icy boughs. On a quiet day, when snowflakes fell in gentle spirals instead of frenzied blizzards, I sat among the ash branches. The household and forest sprites clustered about me as we watched the young man approach across the snow-covered fields.

"What does he want?" I wondered, conscious of the glinting axe blade he carried in frost-bitten hands.

"He is unbending," the sprites confirmed in unison. "We no longer tend the herds or flocks, and most have succumbed to the winter. We do not mend the house nor tend the supplies in the cellars."

"He is here for vengeance, then." I glanced toward the mound near the house yard, fresh but shallow.

"Ash Wife!" the man below demanded, brandishing the axe while he shivered in thin clothing. "You cursed me! Took everything dear to me."

I summoned the wind, whipping the icy gale through the forest, ice-laden branches crashing to the ground where echoes continued throughout the woods. "I took nothing from you that was rightfully yours," I thundered, my voice a snarl of winter's wrath.

In response, the young man roared and lifted the axe. He screamed his outrage into the stillness before throwing the axe at the mighty ash. The tree where his mother had sacrificed to the Folk, a place she had considered sacred, was violated as the axe blade struck. I stared uncomprehendingly at the axe as it quivered with the force of the impact.

Silence hung through the forest before the tentative twitter of small birds began again. I stared at the young man below, watched his too-thin shoulders slump inside his worn winter coat. Without further comment, he turned and stumbled back through thigh-deep snow, anger draining with every passing step. He paused outside the house, staring up at the poorly repaired thatch roof, noticing the many broken shutters hanging crookedly from their hinges. The once-proud son stooped to collect a small pack from the doorstep. He stared at the house once more before slinging the meagre pack across his shoulders and walking away.

By the evening, when I was certain the son's presence had faded, I lifted the curse of winter. My awareness flowed through the fissures in the earth, tree roots of the forest and rivulets of the waterways, awakening the lands and bringing spring.

It was a warm evening in early summer as I drifted formless through the forest. I heard the soft voices of a couple as they stole through the dense woods and, conscious of the other Folk, I focused my attention on these young mortals. I summoned a glamour, taking humanlike form, limbs golden like midsummer sunlight, dark brown hair flecked with silvery cobweb. Dropping silently from a tree branch as the mortals approached, I landed in front of the couple, the young man shouting in surprise. His pregnant wife stepped away from me as I rose from a low crouch. I kept my gaze on the man as he brandished a sword at me.

"Stay back," he stammered, glancing around the forest as though more strange beings might appear.

"You are on my lands," I said, appealing to the young woman, who looked more rational than her protective husband.

"Forgive our intrusion," the young woman began, reaching out to take her husband's arm and gesturing he lower the sword. He glanced behind him quickly, questioning his wife, but did as she bid him.

"You are in need?" I asked, raising my brows.

The woman wet her lips, touching a hand to her swelling belly. "We are," she confirmed. "Our families did not approve our union."

"They cast us out," the young man corrected. "Wouldn't even condone our marriage."

I looked at the young couple. "I have no care for the ways or laws of mortals," I said. "I offer you these lands and the promise these fertile fields and reliable springs can provide. I ask but one thing in return."

The couple looked at each other. "What do you want?" the woman asked me.

"In return for reliable crops and fertile lands, we ask for small offerings from your labours. The returns of your labour ensure the cycle continues."

The young man frowned, confused. "Surely, if these lands are as fertile as you claim, why not take everything for yourselves?"

"Our purpose is to maintain an equilibrium," I explained. "Do you accept the terms of the bargain?"

The young man hesitated, then sheathed his sword, placing his hand on his wife's swelling belly. I watched her gaze linger on his hand before she met my gaze.

"We accept," she said.

'The Bargain' is a fictionalised reimagining inspired by the Celtic folklore and legends surrounding bargains made between mortals and the Fae in order to benefit each other. Offerings were provided by mortals, who relied on the land for their existence, and reciprocated by the Fair Folk, who in turn ensured the land was fertile and abundant. I was intrigued by what might happen if a bargain is broken and the offerings to the Fair Folk no longer provided. The close connection between landscape, crops and domestic abundance is often evident in Celtic folklore and legends where the connection must be maintained or the consequences can be dire.

Publication Acknowledgments

Three Tasks for the Sidhe, *Stories of Survival*, Deadset Press, 2021

A Thief in the Alhambra, unpublished

Three Curses, unpublished

The Black Hare, unpublished

A Handful of Dead Leaves, *Greed*, Black Hare Press, 2020

The Hobgoblin's Lament, unpublished

The Bull of Heaven, *Taurus*, Deadset Press, 2020

The Selkie Twins, unpublished

Them, *Wrath*, Black Hare Press, 2021

Pan's Dance, unpublished

The Monsters We Become, unpublished

Bones and Fur, unpublished

Talismans, *Revolutions*, Deadset Press, 2021

Maidens of the Bloody Brook, unpublished

The Monster, *Gluttony*, Black Hare Press, 2021

A Night on Skye, unpublished

Poisoned Fruit, Poisoned Reign, *Reign*, Black Hare Press, 2021

The Dark Harpist, *New Tales of Old, Volume 1*, Black Ink Fiction, 2021

The Devil's Fool, *April Horrors*, Raven and Drake Publishing, 2021

When Dead Gods Walk, unpublished

A Trail of Corpselights, *New Tales of Old, Volume 1*, Black Ink Fiction, 2021

The Making of Hel, unpublished

The Dark Horseman, *Legends of Night Anthology*, Black Ink Fiction, 2021

Second Chances, *Tick Tock*, Black Hare Press, 2020

The Order Sagittarius, unpublished

Black Wings at Samhain, unpublished

The Grave Robber and the Church-grim, unpublished

The Eldritch Wood, *Watch*, Black Hare Press, 2021

Loki's Choices, unpublished

The Bones of a Dead God, *Bones*, Black Hare Press, 2021

Hildur the Cursed Queen, unpublished

Selene and Endymion, unpublished

The Bargain, *Unnatural Order*, CSFG Publishing, 2020